THE LIES WE TOLD OURSELVES

WILLOWBROOK BOOK 2

PIPER WYLDE

TINY PLANT PUBLISHING LTD

The Lies We Told Ourselves: Willowbrook Book 2

First published in 2025 by Piper Wylde

ISBN: 978-1-917387-27-9

Other works by Piper Wylde can be found at www.piperwylde.com

Cover design by Sarah Kil Creative Studio

Formatted by Zsuzsanna Gerhardt of Midnight Readers PR using Vellum

CHAPTER ONE

REECE

I stared at the little flashing lights illuminating the entire dash and swore.

Of course, this was where my car chose to take its last spluttering breath—in the middle of damn nowhere!

This was what my life had turned into. A failure of epic proportions.

Everything I had left was in this car. All of my belongings were shoved in garbage bags, and I had thirteen dollars left in my pocket.

What was I supposed to do now?

The telltale lump in my throat started to choke me as I tried desperately to hold back the tears. If I started crying now, I wouldn't stop. I didn't have time to fall apart. This wasn't far enough, and I still hadn't figured out where to go.

I couldn't go back. The dulling ache in my ribs was a reminder of why.

It wasn't supposed to be this way.

I...

My head started thumping, and I squeezed my eyes closed, trying to stop the spiral I didn't have time for.

I *had* to do this.

But then a gust of cool air hit my cheek, and a voice growled, "Are you out of your damn mind?"

"I think I might be," I whispered.

My body felt like it was wading through sand as I turned my head to see the owner of that gruff voice. I should probably be scared, but I didn't have the capacity to feel any more than the sorrow and despair that currently filled me.

The sight of the scowling cowboy in front of me didn't register as real. I thought I was in New York State. Yet there he stood, jeans, a flannel shirt, and a Stetson sitting on top of his head.

Maybe I really had lost my mind after all.

He grumbled something under his breath and then reached across me, unfastening my safety belt, and suddenly, I was in his arms as he pulled me from the car.

Most women would probably start screaming at this point. I was fighting the urge to lay my head on his chest and start crying.

Was it so wrong to need someone else to carry the burden, even if it was just for a moment?

He carried me over to a truck that was parked a little way in front of my car, dropped the tailgate, and gently sat me down on it.

When he pulled off his hat and bobbed down to look me in the eye, his expression confused me. He was either furious with me or extremely concerned. It was a strange mix that I'd never seen on anyone's face before.

"You with me, sweetheart?"

My eyes took in his face, his dirty-blond hair, and the beard that only made his chiseled jaw look like it was begging to be touched. I should probably answer his question, but I found myself mesmerized by his stormy blue eyes and the way they were pinched in concern in the middle. It had been too long since I'd seen that expression on anyone's face. At least when it came to me.

"Val. Here," he suddenly barked, and I flinched.

I couldn't help it. It was a natural reaction for me now. One I doubted I'd ever be free of.

When did I become this person?

He raised his hands in surrender as his gaze moved across my face. I'd usually duck my head now, turn away, and try to hide the fading bruises, but there was something about this man that strangely made me feel safe.

Something wet nudged against my hand, and I blinked in surprise and glanced down. A dog shuffled closer to me, staring up at me with big brown eyes before laying its head in my lap. My fingers brushed through the soft brown and white hair on its head, and I felt the tightness in my chest loosen enough for me to take a deep breath.

"Good girl, Val," he grumbled. "I need you to tell me you're back with me so I can put out the fire."

My head snapped up. Fire?

And then I saw it behind him, the black smoke that poured out from under the hood of my car.

"No! Everything I have is in that car."

"I got it." He stepped back, looking at me with concern. "Stay there."

I nodded numbly. Those tears I'd wanted to hold back finally broke free.

He swore softly when he saw them and then reached into the bed of the truck and pulled out a small fire extinguisher. I watched as he jogged back over to my car, popped the hood, and then hit it with a blast from the extinguisher.

I was actually surprised when the smoke stopped. It would be just my luck for the whole thing to explode and take everything I had with it. It had been foolish to think that beat up old thing could have been my escape route, anyway. But it was one more thing that I was clinging to from my past. A reminder that I'd once had the freedom to do whatever I wanted, and I could get back to that if I was just brave enough to try.

The cowboy reached inside the hood and then swore as he burned his fingers. He quickly pulled off his flannel shirt, revealing a white undershirt and more muscles than I knew could possibly exist on a man. I tried not to drool as he wrapped it around his hand and started to do something with the engine.

It was impossible not to stare as he walked back to me. I was even embarrassingly aware that my mouth was hanging open as I did.

"I've disconnected the battery, which seemed to be the problem, but that car isn't going anywhere," he said when he reached me.

My teeth clicked together as I snapped my mouth shut. Now was the time to respond, but I was starting to think I'd forgotten how to form words.

"And for the future, when your car sets on fire, you're supposed to get out of it."

That strange mixed expression of annoyance and concern was back.

"Sorry," I muttered.

"Don't be sorry. Be safe."

I nodded numbly. That was actually pretty sound advice.

"So...what's the plan?" he asked.

I looked back at the completely trashed car and then around me at nothing but open fields, and my heart sank. I had absolutely no idea. I was out of money, without transportation, and had nowhere to go even if I had some. I'd basically just thrown what I could salvage of my life into the back of the car and drove with no destination in mind. I didn't even have a phone, not that I had anyone to call.

"I don't know," I admitted.

This would have been the moment to start crying. The point when I realized I was completely out of options apart from the one thing I never wanted to do—go back. Instead, I took a deep breath and built up the walls inside me. Tears wouldn't get me through this. I needed options.

"Okay, well, you got a place to go? Someone you can call?"

I shook my head and then focused back on the man in front of me. "Thank you for helping me." I hopped down off the tailgate of his truck and patted the head of his dog. "I shouldn't take up any more of your time."

I had a backpack in the car somewhere. I'd take only the important stuff, walk to the nearest town, and see if I could find a job. Anything. Maybe if I pushed the car off to the side of the road, I could sleep in it tonight. Or if there was someplace nearby I could push it to and leave it parked, I might get a couple of weeks out of it. I wasn't above sleeping in my car until I could get my feet under me.

I walked back to the car, but then his hand on my arm stopped me.

"Wait. I can't leave you here without knowing you're going to be safe."

"I'll figure something out. It's okay." I gave him the best smile I could summon, but I could tell he wasn't fooled.

I slipped from his grip and headed back to the car. I could do this. I'd gotten this far, and I wasn't turning back now.

I heard him swear softly behind me before he jogged to catch me up. "Will you just wait a second?"

I turned and looked at him expectantly. I shouldn't be annoyed. He was only being kind. Kindness might be something I wasn't all that familiar with anymore, but that didn't mean I had to be rude to him.

"Look, you're obviously in trouble. And if I had to guess, you're not exactly in a position to get that car fixed. How bad is it?"

Part of me wanted to tell him it wasn't his problem. To say something so scathing that he'd wash his hands of me and leave me at the side of the road. But there was just something about him. I should have been scared of this enormous man, but he'd been nothing but gentle with me. He'd even called his dog over to me when he could see that I was spiraling. Something about him made me think that he'd understand.

So, instead of running, instead of acting like a crazy person to get him to leave, I sighed. The fight leached out of me, and I looked at the stranger in front of me, desperately needing to think that he could be someone I could trust.

Trust.

That had come so easily to me before.

I ignored the pinch in my heart and the ache of my bruises, and I made a decision.

"I'll be fine. I'm heading into town to find a job, and I'll get back on my feet. The car can wait. I don't have the money to fix it right now, but I'll figure it out. That's what you do, right? You figure it out and just get on with it."

He squinted in annoyance. It might have been the truth, but it clearly wasn't the truth he wanted.

I wasn't an idiot. I knew what he was really asking me. He wanted to know why I had bruises on my face, why I couldn't quite stand completely straight. The thing was, I didn't know why he'd care.

The me from before would have just told him the truth. Any truth he wanted to hear. Because that's what you did, right? People were concerned because they wanted to help. They weren't trying to assess your vulnerabilities so they could manipulate them in whatever way they needed for their own benefit.

I'd never seen the potential for bad in people. I'd always believed that, deep down, everyone was at least decent.

And that was the thing he'd taken from me that I hated him the most for.

So I sank down deep inside myself, and I pulled the Reece I used to be back to the surface, and I smiled.

I knew it didn't reach my eyes. Not yet, at least. But I was working on it, and even if I had to pretend for a little while, I'd find that version of myself again one day.

"No," he growled, squinting at me as his massive hands landed on his waist.

Holy crap, this man might be part giant or something. I was getting a crick in my neck just from staring up at him and trying to hold this look of fake confidence on my face.

"No?"

He sighed, and I could have sworn I heard him swear under his breath. Honestly, the fact that he was so annoyed by either me or his own concern for me was getting amusing.

"No, you don't just figure it out. I'm not leaving you on the side of the road with no clue about where you're going and how you're going to get there." He glared at me again, and then he pulled his cell out of his pocket. With a sigh of annoyance, he did something on the screen and then held it to his ear. "Dex, I need you on the road out to the ranch...

No, we're not playing paintball. I need you to come and pick up a car and fix it... Just do it."

He abruptly hung up on whoever Dex was and shoved the phone back in his pocket. "Idiot," he grumbled.

"Erm, while I appreciate all this, I don't have the money to fix my car. It's a piece of junk, anyway. It's probably time for it to go to the scrap heap in the sky."

He looked at me like I was insane, and for a second, I shuffled awkwardly on the spot. This was honestly the strangest situation I'd ever found myself in, and this was coming from the girl who once got her foot stuck in the automatic doors at Target and had to be cut free by firemen.

"I own the ranch up the road. I need some help."

I stared at him and watched as his scowl grew deeper. "Is that a job offer?" I asked.

Obviously, it was, even if it had been done in the strangest way, but I was wondering just how deep this guy's scowl could get.

"Yes. Or you can stay here and die on the side of the road."

"That sounds awfully like a threat," I pointed out.

I wasn't dumb. I could see this guy was trying to help me out, even if it seemed like it wasn't something he was all that used to.

"Considering you were about to set yourself on fire, it's more of an observation."

"I would have gotten out eventually!" I protested.

He raised a single eyebrow in question but, thankfully, didn't say a thing. I wasn't so sure that was the truth, either.

"What's the job?" I asked instead.

"Working on the ranch."

"I might not be very good at that," I said nervously.

My expertise was actually marketing, with a bit of event

planning. There was no way my body would handle manual labor. The will might be there, but my noodle-like arms would definitely fail.

"I've no doubt you'll be terrible." The corner of his lips ticked up in a smirk, and it lit a fire in me.

"Well, that doesn't make you sound like a very good employer or business owner."

"We'll make a perfect pair, then." He turned around and started heading back to his truck.

This was it. A turning point in the downward slide that had become my life. I could take a chance with this guy I didn't know and who could be a serial killer rapist, or I could stand here on the side of the road with no plan, no money, and no one else in the world who gave a crap.

He opened up the passenger side door to the truck and looked at me expectantly.

"What's the worst that can happen?" I mumbled and jogged to the truck.

He shook his head, almost like he was disappointed in me. Hell, I was pretty disappointed in myself, too. The last person I'd trusted was the reason I was in this entire mess, and I hadn't met him on the side of the road.

"It's Reece, by the way," I said as he watched me climb in and clip the seat belt in place. "My name," I clarified.

He nodded. "Booker."

Booker slammed the door and then disappeared. I'd expected him to climb in the driver's side, and when he didn't, I twisted in my seat to see if he was prepping a machete or something for me out of sight. Instead, I found him pulling the bags out of the back of my car and moving them into the back of his truck.

I probably should have thought of that.

I watched as he ruffled the hair on his dog's head and

then leaned forward and softly bumped his forehead into hers. It was one of those sweet moments you weren't supposed to see but told you so much about a person.

When he looked up and saw me watching him through the window, his scowl was firmly back in place. It wasn't fooling me now. I'd had a peek at the soft, fluffy center this guy was trying to hide, and it intrigued me.

"So, just to clarify, murder isn't on the cards, then?" I asked as he climbed into the driver's seat and started the engine.

He looked at me for a moment like he was considering it, but then that smirk was back. "Nah, too much mess to clean up."

CHAPTER TWO

BOOKER

I peered into my living room at the woman sitting on my couch looking like a frightened little bird, even if she was trying to pretend like she had all the answers to the world's problems.

Hiding in the kitchen wasn't exactly the best idea, but then inviting her back to the ranch and telling her I'd give her a job wasn't something I'd ever do, either.

Hell, I had the ranch because I'd take horses over people any day.

But as soon as I'd looked through the car window and seen her bruised and breaking down inside, I knew she needed help.

And for some reason, I knew I was the one who would give it to her.

Which was completely against my nature.

Now, she was sitting in my living room looking so lost, and I had absolutely no idea what to do apart from lecturing her about the dangers of getting into a car with a man she didn't know, even if that man had been me.

I pulled my cell out of my pocket and glared at it.

Maybe Delaney could help. She was a girl. She knew how to talk girl. She might even have a job for Reece.

My eyes moved back to the woman in question as I leaned back to get a view of her through the open door. The bruises on her face were a pretty clear sign that she was in some kind of trouble. From the way she favored her side, I'd say her injuries extended further than her face as well.

I couldn't send her to Trace and Delaney's doorstep if that trouble was going to follow her there.

Which meant that Reece was my problem, at least for now.

"Do you need any help in there?" she called out from the living room, sounding nervous.

She probably thought I was preparing some kind of poison for her while I was lurking out here. It would at least be the first sensible thought she'd had since I'd met her if it was.

"No."

I winced at the gruffness of my voice. Damn it. This was a traumatized woman. I could at least try to be passably nice at first.

"No, *thank you*," I stressed, trying not to grit my teeth as I did.

"Aww, did that hurt, big bear?" she asked, her voice sounding like it was directly behind me, and I was embarrassed at just how much it made me jump.

So, because I was trying to be nice, I turned around and just glared at her rather than saying what I really wanted to say.

I nodded to the kitchen table. "Sit."

She moved without question and then sat down and watched to see what I'd do next.

I should have left her in the dark living room because

sitting on that chair in front of the window, her long blond hair glistened in the sun as she watched me curiously with those warm chocolate eyes, I could feel my heart thump in my chest.

I grabbed the coffee I'd been procrastinating over and moved to the other side of the table, hoping the wooden furniture would block the view of all the curves her sweater did absolutely nothing to hide.

Unfortunately for me, the vision of her was already burned into my memory, and I was feeling like a creep for even having looked.

"So," she said after an uncomfortably long pause. "What exactly is this job that you want me to do? How much does it pay, and for how long do you expect it to last?"

I could feel my lips twitching in amusement as she tried not to squirm in her seat and project the picture of a confident job prospect instead.

This was the point where I was supposed to answer her. The thing was, I didn't want to talk about that. I wanted to know who the hell had done that to her face and demand that she tell me where I could find them.

So I did my usual and reverted to my usual attitude instead.

"Come on." I lurched out of my seat and headed to the back door, leaving the coffee untouched on the table.

It was cold anyway. I'd spent far too long hiding in the kitchen for it to be worth drinking now.

Val jumped out of her bed and trotted to my side like she always did.

"Erm, okay." She followed a few steps behind me as I jogged down the back porch steps and headed to the old bunkhouse.

"This used to be where the ranch hands bunked back in

the day," I told her as I opened the door and then stepped to the side to let her go past.

Reece's eyes widened in alarm at the dark interior, and she hesitated.

Finally, the woman was making a sensible decision for the first time today and questioning her own safety.

I reached around the doorframe and switched on the lights, illuminating the interior. Reece's eyes widened in surprise as she cautiously took another step closer.

"We had it changed into a cottage last year. The ranch hands were happy to get an updated bunkhouse further back on the property, away from the main house. Don't feel like they're being watched over all the time then," I added, so she'd at least know that she'd be safe out here even if she was on her own.

Reece smiled and walked inside, looking around at the cozy little living room and kitchenette that had been added.

The cottage was a single-story structure, but we'd been able to squeeze in a bedroom on either side of the living room and a small bathroom. It was the only finished one on the property at the moment. The plans for building the others were moving slowly but surely, but they wouldn't be habitable for a while.

"This is for me?" she asked as she peered through the bathroom door, her eyes wide in surprise.

"It's the best I can offer. I'm sure you can make do for now."

When she turned to look at me again, there were tears pouring down her face, and I froze.

Shit.

Val moved to Reece's side, sat down, and leaned against her leg like she did whenever someone was upset. I could have sworn the dog was staring at me accusingly.

Was this too much? I didn't think she'd want to stay in the house with me. It felt a bit too much like I was trying to say there were strings attached to the help I was offering.

There definitely weren't.

I didn't even know why I'd offered. I liked my space. My own company, if you didn't count Val. But she'd looked so lost and broken sitting in that car at the side of the road, and I wasn't about to just abandon her out there when she was so obviously in trouble.

"This is..."

I braced myself for the criticism. For that thing people do when they try to manipulate you into giving more than you're prepared to do.

"This is the nicest thing anyone has ever done for me." She sniffled and then moved toward me.

I saw it coming. It was hard not to when she was walking across the room with her arms opened wide.

A hug.

One of those human gestures that was completely unnecessary for anyone over the age of twelve. Or four if you grew up in the house I did, and even then, it only ever came from the nanny.

Reece wrapped her arms around me as much as she could and squeezed. I heard the hitch of her breath, and I knew it had hurt her. For some reason, that was what made me move. I might have just awkwardly patted her on the back, but it was the warmest gesture I'd ever made for a stranger.

"It's nothing," I said quickly, gently taking her arms and unwrapping them from me, not wanting to hurt her anymore.

I awkwardly cleared my throat and then stepped back out of the door. Val looked at Reece and then followed me.

"I'll leave you to get settled in. We can look around the ranch tomorrow and talk about the job." I kept backing up as she watched me awkwardly. I should have remembered the low deck we'd put on the front of the cottage in place of a porch and stumbled down the small step instead. "I'll get your bags from the truck."

I turned and strode away, my hands rubbing against my arms like I could erase her touch if I tried hard enough.

This was going to be an issue.

She was going to be an issue.

This was just my luck. You try to do a nice thing, and you end up with someone wanting to act like a human being around you. It would have been easier to pick up a stray dog from the side of the road. I should have known better than to rescue some damsel in distress.

CHAPTER THREE

REECE

It felt like someone had stretched out my muscles to the point where they'd all recoiled and then turned to stone.

I swung my feet over the side of the bed and forced myself to sit up.

"Ohhh, that's not good," I grumbled as the pain lanced through my side.

It had been two weeks since the incident that had left me with these bruises. Watching them slowly fade was the only thing that kept me going while I was planning my exit. I'd managed to get to a clinic before leaving my old life behind, and knowing I'd only bruised my ribs had been a relief I hadn't been expecting. I knew I couldn't leave until I'd been checked out. I didn't want to risk being registered in the system anywhere that could help him trace my location.

The system.

What was I? Some kind of spy?

I looked around the cute little bedroom again in

wonder. Turning up here was the best thing that had happened to me in a long time. I might be okay with being murdered in my sleep if this was where it happened.

Getting into the car with Booker had been possibly the stupidest and yet the best thing I'd ever done. Lying low on the ranch to recover and build up some savings was exactly what I needed. But I could also have easily ended up in the basement, tied up, and making friends with the rats.

Desperation made people do stupid things, and I needed to make sure I never put myself in a situation like that again.

I stood up with a wince and headed into the bathroom. This place was clearly set up as some kind of holiday cottage, and I was surprised that Booker would be happy to have something like that so close to his own house. He didn't come across as the most social person in the world, but there was clearly a big heart hiding underneath all that barbed wire he liked to pretend was there.

Hugging him might have been a mistake. I chuckled at the memory of the Booker-shaped hole he'd nearly left in the wall. The poor guy couldn't get away from me fast enough.

I turned on the shower to let the water heat while I brushed my teeth, all the while staring at my face in the mirror. The black eye was changing to that horrible green color, but at least that meant it was healing.

I rushed through the shower. Washing my hair was getting easier, but I never wanted to experience agony like that again, and I made that vow right here and now.

Never again.

I would never let myself get in a situation with a man where I was too blind to see the signs. Where I was too isolated to feel like I had anyone who could protect me. Where I didn't have some kind of escape route.

My eyes locked onto my reflection as I examined the job I'd done with the few makeup supplies I had. It wasn't good. I looked like a woman with a black eye who'd tried—and mostly failed—to cover it up. Then I sighed. This was as good as it was going to get. At least it was fading now and, hopefully, wouldn't be a problem for much longer.

My stomach grumbled as I quickly pulled on some jeans and a shirt. I didn't really have any work clothes, not that I had any idea what work I'd be doing, so I slipped on my sneakers just as there was a loud knock on the door.

I pulled it open to find Booker scowling on the other side. He looked down at his watch as if I was supposed to know what that meant.

When I said nothing, he sighed.

"What are you still doing here?"

"Erm, you said I could have a job and stay in the cottage." I couldn't lose this place already, and I was ready to beg for that job if that was what it took.

He sighed again. "It's already nine a.m. Why are you not in my kitchen for breakfast?"

My back snapped straight, and I immediately regretted it as a flash of pain surged from my ribs, taking my breath away. Booker must have noticed because his scowl deepened before he turned and stormed back to the house.

I swore softly and hurried after him. I should have realized that this was my job. Even if it wasn't, it was the least I could do, considering he'd essentially pulled me out of a burning car.

Damn. Booker was literally my hero, and I couldn't remember if I'd actually thanked him yet.

I hurried through the back door and then came to a stop so suddenly my sneakers squeaked on the floor.

The kitchen table was set and laid out with enough food for a whole family. There was a pot of coffee and a jug of orange juice. My mouth was already watering from the delicious smell of bacon floating my way.

"Sit," Booker said as he pulled out a chair.

I scurried into it, my eyes fixed on the food like I was afraid it would disappear if I looked away. My stomach grumbled embarrassingly, and Booker's gaze dropped to my abdomen before returning to my face.

Booker pushed a tube of cream toward me, and I looked at it curiously. Arnica.

"I'll make you an appointment with the doc in the next town over for this afternoon," Booker said, like it was already a done deal.

"No need." His head snapped up, and I could tell he was getting ready to fight me on this. It was kind of endearing. I quickly added, "I went to the clinic last week. I'm healing nicely, and there's nothing to do but ride it out."

This was a conversation I didn't want to have. Judging from Booker's face, he didn't either. Or rather, he hated it was even a conversation to begin with.

"Thank you for this," I said, taking the tube of arnica and sliding it a little closer to me.

I didn't really need it at this stage, but I could see that it made Booker feel better, and it didn't cost me anything to do this for him.

"When did you last eat?" he asked a little less angrily as he took his own seat.

I shrugged, even though I actually did know when it was. I just didn't want to admit to him that I was a grown woman who'd gone more than a day without eating. I didn't want to continue to be this charity case he needed to save. I wanted to get back to the person I used to be, and part of that would happen by taking control of my life again.

Booker leaned back in his seat and crossed his arms across his chest like he was getting ready to wait me out. Thankfully, Val chose that moment to drop her head on his leg and whine until he relented and gave her a sausage link, which she took to her basket.

"She's a good dog," I murmured, watching her fondly. "What breed is she?"

Yes, it was a pathetic attempt to change the subject, but I wasn't ready to tell Booker my sad stories. I wanted to just be me for a moment. That shouldn't be too much to ask for.

"Australian Shepherd," he muttered, reaching for the coffeepot and holding it up as he looked at me in question. I nodded as he gestured to the plates of food on the table. "Eat."

I was so hungry I could feel that pinch in my stomach that I'd been able to ignore, thanks to the pain in my side. I only put two pieces of bacon on my plate and some scrambled eggs. There was an awkward part of me that didn't want Booker to think I was using him. I wanted to prove to him that taking me in wasn't a mistake.

Booker slammed the coffeepot down with more force than necessary, and I peered up from my plate in concern.

"Eat properly," he growled, nudging a plate closer to me.

It was exactly what we needed for the awkward tension to snap, and I heaped the food on my plate, tucking in with a happy hum.

When I glanced up at him between mouthfuls, I saw the slight smile on his face and felt a little more of the tension drain out of me. Booker's attitude would probably annoy some people, but I appreciated him not treating me like I was some kind of broken bird.

"This is the smallest barn on the property," Booker said as we walked through the sliding doors, which were already open. "It's closed up at night or if the weather turns."

I wandered inside, looking around with interest. Should I confess that I'd never been in a barn before, and the only stables I'd ever seen had been in movies?

This place was impressively clean, and even though there was the smell of the ranch in the air, it was nowhere near what I'd expected it to be.

Booker wandered down the open central walkway with Val on his heels. I could almost see the tension leaking out of his body as we walked into what was clearly his favorite place.

"Are there other barns, then?" I asked.

"Yes. There are two more, one we're renovating at the moment. This one will be your concern, though."

I nodded, trying to look like I knew what I was doing.

"This is where the horses come when they first arrive."

I looked into the nearest stable only to find it empty but lined with clean sawdust on the ground. In fact, from the sound of it, there weren't any animals in the barn right now.

"Are the horses in the fields already?" I asked, hoping that didn't sound like a stupid question.

"Yes. But this barn is empty because we haven't had any new arrivals for a while. They stay here to be quarantined and heal before they mix in with the rest. There's also a foaling stable set up here, not that it gets much use."

That made sense. I guess.

"Why do they all need to heal?"

"I take some in on a private contract basis for training. People send problem horses to me that haven't been trained properly or are too reactive," Booker said, looking inside one of the empty stalls and then nodding in satisfaction at whatever he saw there. "Most of the horses that come to the ranch, though, come from kill pens. They're in bad shape when they get here."

My mouth dropped open in horror. "Kill pens?" I whispered.

Booker apparently rescued horses as well as broken women on the side of the road. He might actually be some kind of saint.

He shrugged like it was no big deal, and I could see that he was the kind of person that thought it wasn't.

He also genuinely looked uncomfortable to be receiving any kind of praise, so I ducked down and scratched Val behind the ears. I swear she smiled as she looked up at me with her tongue hanging out of her mouth. Her coat was so soft that I had to resist the urge to lie down on the floor just to snuggle with her.

"Your job is to keep this place clean and ready to go," Booker said, turning back to the doors and heading back outside. Apparently, we were done with the part of the conversation about how impressive Booker was.

"Okay, I can do that."

Probably.

"I'll give you a list of what needs doing every day, and I can be around for the first couple of days to show you the ropes. We have a new horse arriving tomorrow, so it's good timing."

Hopefully, I looked like I was confident I could do this.

"Grab your stuff," Booker called out as he walked out into the sunshine. "We're going into town."

I found myself jogging to catch up with him again and fighting the urge to swear with every step I took. Val ran alongside me, looking up at me with concern.

"What stuff?"

Booker was already at the door to his truck, squinting at me from under the brim of his hat. I was literally five steps behind him. He couldn't be annoyed with me already.

"Your girl shit," he said, and then when I didn't move from sheer confusion, he huffed, "You know, like your bag or whatever you carry around with you."

"Ooooo-kay."

Rather than argue, I did what he said. It seemed like the easiest option in this fever dream of reality I'd found myself in.

It took me less than a minute to find my bag and get back to the car, but Booker was still standing at the door, watching me impatiently. It was pretty easy to see that this was his default setting when it came to other people. Rather than taking it personally, I pasted a huge smile on my face and climbed into the truck when he opened the door for me.

I was going with the tactic my mother had always told me. I'd wear this big bear of a man down with kindness, and then, to repay him for everything he'd done for me, I'd show him that having people around you wasn't so bad after all.

Maybe I'd be able to find myself along the way. The version of me that had slowly faded away over the past couple of years and the version I was so desperate to have back.

As Booker threw the truck into drive and set off down the gravel driveway, I wrapped an arm around Val, who'd squeezed between us, and threaded my fingers through her soft fur as she snuggled against me.

I could do this.

I could rebuild a life that I wanted. A life worth living, and it would all be possible because the man sitting beside me had the kindness to stop when he saw a stranger stranded on the side of the road.

CHAPTER FOUR

BOOKER

My hands tightened on the steering wheel to the point where the leather creaked beneath them. I couldn't stop sneaking glances at Reece out of the corner of my eye as I drove us into town. She was staring out the window, her fingers lazily threading through Val's fur, and for the first time in my life I was jealous of a damn dog.

And that didn't make me feel good.

Not because I wished I was a dog, but because I wanted to feel her fingers lazily drifting across my skin, and that made me a huge goddamn creep.

I wasn't that guy.

But there was something about her.

I could see the pain, the broken parts of her she was desperately trying to hide. But I could also see her sheer determination to get through it, no matter what. And that was the part of Reece that drew me in. She was strong, even if she didn't feel like it right now. She was fighting in her own way, with that bright smile that didn't quite reach her eyes and would usually have annoyed the hell out of me.

"The ranch hands make $2000 a month with accommodation," I said, desperate to find something to take my mind off my dick. "The days can be long, but the new horses will be coming in slowly so you can work up to a full day."

I didn't really want her to work at all. I was needed out on the trails this week to make sure they were all still passable, but I wasn't about to let Reece do any heavy lifting when she was clearly in pain. Despite what she said, I wasn't convinced that she didn't have a couple of broken ribs. Whoever had done it to her and been thorough, and that thought alone made my blood boil.

"That's...Wow, are you sure?"

"Yes, that's definitely what I pay them."

"That's not what I meant!" She stopped when she saw the corner of my mouth tick up in amusement. "Oh, fine. Be obtuse about it."

"Obtuse?"

She stuck out her tongue, and I rolled my eyes.

"I think you should cut the pay down to match my decreased hours," she said reasonably.

"No."

"No?"

"Agreed." I was purposely aggravating her now, but the little wrinkle in her nose that she got when she was annoyed verged on adorable.

"I don't know what to say," she muttered.

I didn't respond, and we drove the rest of the way into town in silence. I knew what it was like to be in a situation you didn't see a way out of. I also knew what it was like for someone to step up and give you a solution. My grandfather had done it for me when I inherited the ranch and enough money that I'd never have to worry about how to run it. I swore there and then that I'd work to pay it forward in any way I could, and that was why the ranch was changing into what it was.

I pulled the truck into a spot near the grocery store, and we both climbed out. I told Val she needed to stay in the back of the truck and then gave her some fuss to take the sting out of it. She'd probably nap the entire time, but that didn't mean I wouldn't feel bad for leaving her behind. We went everywhere together, but she wasn't allowed inside the store.

"Will she be okay in there?" Reece asked, looking back at Val sadly, who'd already laid down on the blanket I kept in the flatbed for her.

"She's already asleep."

"She won't jump out and run away?"

"No."

Reece pouted for a second, but then her attention was fully on the town as we walked to the store. "Wow, this place is so pretty."

I guess it was. Growing up around here probably meant I didn't appreciate Willowbrook as much as I should. For a small town with little tourist traffic, it was clean, busy, and surviving from the local community alone. For now. My brother and his fiancé were on a mission to change that, though. They had big plans to bring in the tourists and get the town's economy booming.

It needed it. Because as pretty as Willowbrook might have been, the signs were showing that we were slipping in the wrong direction. Starting with the fact that the local doctor had retired, and no one had taken up the practice. The dark windows concerned more than just me, but the townspeople seemed in denial, if not completely oblivious, to what it could mean.

I held open the door to the grocery store, and Reece

stepped inside. I watched as she tensed, looking around at her surroundings as she made sure she knew the layout and who was inside.

She walked straight past the carts, so I grabbed one. I wasn't here to be her damn bag boy.

Reece wandered the aisles of the grocery store, every so often glancing over her shoulder at me as if to check I was still there. By the time we'd made it to the end of the third aisle, there wasn't a single thing in the cart, and I'd had enough.

"What is wrong with you?" I growled.

She came to an abrupt halt and looked at me with wide eyes.

I nodded at the empty cart. "Why is this empty?"

Reece looked confused for a moment. "I don't know. Why are you following me and not putting anything in it?"

She sounded annoyed, and I'd have smiled at the glimpse of fire inside her if I wasn't so annoyed right now.

"I'm not shopping for you. I don't know what you like. You need to do it yourself."

"Shopping for me?"

"Why else would we be here?"

"Because you told me I had to come." She looked confused again, and I cast my mind back to earlier. Surely she knew we were here because she had nothing to eat in the cottage.

"You don't have any food, and I'm not watching you starve." I grabbed her hand and pulled her back to the first aisle before I turned her to face what was offered. "Shop," I said, nudging her in the direction she needed to go.

Reece looked at me with a bemused look on her face, pulling her bag tighter to her side, and then slowly walked down the aisle, actually looking at the shelves this time.

When we made it to the end, and she still hadn't put anything in the cart, I was ready to shake her.

"What's happening now?" I asked through gritted teeth as I stopped the cart and refused to go any further.

There was barely any meat on the woman, and if I had to sit her down for every meal and watch her eat, I'd do it.

"I just need bread, peanut butter, and maybe—"

"No."

"No? Is that your favorite word or something?"

"No." The corner of my mouth ticked up again, and now I was ready to shake myself. "You need proper food."

Reece shuffled awkwardly. "I don't really have much. I can survive for a while with just—"

"No."

When her eyes flicked up to me, I could have sworn she was getting ready to punch me. It lit a fire in me in response that I didn't want to acknowledge.

"I'm paying," I told her. "Think of it as an advance."

Reece opened her mouth to argue, but then it slowly closed before she said a word. She knew she needed this, and I could see how hard it was for her to accept it. Instead of waiting for her to say something, I headed back to the beginning of the aisle again. This had better be the last time today because people were already looking at us funny.

Reece followed quietly, and then she finally shopped. Every time she picked something up, checked the price, and then put it back on the shelf, I grabbed it and put it in the cart while she wasn't looking.

She didn't notice until we'd made it to the end of the aisle, and when she went to thank me, Marie from the bakery stepped into view.

"Booker! Why don't you introduce me to your lovely friend," she said warmly.

My presence in the grocery store with an unknown woman would be all over town in less than an hour. The gossip would go wild with this.

"Hi! I'm Reece Graham," Reece said, stepping forward to shake her hand.

It probably wasn't a good sign that this was the first time I'd learned Reece's last name.

"It's a pleasure to meet you, dear. That's a nasty bruise on your face."

Oh hell, I really hadn't thought this through.

"Erm, yes," Reece said awkwardly, her fingers coming to her eye as if to remind herself it was there. "Hopefully, the last one I get."

I hated the sight of that thing on her face. It made me want to punch something every time I saw it. It was definitely the last one Reece would ever get because as soon as I found out the name of the guy who'd given it to her, I was breaking both his arms. And there was no doubt in my mind this had happened at the hands of some guy.

Marie looked at me, her head cocking to the side as she thought. The scowl on my face actually made the strange woman smile. "Well, by the looks of it, Booker is going to make sure of that. Now, my name is Marie, and I run the bakery in town. Make sure you stop by soon, and we'll have some cake and a chat."

Reece thanked her, and then they hugged before Marie walked away. What was with this girl and hugging random strangers?

The rest of the time we spent in the store was a test of my sanity and patience—of which I had none.

Every person we came across stopped and introduced themselves to Reece, and she had a standing invitation to four people's houses, the bakery, and apparently a discount at the beauty salon waiting for her.

Every. Single. Person.

I was pretty sure I was about to crack a molar with how hard I was grinding my teeth. The whole while, I'd pushed the cart silently behind her, praying that the world would end.

When we finally approached the register, Reece turned to me with a smile. It was the first genuine smile I'd seen on her face, and it made her breathtakingly beautiful. A simple trip to the grocery store shouldn't be able to have this effect on a person.

"If you grumble any louder, people are going to talk," she quipped.

"You've never been to a small town before, have you?" I asked, and she frowned in confusion. "They're already talking. They never stop talking."

She grinned again, and I rolled my eyes. This couldn't be a normal response.

"I think I like it here."

That simple statement shouldn't have made me as happy as it did, so I grumbled in annoyance just to balance it out in case this happy shit was catching.

"Do you know if they have any magazines?" Reece asked, looking around. "I was hoping to get something for the cottage."

I could have cursed then. She didn't have a TV. In fact, the cottage was lacking in most things electronic because I hadn't had time to set it up. There wasn't even a coffee pot. Damn.

"I know a place," I said, internally cursing myself for forgetting something as simple as that.

I had enough stuff in my kitchen to stock her up with

the pans and stuff that she'd need, but I'd need to order her a coffee pot and some other things. Reece wouldn't like it, but the cottage needed it, anyway. Maybe I could just put it in the kitchen without her noticing.

When Reece squinted at me in suspicion, I almost smiled. At least she had some vaguely normal reactions. So I did what any other normal person would do, and I turned my back to her and loaded the groceries onto the register.

It could be a surprise. She'd probably like it. And I refused to acknowledge how happy that made me.

CHAPTER FIVE

REECE

Booker loaded the groceries into the back of his truck, then waved me to follow him down the sidewalk. I took a moment to marvel that he wasn't even slightly concerned someone would steal them and then followed with one last look back at Val, who had only cracked open one eye and then immediately gone back to sleep.

Where were we going?

I'd tried not to listen to how much the groceries came to. The guilt over the fact that this was one more thing Booker had to do for me was nearly more than I could take.

I had to admit though, knowing that the cottage was set up for me to look after myself was helping. Especially with how much being out in public was freaking me out.

Stepping into the grocery store had been tough. The first person I saw commenting on the bruise on my face was nearly enough to floor me. But I'd pushed through. I kept the smile on my face and forced myself to act like I used to. Maybe if I tried hard enough, *one day* it would feel real.

And it had.

By the time we got to the register, the warmth I'd found in every person I'd met was starting to sink in. Everyone had been nothing but nice to me. The comments on my bruise were genuine concern. I hadn't experienced anything like this before, and the way that Booker had been so ready to help me was making more sense. This was just how people seemed to be around here.

"Where are we going?" I asked, quickening my steps to catch up with Booker and hoping it didn't look like I was running after him.

Why were his legs so unreasonably long? Who walked this fast?

"We're going around the corner," Booker said, and I mimed throttling him from behind.

This was past the point of cute now.

Booker came to a stop and then looked at me from under the brim of his cowboy hat as he hooked his thumbs in the pockets of his jeans.

He had to know what he was doing.

Then he nodded to the door beside him, and I looked up at the sign. Books and Beans.

My heart thumped in my chest, and a squeal built inside me that I tried to swallow down.

"A bookshop!"

Booker looked at me warily, and when I took a step toward the door, I swear I saw him flinch.

"What is wrong with you?" I laughed.

"I thought you were going to hug me," he complained, then he grabbed the door handle and held the door open for me.

"We can save the hugs for later," I told him, patting his arm as I squeezed.

Holy biceps!

I should have been scared of Booker. He wasn't exactly the most open person in the world. In fact, most people would probably say he was an ass. But this was a guy who helped when he saw I needed someone. He rescued horses no one else wanted and rehabilitated them.

And the most important thing was that he was absolutely nothing like my ex.

That beautiful bookshop smell hit me as I walked through the doors, and I felt actual tears in my eyes. The coffee machine bubbled to life with the sound of milk being steamed.

"This is amazing!" I whispered as I took in the cozy coffee shop vibes with the neat lines of bookshelves at the back. "Can I..."

"Knock yourself out." Booker laughed at the look on my face, and my eyes widened in awe. An actual goddamn laugh. "How do you want your coffee?" he asked.

"I'll take a caramel latte, please?" I asked politely, making sure that I kept a tally in my head of everything that Booker spent. I wouldn't let him try to wave this off as nothing, which I had a feeling he would.

I headed to the romance section and got lost among the spines of second chances and love at first sight. I'd stood there for far too long looking between the books I held in each hand when I felt a presence behind me.

"What are you doing?" Booker growled, and I jumped about a foot in the air with a squeal.

"You scared the bejeebers out of me!" I swore, and the corner of his mouth ticked up again in that way I was starting to crave.

"Booky bear!" someone gasped behind us. "Are you harassing that poor woman?"

"Oh lord, what did I do to deserve this?" Booker

muttered before he turned to look at the pink-haired woman standing and grinning behind him. "Blake."

"Booky bear!" she cheered and then threw her arms around him. "I didn't know you came into bookshops," she whispered, looking from side to side dramatically like she was in on some kind of secret.

I looked around Booker to get a better glimpse at the woman I was pretty sure was destined to be my friend. He practically squirmed with discomfort.

"Ooooo, new friend!" she squealed.

"I'll be with the coffee," Booker growled, taking the books from my hands and then storming back to the table he'd found.

"Hi, I'm Reece."

"Blake." She smiled gently and shook my hand. "Booker will look after you," she said.

I frowned, confused, and she shrugged. "Whatever you're running from, whoever did that to you, Booker will make it right."

"It's not really his..."

She hugged me before I could finish. "That doesn't matter. We look after our own around here, and I have a feeling we'll be seeing a lot more of each other."

"Thanks, Blake."

She smiled and then pointed in the direction of Booker, who was sitting down again with a small bag that he put next to my coffee. Of course, he'd bought them both. "I've never seen him out in the wild like this before," Blake told me. "Maybe you can help each other."

"I don't think Booker needs any help. He's the most put-together person I've ever met."

She laughed then. "Not everyone wears their bruises on the outside, Reece."

I really looked at Booker then, but I already knew what she was talking about. Booker was closed off from other people for a reason. His gruff attitude was a defense mechanism he'd used to protect himself, and that was how I'd repay him for pulling me out of that car.

I'd show Booker that he didn't have to be alone anymore.

"You should have a coffee with us," I told her as we moved to the table.

I saw the way Booker tensed as he overheard us and then wilted in resignation.

"That sounds like a perfect idea," she crowed, moving to the counter and the man standing at the register who couldn't take his eyes off her. What should have just been a quick order turned into a whispered conversation, and then she turned back to us with a grin.

I smelled a secret brewing. Hey, I was transitioning to small-town life like a pro.

CHAPTER SIX

BOOKER

Breakfast was strange because I couldn't stop looking at the empty seat in front of me where Reece sat yesterday. The whole point of taking her to the grocery store was so she could cook for herself, and yet part of me wanted her here.

And I didn't know why. It's not like I hadn't had breakfast alone before.

No. I knew why. I just didn't know when I'd become such a freak that I was obsessing over a woman who needed my help.

There was no time to sit inside and avoid the woman in question. Hank was on his way with the new horse, and they'd be here any minute. Reece wouldn't stay inside the cottage when she saw the new horse turn up, given that it would be her job to help with its care.

As if I'd summoned them, I heard the crunch of gravel under tires. Swearing, I abandoned the rest of my coffee and stood with a sigh of resignation. Val's head popped up at the sound, and she peered at me over the edge of her dog bed. I could have sworn she rolled her eyes at me, but it was probably my subconscious trying to make a point.

"Come on, Val. Time to welcome the newcomer."

I stood on the porch with Val at my side as Hank pulled the trailer around and then backed up toward the open barn doors. It was easier on the horses to get them into the biggest stable at the end as quickly as possible. They were already pretty stressed out from the journey and everything they'd been through.

"Morning, boss," Hank called out as he climbed out of the truck. "I don't think this one will be any bother. She got in the trailer as calm as anything."

That wasn't always a good sign. Some horses who'd lost their fight didn't make it. It was like they'd already given up and were just waiting for the end.

"Let's get her out and see what we're working with."

Hank nodded, ducking down to fuss over Val when she ran to his side and then reached into the truck for his hat. The sun glinting off the metal of the horse trailer could be enough to blind you momentarily on a sunny day, and it was never a good idea to take your eyes off an unpredictable horse. Especially not on arrival day.

Hank and I worked together to get the barn set up and ready. How this stage went very much depended on how much the horse cooperated with us. The hope was to get it into the stable, which already had the door open, and ready to close behind it. Worst-case scenario, though, she'd be in the barn until we could calm her down enough to lead her in.

We'd done this enough times now that we could probably do it in our sleep, so when Hank lowered the horse trailer's door down, I wasn't worried.

I peered inside and saw the mare standing calmly at the

end, the halter secured loosely enough that she could move a little if she needed to, but not enough to hurt herself in transit. With her head hanging low, I could already see that Hank was right about her. She didn't even flick an ear as he came in through the side door to get her out.

"She's been through it, this one," Hank said softly as he stroked the mare's nose. "But she's not given up yet. We're gonna show you how beautiful life can be, little one."

Whispering in soft tones, Hank backed the mare down the ramp. I heard a soft gasp behind me I knew had come from Reece. I'd seen enough horses in this state that it didn't shock me anymore. It still had me gritting my teeth and wishing I could get my hands on the previous owner, though. That never left me.

The mare stumbled, and it was hard not to react. If she went down now, I doubted we'd get her back up again.

The poor thing was so emaciated that she looked like a skeleton covered in skin. Patches of her hair were gone, and angry ulcers glistened with infection in the sun. The smell was something you couldn't describe. I shook my head as Hank slowly walked the mare to the stable. Her hooves were so overgrown that they'd curled up on themselves, and I knew every step must have been agony.

"Why would someone do this?" Reece whispered as she came to my side.

"Unfortunately, that's not the worst case I've ever seen," I told her as we followed Hank and the mare at a safe distance.

It was being overly cautious. This poor girl didn't have the strength to fight anymore.

"What do I do?" Reece asked, her voice sounding stronger with determination.

I stole a glimpse of her out of the side of my eye, and I

saw the anger in her eyes. Her hands were balled into fists, and for the first time since I'd caught sight of her, she stood with her back completely straight as if she was prepared to fight the world. I knew she wouldn't have recovered enough for it not to hurt. She was just angry enough that she didn't feel it right now.

"There's nothing to do for now. We'll give her some food and let her rest for a bit. She's not showing it now, but she's stressed, and it will take time for her to know she's in a safe place."

Reece nodded, looking around like she was trying to find something. I could sense her need to do something, probably because it burned inside me, too.

"If you want to do something, you could see if you can get her to drink. I've prepared some salt water in a bucket in the kitchen."

"Salt water?"

"She's severely dehydrated. To get her hydrated as fast as possible, we give her small amounts of diluted salt water every thirty minutes until she's not thirsty anymore. Then she can have normal drinking water."

Reece nodded and headed to the back of the barn where I'd shown her the feeds and supplies were kept. The determination in her walk was new. She wasn't trying to fold in herself. She'd need some boots and a hat. She probably didn't have suitable work clothes, either. Getting her to accept those wouldn't be easy, and there was no way I was going shopping for her. Unfortunately for me, that meant I'd have to enlist some help. They'd know by now, anyway. Even if they hadn't heard it from the town gossip, Blake would have told Delaney all about Reece within seconds of us leaving her yesterday. I was actually surprised they hadn't turned up already. My brother and his soon-to-be wife would love everything about this.

Reece came back with the water bucket and then walked into the stable without even waiting to see if it was safe. That was a conversation we'd need to have later. Hank had taken the mare's lead rope off but left her in the halter just in case. It was loose enough not to rub against the sores on her face, but I wanted it off her as soon as possible.

I stepped forward, ready to jump in if Reece needed me. But she calmly approached the little mare, murmuring soft words to her as she held the bucket close enough that she could drink. The mare backed up a step, eyeing Reece cautiously, and I froze, watching for a twitch of a muscle that could mean Reece was in danger. But she stood still, murmuring to the mare and reassuring her she was going to be all right.

Hank came to my side, watching Reece carefully. His hands were shoved in his jeans pockets, but I knew he was ready to move if necessary.

Hank had been with the ranch for nearly ten years now. He was one of the first hires I'd ever made. I only had two ranch hands at the moment. There wasn't a huge amount of work to be done. We were down to just the horses now, and renovation works were underway for my new project. Hank and Cliff were helping maintain the acreage until the real work started.

"I didn't know we were ready to take on guests," he said quietly.

"We're not," I admitted. "But she needed help, and I was in a position to give it."

Hank hummed thoughtfully, then fell silent as we watched the mare stretch out her neck toward Reece to sniff at the bucket.

This was a crucial point when a new horse arrived. If it wouldn't drink, it would need fluids intravenously, and it usually meant we'd have a hell of a fight on our hands to get it healthy again.

Reece stood completely still, letting the mare make her own decision, and we all released a collective breath when she took a step forward and finally drank.

Reece smiled gently, watching over the mare as she drank the small amount of water I'd prepared. When she'd finished and Reece came out of the stable, I could see the tears in her eyes.

I reached down and grabbed the hay net filled with leafy alfalfa hay and closed the stable door, hanging the net high enough at the side for the mare to reach without having to stress her weak muscles.

"What now?" Reece asked quietly.

"We wait." I wanted to caution Reece that not every horse made it, but I could already see that wasn't an option for her. "We get her hydrated and then see if we can get close enough to assess her condition and the sores."

Hank clapped me softly on the shoulder. "I'm going to take the trailer down the yard and sanitize it. Holler if you need me."

"Thanks, Hank."

Reece moved to the other side of the walkway and slid down to sit on the floor, her eyes never once leaving the open half of the stable door. A soft smile came to her lips as the mare moved to the net and pulled some alfalfa free.

There was a lot to do. I needed to update the vet and get confirmation on when they were coming by. I should probably get hold of Cliff too and get him to ride the trails I still hadn't gotten around to. Instead, I moved to Reece's side and sat down on the ground, pulling the hat from my head and running the brim through my fingers just for something to do. Val went to her other side, lying down and putting her head on Reece's lap.

"I inherited this ranch from my grandfather," I told her. "My parents had high expectations for me when I was a kid. My dad's in the property development business, and they expected me to work with him. Take over the business one day. Turn their millions into even more millions. But that wasn't me. This place. This was where I was always supposed to be, and they hated it."

Reece turned her head to look at me, and I could see the sorrow in her eyes. I didn't want it, but I knew if she was ever going to trust me with her story, then I needed to give her mine.

"That must have been hard," she said quietly.

I shrugged. "It is what it is. I love this place. I always have. It's in my blood in a way that I can't describe. I spent as much time as I could here to get out of their house. It was always the horses for me. My grandfather used to raise cattle, but we don't have any on the ranch anymore."

"How come?"

I hesitated. I'd never actually told anyone about the next part. The plans I had for the ranch or the fact that they were already underway.

"One day, my grandfather brought a plow-horse back to the ranch. It was in a terrible state. Worked until it couldn't work anymore. I helped him nurse that horse back to health. I used to sneak out of the house at night so I could sit in the stable and watch over it. Then, when it was healthy again, I used to sneak out to sit with him for different reasons. A lot of stuff went on in my parents' house that...we don't talk about."

Reece reached out and took hold of my hand, which I'd

balled into a tight fist. She gently opened my fingers and then threaded her fingers between them, holding my hand.

"And now, you want to help as many horses as you can," she said.

"Yes. But it's more than that. That old horse saved me. He gave me purpose, a reason to assess the bad stuff in my life and choose whether I was going to let it keep holding me prisoner. I want to help other people find that."

"Is that why you brought me here?" she asked softly.

"I saw something in you I hadn't seen since I was a kid. You need this as much as I did."

She nodded, her eyes going back to the mare, who was slowly eating now. "You know, this is the most you've said to me in one go since we met," she pointed out.

"I'm not the best with people," I admitted.

"You could have fooled me." Her head tipped to the side and gently laid on my shoulder, and I fought the urge to move.

Not to escape her, but to slide closer. To wrap my arm around her shoulders and draw her into the side of my body. To give her the shelter I craved.

"It's such a cliché that I couldn't believe it was happening to me until I was so deep I didn't know how I'd got there. He seemed like the perfect guy when I met him. I was fresh out of college and in my first proper job, doing exactly what I wanted to do with my life. I was flattered, you know? He saw me, he wanted me. And it wasn't bad at first. He took me out for fancy meals, bought me expensive gifts, told me I was the only woman in the world for him. I can't believe I fell for it."

She fell so quiet I was sure she could hear the creak of my teeth as I clenched my jaw.

All I needed was a name. The name of the dirtbag

who'd taken this beautiful woman and broke her just because he could.

"We moved too fast. I should have known better," she whispered, laying the blame on herself and not where it belonged. "I was so flattered when he asked me to move in with him. We'd only been seeing each other for a few months, but I was so completely in love with him. Everything changed once he had me in his house. It started with cruel comments at first, then he slowly manipulated me into cutting out my friends. If I loved him, I wouldn't need them. Why did I want to go out with someone else when I had him at home? Didn't I love him the same way he loved me? It all came to a head a few weeks ago. He wanted me to leave my job to be at home for him whenever he needed me, and I suddenly looked up and realized what had happened. How alone I was. How my life was slowly slipping off the tracks I'd put it on. And for the first time, I said no to him."

My hand squeezed hers gently when she hesitated. I wouldn't push her, not yet. There were so many details she was leaving out, and I needed them all. But she'd never give them to me if I tried to force her now.

"He completely changed in an instant," she whispered. "It was like his mask fell off, and I saw him for who he truly was. I said no, I didn't want to lose the independence that my job gave me, and he flew into a rage. I'd never seen him like that before. He punched me, and I fell to the ground. It was so unexpected. He'd never done anything like that before. But then it was like he snapped. He was screaming at me that I was his, kicking me. I tried to stop him. I begged him to stop, and then...at a certain point...I gave up. I thought he was going to kill me. But then he stopped. He stared down at me on the ground, and there was nothing on his face, no emotion, nothing. He told me to clean myself up, and then he left. I knew if I didn't leave then, I would never get away. So I made a plan. It took me a couple of weeks, but I slowly packed all my old things and moved them into my car without him noticing. I didn't need anything he'd given me. I didn't want it. Then, at the first opportunity I had, I drove away. I guess you know the rest."

Reece shrugged then, like it was no big deal.

"I'm sorry that happened to you," I finally said when I couldn't take the silence anymore.

It wasn't enough. I wanted to swear to her that I'd hunt him down and tear him limb from limb, but violence wasn't what Reece needed right now.

It was what *I* needed.

"Will you show me how to make the salt water she needs?" she asked instead.

"Sure."

We both got up and headed to the back of the barn, and Reece listened intently while I took her through the water and feeding routine for the mare. She didn't say another word about what had happened to her, and I didn't ask her any questions. It was harder to resist pulling her into my arms and promising that I was going to make it all better.

She didn't need that.

She didn't need *me.*

Reece needed compassion and a safe place where she could heal, and I wouldn't be the creep who took that away from her.

CHAPTER SEVEN

REECE

It had been a long day and night of watching over the little mare and making sure she had everything she needed.

Booker had told me about re-feeding syndrome, and I hadn't slept for more than half an hour the entire night from worrying about it.

"We need to give you a name," I murmured as the little mare nudged at the empty hay net with her nose. "You're going to have to wait an hour before you get your next net," I told her, taking down the empty one.

She was so thin that part of me didn't see how she could survive. I'd never understand how a person could do something like this to an animal.

The vet was due to come tomorrow to do some tests, but Booker had done this enough times that he knew what he was doing by now. His primary concern seemed to be the sores and getting the mare calm enough around us that we could bathe and treat them.

I moved closer to the stable door, and she eyed me warily. "You'll feel so much better once we get you some medicine," I told her softly, slowly moving one hand out in front of me. "I'm going to make sure that you get better. We've got you now. This is a safe place. Booker looks after us all."

The mare stretched her neck and sniffed my hand. I felt the gust of her warm breath against my skin and smiled.

She was starting to trust me.

I couldn't believe I'd told Booker what had happened to me yesterday. Talk about a show of trust. It wasn't so much that I didn't trust him with my story. I think it was more that I was ashamed it had happened. That I'd been stupid enough not to see the situation I was getting myself into.

But when I looked at Booker after my confession, he didn't stare at me like I was the broken, pathetic thing I felt like. There was an anger in his eyes, and I liked it.

I liked that there were still people in the world who cared if I was hurting.

My hand came to my side, and I touched the faded yellow marks. It wouldn't be long until they were gone now, and something about that made me sad. These were my reminders. The price I'd paid, and a part of me was afraid that once they were gone, I'd forget. I'd whitewash over the pain and walk straight into the same mistake again.

My mind immediately went to Booker. I should have been afraid that the past was repeating itself with him. After all, when I'd first met Camden, there was nothing about him that made me think he was capable of what he'd done. Not at the time, at least. Of course, there were signs. I'd just been too naïve to notice them.

What if I was making all the same mistakes again? What if Booker wasn't the person I thought he was?

But then I looked around the barn and at the little mare who cautiously watched me and knew it couldn't be true.

Booker was exactly who he seemed to be. He couldn't have created all this if he wasn't.

"It looks like we're both on difficult roads," I said to the horse.

"Why are you talking to a horse?" a small voice asked from beside me, and when I looked down in surprise, there was a boy standing there. He had to be around ten, and I had absolutely no idea if he was supposed to be here.

"Erm." I looked around, but there was no one else about. "I guess because I wanted someone to talk to, and she was here to listen."

He nodded sagely. "That makes sense." Then he looked me up and down. "Did she do that to your face? My mom says horses are demons and that no one should ride them because their feet are fitted with murder shoes."

I snorted with laughter. Someone didn't like horses.

"No. Someone else did this to me."

He frowned, and then he reached up and took my hand. "That's not very nice. But you're safe here. We'll look after you."

"Do you know Booker?"

"Yeah! He's my uncle. He's so cool. He rescues horses, and he's going to teach me how to ride one and buy me one, one day. And he has these amazing quads in the barns that we go out on, but I'm not allowed to ride one of my own yet. It's still cool, though."

"It sounds really cool. I'm Reece."

"I'm—"

"Cade, are you in here?" a male voice called out, and the kid turned and grinned at me.

"We should hide," he whispered.

"We could," I whispered back, ducking down to talk to him. "But I'm too pretty to go to prison."

He nodded again and then turned toward the barn doors, shouting, "I'm in here, Dad."

Cade's dad walked down the center of the barn, his face going from puzzled to happy to grinning in glee.

"Hi! I'm Trace." He held out his hand for me to shake, and I took it. "You're a girl."

"You know, I think you're the first person to ever notice," I told him as he continued to shake my hand.

"But you're so pretty!" Cade gasped, clearly not understanding the joke.

Trace laughed and wrapped his arm around his son. "She's joking, kid." He ruffled his hair and then turned back to me, nodding toward the barn door, so I followed him. "I can't believe Uncle Booker has a real-life girl at the ranch."

"I feel like I'm missing something," I mumbled as we walked out into the sunlight where a woman was standing by an SUV I hadn't seen before.

"Delaney!" Trace shouted. "There's a girl!"

"What?" someone shrieked, and I ducked down next to Cade.

"What's happening right now?" I whispered dramatically.

Cade rolled his eyes before loudly whispering back to me, "My parents are so cringe."

"I am not!" Trace gasped. "Take that back!"

"I call cringe when I see cringe," Cade said back, crossing his arms as he stared his dad down.

I might not have had any idea what was happening, but it didn't take a genius to figure out that this guy was Booker's brother. He was obviously younger, and he wasn't as heavily built as Booker, but apart from that, they looked so similar. It was like getting a glimpse of Booker from ten years ago.

Booker appeared on the porch of the ranch house, and I swore I heard him swear all the way from over by the barn before he stalked his way across the driveway.

"Oh, you've done it now. Hi, I'm Delaney!" she said as she stood at my side, and we all watched as Booker stormed closer.

"What is wrong with you two?" Booker snapped.

"Too cringe," Cade and I said at the same time and then started to giggle.

Delaney looked at me and grinned. "I like you." She turned to Booker. "I like her, Booker."

"Someone call the papers," he snarked. "Now stop traumatizing Reece. You're supposed to be here for a riding lesson."

Delaney shuddered, and Cade patted her arm in solidarity. She must be the one that thought horses wore murder shoes. Trace just snickered at her distress, and she threw him a dirty look before an evil grin came across her lips.

"That's a fantastic idea," she beamed before she linked her arm through mine. "You guys go and do that, and Reece can keep me company on the porch. You know, for emotional support."

And then she tugged on my arm as she started walking toward the house.

I glanced back at Booker, who was scowling in our direction. This clearly wasn't going how he wanted, but his family seemed really nice, and I couldn't lie. It was kind of funny how much fun they were having messing with him.

"So," Delaney said, as she led me over to some seats on the porch. "My son is about to get onto a death demon, and I need someone to distract me. Tell me all about you and how you caught the eye of my lovely soon-to-be brother-in-law."

I laughed, watching as Cade was helped onto a horse that didn't move even a fraction of an inch as he did. It stood completely still until it lowered its head to sniff Val sitting patiently at its feet.

"See!" Delaney hissed. "I don't know if I can watch this."

I turned to laugh at her, but when I saw how gray her face was, I realized she was actually being serious. She was terrified for her kid right now.

"Booker rescued me from the side of the road," I blurted out, and she looked at me with wide eyes. "My car broke down, and I was freaking out about what to do and kind of didn't realize that it was on fire. He knocked on my window and hauled me out of there."

She blinked, her lips parting in surprise. "Wow, that's... kind of dreamy," she admitted, and I laughed.

"Yep, my real-life knight in shining armor."

I looked across at Booker, who was giving Cade instructions on how to hold the reins. He looked different. More relaxed. Happier even.

"He's a good guy, you know," Delaney whispered, almost like she thought we'd be overheard. "He's a grumpy ass sometimes, but it's only because he's too used to being alone."

"Being alone isn't so bad."

"Don't let one person break your view of the world."

I looked across at Delaney, who was watching the guys. Booker had the horse walking, and Cade was chatting away from the saddle as Trace watched on proudly. He was clearly having the time of his life. She didn't make any sign that she was talking about anything as serious as we were. I could appreciate that. Having control of my situation and how everyone dealt with it was something I needed, and she seemed to sense that.

"I won't. I just need to get back to the me I was before all this happened."

"Hmmm," she hummed, still not looking at me. "It's not so bad to be changed by your situation. Something happened to me. Something awful. I...I got pregnant with Cade when I was sixteen. Our parents worked together to separate me and Trace. Trace's mother even got his brother, Gage, to help her. He never forgave himself and, as soon as he was old enough, he left and never looked back. Trace and Booker lost their brother, and Trace never knew his son existed. They convinced me that he wanted nothing to do with us. I lost ten years with him because of them."

"That's awful!" I gasped.

Booker had said something about his parents not being good people, but that was truly evil.

"It is what it is. Sometimes I think it might have even been for the best." She could see I was about to argue with her, and Delaney patted my arm lightly. "I know missing out on all that time was terrible. And for Trace to have missed out on all of Cade's life was truly horrific. But we're different people now. We're stronger because of the things we've been through, and I'm not sure we'd have survived if we hadn't had that time to grow."

Delaney had obviously had time to work through this thing that had happened to them, and it was good to see that she was on her way to a good place. She was proof that it was possible.

My situation, compared to hers, didn't seem so bad. I was one bad dating decision from losing myself, but I pulled myself out when it turned south. I'd escaped where many before me hadn't been able to.

"What's it like living in Willowbrook?" I asked, changing the subject.

"It's strange and unusual and honestly the best" Delaney laughed. "I was so reluctant to come back here, but it's the best place on earth. They look after their own around here. We have our problems just like anywhere else, but they won't abandon you if you need them."

"That must be nice."

Delaney hummed in agreement, and we went back to watching the guys. Every time Cade made even a slight movement, Delaney flinched. I ended up reaching out and taking her hand because I couldn't take the stress of watching her suffer through it.

"How come you don't like horses?"

She shrugged. "It's stupid. I went out riding as a kid and got dumped into a patch of stinging nettles. I've never been able to look at the damn things ever since." She turned to look at me with a wince. "I can see them plotting against us every time I meet their gaze."

I swear I tried not to laugh. My lips pursed together, and she squinted even harder before sighing. "Go ahead. Laugh at my pain."

And I did.

It burst out of me in joyous peals, and then it just kept on coming. After a minute, Delaney joined in as well, and we laughed until my side ached more than I could ignore.

"Oh my god, I needed that so bad."

"You're welcome. Do you want something to drink? We should totally raid Booker's pantry. He always has the best snacks, and I know all his hiding places."

I glanced over at the guys and found Booker and Trace

watching us intently. I found myself locked in his gaze, unable to look away. There was just something about Booker that drew me to him. He had this intensity that should have scared me, yet it didn't. If anything, I knew this man would do everything in his power to keep me safe.

I just didn't know why.

Val yipped and darted out of the training ring Cade was riding in, moving closer to the house with a bark.

Delaney surged out of her seat in panic, but the horse that Cade was riding didn't even flick an ear at the sound.

"Val!" Booker barked. "Leave it. Doc's fine, Delaney. He's used to her yapping."

Delaney nodded grimly, her eyes not leaving her son. "I knew I shouldn't have come to watch this, but Cade was so excited. What's she barking at, anyway?"

"I don't..." My eyes moved to Booker's faithful friend, and as they did, they drifted across the driveway leading to the house and the shiny sports car glinting in the sun as it slowly made its way across the gravel. "No," I whispered in denial.

My body locked up in fear as I took in the black sports car that definitely wasn't suited to the roads around here. It slowly made its way around the potholes and crept closer to the house. Closer to me.

He'd found me.

I should have run farther. I shouldn't have stayed. I knew I wasn't out of his reach, staying so close to the city. Only by putting states between us would I ever be far enough away.

"Val!" Booker barked, sounding closer than he had before. "With me."

The dog skipped to Booker's side as he stood strong in front of the house. His shoulders were squared as he stood ready to defend. "Trace, take Cade and the girls inside," he shouted at his brother, locking eyes with him as he did.

Trace pulled a confused Cade off the back of the horse and jogged toward us, with Cade giggling under his arm.

"Delaney, get inside!" he shouted, putting Cade on his feet at the bottom of the porch and giving him a little push of encouragement. "Protect your mom and Reece for me, kid."

Cade came charging for us, his eyes glinting with determination. He'd sensed the change in the atmosphere and was ready to do exactly as his father had said.

My little hero.

Delaney was right about the people around here.

But I couldn't move. My body was frozen in fear, and I hated that this one insignificant man could elicit such a reaction in me.

This wasn't how it was supposed to be.

I never meant to bring him here after me.

CHAPTER EIGHT

BOOKER

If this fucker thought he could come here and hurt her again, he was sorely mistaken.

Val bristled at my side. She could feel the anger running through me, and she was ready for whatever happened next.

"I need details," Trace said grimly as he stepped up beside me.

"I don't know who he is, but I know he hurt her."

Trace grumbled under his breath. "Then let's show this fucker what happens when you mess with what's ours."

I glanced at my brother out of the side of my eye, impressed that he was standing beside me right now. Trace had never been the one to get into trouble when we were kids. Well, if you didn't count the fact that he got his teenage girlfriend pregnant. He'd changed since she'd come back into his life, though. He knew what it was like to lose something precious, and it had awoken a different side of him.

The sports car pulled up a short distance away from us,

and the sun glared off the windshield, obscuring whoever was inside.

"I've got your back, Book," Trace told me as I stormed forward, ready to rip whoever had dared to come here out of the car.

Val growled softly as she stalked forward with me. She was low to the ground and ready to go. And she was getting the biggest damn steak for her dinner tonight.

I braced as the car door opened, the need for violence running through me.

This man had hurt Reece. He'd beaten her until she'd thought she was going to die. She was scared of him. He wasn't walking away from this place until he knew what that felt like.

As the fancy leather loafers stepped down with a crunch onto the gravel and he stepped out of the car, I was moving. I didn't even look at his face. What was the point? He wouldn't look the same once I'd finished with him.

But Trace's gasp behind me had me coming back to my senses, thankfully, before my fist flew for this guy's face.

"Xander?"

I blinked, coming to a stop as I took in the sight of the brother I hadn't seen for two years.

Val growled at my side, hunching down further as her fur bristled in agitation.

"Fucking hell, Book. I know I haven't been around much, but are you really going to set Val on me?" Xander asked, sounding confused.

At the mention of her name, Val sat, her tail wagging and her tongue drooping at the side of her mouth as she panted happily. Yeah, she wasn't really much of a fighter, was our Val, but she had my back whenever I needed it.

"What are you doing here?" The question came out as a

growl. I hadn't quite pulled my mind back to where it normally was yet.

My heart thumped in my chest, and I squeezed my fists in time with it, hoping the adrenaline would leave my system soon.

"Wow, I know it's been a while, but I didn't think you'd hate seeing me quite this much, Booker."

I should have reassured him it was fine, that I'd missed him even. Xander and I were the closest in age of all our siblings, and we'd naturally banded together against Trace and Gage. But I couldn't open my mouth.

I couldn't say a word.

Because all I could think was, had it been my brother that hurt Reece?

My head slowly turned as I sought her out. Somehow, I knew she hadn't gone inside the house. She'd looked so scared when I saw her standing frozen to the spot on the porch. It had been her wide, frightened eyes that made me snap. That had the urge to protect roaring to life inside me.

And now I was dreading looking at the woman who had me so intrigued.

I didn't know how I'd ever make it up to her if Xander had been the one to hurt her.

"Trace?" Xander sounded so confused as he turned to our other brother for answers.

I didn't catch our youngest brother's response because I was too busy looking at Reece standing on the porch. Delaney had an arm wrapped around her shoulders in support as she sagged against her. Tears trailed down her cheeks, but she looked so relieved. Her hand lay gently on the back of Cade's head as he wrapped her up in a hug.

She looked so right standing on my porch, part of my family, that it was impossible for me to stay away from her.

"It's not you, man," I heard Trace say as I strode toward the house. "We've got some stuff going on, and we thought you were someone else."

I faintly heard the car door close as I took the porch steps two at a time. Delaney smiled happily as I crossed the wooden planks with a purpose I didn't quite understand.

I pulled Reece from Delaney's side, wrapping her tightly in my arms as I crushed her to my chest, cautious not to put any pressure on her ribs. My cheek laid against her hair, and I breathed in the sweet smell of her coconut shampoo.

"I've got you, baby. It's not him. No one's going to hurt you here."

Reece's breath hitched as she clung to me, soaking up whatever strength I could give to her.

I knew I shouldn't be hugging her. It wasn't right. I'd offered her help, and I didn't want her to feel like she owed me anything for it.

Yet still I couldn't step back. I couldn't let go of her.

Reece and I barely knew each other. We'd spent such little time together, and I wasn't exactly the friendliest guy.

But more than that, she was here to heal, and she didn't need me panting after her like she was a dog in heat. I shouldn't be clinging to her now because I knew this could be the only chance I ever got to hold her. I shouldn't be thinking about how well she fit against me, how perfect she felt in my arms.

So I gritted my teeth, and I forced myself to step back. To put the distance between us that there always should have been.

"I'm sorry..." she started.

"You have nothing to be sorry about. None of this is your fault."

She shook her head sadly, and I shoved my hands in my pockets in an effort to keep them to myself. "I'm going to feed the mare. She's due another hay net."

I let her go. I hated it, but I knew Reece needed the space.

"Booker, you should go with her," Delaney said softly from behind me.

"No."

"She needs you."

I turned to look at my soon-to-be sister-in-law then and shook my head sadly. She wouldn't understand. She had her happily ever after already. Delaney was too far into her happy life to realize that it didn't turn out that way for everyone.

"I'm just the guy who found her on the side of the road and gave her a place to stay."

This was the best thing for Reece.

I'd get over this stupid infatuation in time, and she'd go on to live the life she deserved.

CHAPTER NINE

REECE

Booker never came to find me after the disaster of his brother turning up and my having a breakdown on his front porch.

I could still feel his arms banded around me, the safety I'd felt as he held me. I'd never had that with anyone else. Never had the certainty that nothing could reach me when this man would willingly stand in the way.

But then he'd avoided me for the rest of the day. I hadn't caught a single glimpse of him, and given that the new mare in the barn needed so much attention right now, he had to be working hard to achieve that.

My feelings for Booker weren't the only surprising thing to come out of yesterday, though. I hadn't realized how much my ex still affected me. That the mere thought of him being here could elicit that amount of fear in me.

I thought I was in a better place in my head. That the distance I'd put between us had given me the perspective I needed to assess the things I'd been through and accept that it was a season in my life I was leaving behind.

But it wasn't as far behind me as I'd tried to tell myself.

And I needed to make that happen.

Because something had happened yesterday when Booker held me in his arms. When he'd whispered in my ear that he had me. It was the single most hard-hitting truth that anyone had ever told me.

And something had shifted inside me.

But what did that mean for me and Booker? Was there even a Booker and me to begin with?

So I made a decision.

I washed my breakfast dishes quickly and then pushed my feet into my sneakers. Booker might be avoiding me, but there was one thing he couldn't avoid that was happening today. The vet was scheduled to check in on the new mare today.

Apparently, I wasn't above ambushing a guy and forcing him to talk about his feelings. And if there was ever a guy who needed to be forced to address his feelings, it was Booker Farrington.

I was out the door before I could even consider if this was a good idea. I didn't even let myself think about whether I was ready to confront my own feelings. All I could think about was getting to him.

My feet skidded on the gravel as I turned the corner into the barn and then slowed my steps as the two men in front of me looked up in surprise.

"Morning," I chirped, trying to pretend that nothing unusual was happening.

"Morning," the guy I didn't know responded. Presumably, he was the vet Booker usually worked with.

The man in question was leaning against a closed stable door, his arms crossed, and the brim of his hat pulled low enough that I couldn't see the scowl I already knew was on his face. It was actually kind of endearing now. When

Booker was scowling, all was right in the world. It would only be when he lost that expression and didn't look like he cared anymore that I'd be worried.

The vet looked over his shoulder at Booker when he didn't say anything and then shrugged. "I'm Cole Harrison," he said, smiling at me. "It's a pleasure to meet you."

"Reece Graham." I reached out and shook the hand that he extended to me.

Cole moved over to the stable and quietly slipped inside. "Hey there, beautiful," he murmured, reaching out a hand to the mare, who watched him carefully.

"She's been really quiet since she got here," I told him. "I don't know if that's a good sign. I'm kinda new when it comes to horses. But Booker is teaching me."

Cole stroked the mare's nose, and she blinked slowly, her tail flicking to the side. "You're a sweet girl, aren't you?" he crooned. "But you've been through a lot."

He ran his hands over her back, careful not to touch any of the sores. Booker had treated them with antiseptic the day she arrived, but they still looked bad.

"Has she put any weight on since she arrived?" Cole asked, looking up.

He wasn't looking at me, and when I glanced over my shoulder, I saw Booker had moved to stand behind me.

"Only about ten pounds," Booker told him. "She's still on the alfalfa every four hours. We're four days in, but I'd hoped she'd gain quicker than she is."

"She's chewing okay? Drinking enough?"

"Yep."

Cole stepped back and frowned. "I'd recommend introducing some calorie heavy feeds to see if we can step up the weight gain. Let's alternate for now, but don't increase her alfalfa until you're sure she's tolerating the new feed."

Booker hummed in agreement, and Cole took a step back, frowning before going to a box of supplies and pulling out a stethoscope.

"Damn," I heard Booker mutter under his breath. "I was really hoping you didn't think that as well."

Cole shook his head sadly and then listened to the mare's stomach carefully.

"What? What's wrong?" I asked.

I could feel a sense of panic building. Especially when Cole sighed sadly, his shoulders drooping.

"She's in foal," he said, stepping back and shaking his head.

Cole made some notes on a clipboard.

Booker moved to the mare, running a hand over her muzzle.

I felt so out of the loop here. A complete novice with no idea of how to help, and I hated it.

"Try getting some fat-added feed into her diet as soon as she's balanced out. I know I don't need to warn you, but I'd be remiss not to remind you to keep an eye out for re-feeding syndrome." Cole finished writing and shoved his pen in his box before he packed up his things. "She's good for an antibiotic wash over those sores, and I'd like you to get her hooves trimmed as soon as you can. She's calm enough that it's not going to be overly stressful for her."

Booker hummed in agreement and walked out of the stable, closing the door behind him. I was left standing in the middle of the barn, silently watching the people who could actually help her.

"It was nice to meet you, Reece. I'll be around in the next few days, but call me if you need anything, Booker."

Cole and Booker shook hands, and then Booker walked him out to his car. I'd never felt as alone as I did right then.

A soft gust of warm breath tickled the back of my neck, and I turned to see the mare with her head over the stable door for the first time since she'd arrived here.

"Hey there, girl," I whispered, turning to her and running a hand over her soft muzzle. "I'm so sorry this is happening to you."

She nudged me gently with her nose, and a sad laugh bubbled out of me. "You getting ready to eat already? Hey, that's got to be a good sign."

"It is," Booker said from behind me.

I couldn't bring myself to look at him. I'd been filled with all these plans of making him talk about yesterday, but in the grand scheme of things, it didn't feel all that important now. Not when we were standing here trying to figure out if we could save the sweet girl in front of us.

"She's going to lose the foal, isn't she?" I asked.

Booker sighed, and I felt him move closer, the heat of his body warming my back. "She will. We just have to hope we don't lose her with it. Her body can't sustain them both, but it's going to try."

"There isn't any way?"

I wanted him to reassure me. To tell me it was all going to be all right. I already knew he was a man who'd fight for what was right, and I didn't think he'd ever lie to me. If I could just get Booker to tell me we could save them both, then everything would be okay.

"I'll get her hay net," he said softly. "I need to work out her new feeding regime, but then I'll talk you through it," he said instead.

It felt like a sign. Like the loss of the foal hanging over us symbolized more than us failing the mare I'd come to love. It felt like the beginning of an end.

But I was done giving up on the things I wanted.

I was done letting life drag me down and then kick me for good measure.

Maybe I was setting myself up for a broken heart.

Maybe I was trying to save more than just this little horse.

It didn't matter.

I was going to save us all.

I heard Booker coming back with the hay net and asked, "Do you have a computer I can borrow?"

He hesitated for a second, reaching around me and securing the net at the stable door. "I've got an old laptop you can borrow. It's old and slow, but it works. Wi-Fi should reach the cottage."

"Good."

He turned around then, leaning against the side of the stable and crossing his arms again as he watched me carefully. "What are you up to?"

"I'm going to find a way to save her."

I could already tell from his eyes that he was trying to let me down gently. To explain to me that the world just didn't work that way.

"Don't," I said. "Don't tell me it's not possible. Just help me find a way."

Booker's tongue ran across his bottom lip as he weighed his options, and then finally, he nodded. "Fine. But if you're going to save her, then you'd better give her a name. Doesn't feel right to keep calling her, 'her.'"

"Will you show me how to clean her sores, too? Show me everything."

He nodded, pushing away from the barn. "Let's get to work."

CHAPTER TEN

BOOKER

This was a feeling I was totally unfamiliar with, and while I grabbed another beer from the fridge, I couldn't help but look out the window toward the cottage.

The lights were on, illuminating the yard between us with a soft, inviting glow.

And I actually wanted to go over there.

Damn it.

Reece was a complication in my life that had blown in here and knocked me sideways. I'd never been the type of person who would have left her stranded. But when I offered her a job, I never thought it would be this distracting to have her on the ranch.

I stalked back into the living room, dropping into my favorite chair with a huff of frustration.

I'd tried avoiding her. Tried acting like nothing was different, like she was just a regular employee.

But I couldn't.

I had an itch just beneath my skin that screamed at me to go over there and talk to her.

Talk to her!

This was me. I didn't do talking. Not to people, at least.

Everything was different when it came to Reece, though.

I wanted to see the smile that came to her lips whenever she thought of something she wanted to share. The light in her eyes that always followed her smile.

When I closed my eyes, I could feel her against my body again. Her soft curves pressing into me, the smell of her coconut shampoo.

Everything about her overwhelmed my senses, and I wanted it so bad I couldn't sit back and do nothing anymore.

So I drained half the beer in my hand, kicked my feet up onto the coffee table, and grabbed the book I'd been reading, feeling like a total idiot. It was the same sappy romance novel that Reece had bought at Books and Beans, and I'd gone back to get my own copy for some stupid reason.

Even Val was fed up with listening to me storm around the house and had retreated to her bed in the kitchen.

My phone chirped on the table, and I gladly reached for it, dropping my book on the seat beside me even though I really wanted to know if this guy was going to realize that his best friend was the perfect woman for him.

It was only a text from Dex, and I was about to ignore it until I saw what it was about.

Dex: I'm nearly done with Reece's car. I'm just waiting for a couple of parts. Should only be a few more days.

Me: Thanks. Let me know how much I owe you.

Trace: Excellent segue, Dex. So…Reece?

Xander: I, for one, think I deserve the full story. I nearly lost my life to your dog.

Dex: Don't slander Val. She's a sweet baby.

Xander: You only think that because you're responsible for the mutt.

Dex: She's not a mutt! And Val was the best present I've ever bought anyone.

I was tempted to let them argue it out between themselves, but Dex was right. Val was the best thing anyone had ever done for me. I was in a dark place that I didn't want to admit to when Dex decided he was going to be my Valentine and left me a gift on the porch one Valentine's morning.

Don't get me wrong. I was so pissed at him at first. At least, as far as he knew. But one look into her brown eyes, and I was a goner. She'd been at my side ever since, well, apart from when I was sulking around the house and annoying her. Then she didn't want to be anywhere near me.

Me: Stop shit-talking about my dog.

Trace: See, if Booker loves her, then you know she's special!

Xander: You'll notice he still hasn't answered the question.

Me: Reece needed a job, and I gave her one. That's it.

Even as I sent the message, I knew it wouldn't work. Not when the brother-wives got together and started gossiping. This was so much like it had been when we were kids it made my chest ache. I'd missed this. Enough so that I was actually considering asking for their advice. I'd never hear the end of it, though.

But as my gaze drifted to the window, just like they had every night since she'd been here, I couldn't help but wonder if it would be worth it.

Trace: And a hug. She needed one of those too.

Dex: I can't believe I missed it. The one time Booker was a normal human. It's like an eclipse. It probably won't come back around for another forty years.

Xander: I nearly missed it. I was too worried about his rabid dog tearing my face off.

Trace: You've gotten dramatic since you moved to the city, brother.

Me: Fine. She's nice.

Nothing came through for a minute, and I rolled my eyes at the idiots.

Dex: Is everyone else as shocked as I am right now?

Trace: I just nearly fell out of bed.

Dex: What are you doing in bed, you old man?

Trace: 😏

Xander: Stop distracting him!

Dex: Sorry, you're right. Tell Auntie Dex everything, Book Book. We'll make it all better.

Me: Idiot.

My thumbs hovered over the screen. It was more that I didn't know how I felt rather than me not wanting to tell them.

Trace: Whatever happens in the text chain, stays in the text chain.

Dex: True dat!

Xander: Idiot.

Dex: You know, I'm feeling really underappreciated here, guys.

Fuck it!

Me: I like her. But I found her after her ex beat the crap out of her, and I won't be the guy that pushes her into something she isn't ready for. I'm not that creep. So I'm sitting in my chair, drinking beer, and being miserable because everything I want is sitting in my cottage, and I can't have it.

I pressed send before I could second guess myself and just delete the word vomit I'd spilled into my phone.

Damn, talk about emotional revelation.

I had another longing look out the window until I felt my phone vibrate in my hand. I looked down, dreading what I was going to see, knowing it would be them telling me that everything I was worried about was true. I was a complete ass for even thinking about her that way.

Trace: How do you know she isn't ready for it?

Me: Because she just went through a trauma.

Trace: And it's up to her how she wants to deal with that.

Xander: You need to talk to her, Booker.

Dex: Better yet, take her on a date. You gotta woo the lady.

Xander: For once Dex makes a good point.

Dex: Hey! I make good points all the time. I wouldn't put up with this if I didn't know you all really loved me, you know.

Me: What if she says no?

Trace: Then you know it's too soon, and you'll be her friend.

Dex: Damn, Trace got all wise when he got all loved up.

Me: How do I do that?

Now I just sounded like an idiot, but I might as well get what I could out of this, and then, hopefully, we'd never speak of it again.

Dex: Well, I think you have to fall in love with someone.

Xander: He means how does he talk to her, idiot.

Dex: Words hurt guys. I'm just saying.

I laughed at their bickering. Damn, I'd missed this so much.

But that happiness came with a sting because we were still missing a brother, and we needed to get him back.

The only way that was happening, though, was for one

of us to talk with our father, and I knew without a doubt that was how I was going to repay them for this. I'd throw myself into the firing line of our parents' crap. Not that Trace was talking to either of them, and rightly so. Xander hadn't been back to Willowbrook for years because of them, and I didn't want to risk losing him for another two years.

That only left me.

> Trace: You know how to do this, Book. You were always the one we came to with our problems. You always knew the right thing to say. Just be honest with her.

And that was exactly the problem right there. Honesty meant vulnerability, and I'd been so closed off all these years because vulnerability was always exploited in our family. I'd learned how to raise my shields at a young age, and I'd not put them down since. I wasn't even sure I knew how anymore.

CHAPTER ELEVEN

REECE

Yesterday had definitely not gone to plan. I'd been so determined to talk to Booker, but the news about the foal had completely thrown me off track, and I'd got lost in the work instead.

Part of me was grateful for that. Not because I hadn't got the chance to tell him how I felt, but because I'd finally felt like I was some use around here.

I still hadn't thought of a name for the mare yet. It felt like something I needed to put a lot of thought into. She'd been through so much that she deserved a good name. I just couldn't figure out what that was.

She'd been so stressed out and tired after we'd washed her down and treated the sores again that Booker said we needed to wait until today to deal with her hooves. I had no idea what that entailed, but I was ready to get to work again.

I slipped my feet into my soggy sneakers and winced. They still hadn't dried out from the horse bath we'd all ended up having yesterday. My skills were a little lacking in that department, but Booker hadn't once lost his temper with me, and we were both as wet as the horse by the end.

I needed to get some more shoes, something more suited to working outdoors. It would have to wait, though. I didn't want to take anything else from Booker that I hadn't earned yet. I hadn't even been here a week, and I was still learning so much that most of the time I figured it would have been easier for Booker if I wasn't here.

I'd yet to figure out what time Booker started work, and I was leaving the house half an hour earlier every morning until I found out. Which was why I slipped out the door of the cottage at seven thirty a.m. and headed to the barn.

I was still too late, though, because Booker was already set up with the mare just outside the barn, and my feet stumbled to a stop when he came into view.

Holy hot cowboy!

I was pretty sure my ovaries just exploded, and I knew my mouth was most definitely hanging open, but I seemed to have lost control of all of my muscles at once as my brain latched onto the sight in front of me.

There was a van I'd never seen before pulled up in front of the barn, and the back doors hung open, revealing an array of tools.

That wasn't what had made my hormones go haywire, though.

Because Booker was already hard at work and, judging from the sheen of sweat coating his muscles, he'd been at it for a while already. He'd stripped down to a white tank, had a pair of wide leather chaps over his jeans, and his usual hat perched on top of his head.

And it was glorious.

Booker reached down, running his hand down the mare's leg before she lifted her hoof for him. His muscles flexed as he inspected the curled hoof that was causing the mare so much pain.

Booker was so gentle with her. His big hands ran carefully over her skin as his muscles bunched and flexed, gleaming in the sun.

"You started without me," I gasped when I saw one perfect-looking hoof on the mare. "Oh, that looks so much better. Does that feel good, girl," I cooed as I moved to her head.

The mare nuzzled her face against the flat of my hand, and I smiled, my mind mostly on the beautiful man in front of me.

"I wanted to get started before the day heats up," Booker said, not lifting his head to make eye contact with me until he gently put the mare's hoof back on the ground.

"I could have helped."

"I don't need your help with this bit."

My fists landed on my waist as I squinted in annoyance at him. "I need to learn this stuff if it's going to be my job."

"It takes years to learn the proper farrier skills to deal with something like this. What you need to do is rest and heal." He glared back at me, almost daring me to deny it.

"I'm fine."

"Then lift your shirt and show me your ribs," he challenged, picking up a saw off the ground and balancing it on his shoulder as he raised an eyebrow at me.

He probably wouldn't be saying stuff like that if he knew I'd just been drooling all over him. Still, part of me wanted to pull all my clothes off just to see what he'd do. I still wouldn't be winning the argument we were having right now, though, because he was right. The bruising on my ribs had turned that mottled yellow of its final stage, which inexplicably seemed to make it look even worse.

"I'm fine," I stressed, apparently deciding that the best

way out of this was to dig this hole even deeper. "It doesn't even hurt when I breathe anymore."

Booker snorted out a laugh at that. "Really? That's the level we're measuring fine up against now?"

He had a point.

"I'm not broken, Booker. I might be down and a bit bruised around the edges, but I'm still the same person I always was. I don't need you to treat me like a delicate butterfly that's going to be crushed in your hands."

He blinked slowly, his tongue coming out to run along his bottom lip, and I realized what I'd said. The implication beneath my words.

Because I wanted to know what it felt like to have his hands on me.

"Stay at her head. Keep talking to her," he said, running his hand down the mare's leg again to pick up her foot.

But when he moved the saw to her hoof, I panicked. "What are you doing?"

He peered up at me with a wry smile on his face. "I'm not cutting her leg off. I'm trimming her hooves."

"With a saw?"

"It's too thick to get the nippers through, and it would take too long. I cut here and take the bulk of the hoof where it's curled back on itself, and then I can shape it with the file and the nippers."

I nodded like I had any idea what he was talking about, not entirely sure that I had the guts to watch what he was about to do. What if the saw slipped, and he cut her leg?

"We're going to be brave, okay?" I said, turning back to the mare and running a hand over her neck. "I'm pretty sure Booker knows what he's doing."

I heard his snort of laughter and then the sound of the saw cutting.

"Maybe don't look," I whispered to her. "If you need me to, I'll look for you."

The mare blinked, and I swear I saw some judgment in her eyes. "I'm only looking out for you," I objected.

I scratched behind one of her ears, and the mare leaned into me. She was such a sweet thing. I didn't see how anyone could have treated her the way they had. How they could have hurt her and then thrown her away like she was nothing.

We had more in common than I really wanted to admit. Except I hadn't been fortunate enough to be thrown away.

It felt like hours passed as I gently ran my hands over the mare and whispered words of encouragement to her. All that time the steady sound of the saw working through the hoof that hurt her so much scratched across the background, proving that Booker was the type of guy who would do what was needed to fix the things that hurt you. Not that I'd needed any more proof of that. I was proof enough.

"Have you spoken to your brother since he came to the ranch?" I asked, probably to distract myself.

"Yes."

I could hear the strain in his voice and peeked around the mare's head to see how much further he had left to go. As I did, he finally made it through, and the gnarled end of the overgrown hoof dropped to the ground.

"Wow."

Booker looked up with a grin, and it hit me full force. Damn, this grumpy man didn't smile often, but when he did, it was beautiful.

"Will you pass me that rasp?" he asked, nodding toward the back of the van.

"Erm." I stepped over to the open doors and looked at

the array of torture equipment, completely lost what any of it was for, let alone what it was called.

"The file. On the left," Booker added.

"This giant nail file thing?" I asked, holding up what I was pretty sure he was asking for.

"Sure." He laughed. "Pass me the nail file."

I passed the tool to him as he shook his head and then, with both hands on the rasp and the hoof held between his thighs, he started to file it down.

"Is he okay?" I asked.

Booker paused and looked up at me with a frown. "Who?"

"Your brother?"

"Xander? Yeah, I think so. Why?"

"Just seemed like if you didn't know he was coming, and he came over, and that he might not have been okay, you know?"

Booker's frown deepened, and he seemed to think for a second. "He didn't say anything."

I could tell he was uncomfortable as he went back to work. But this was what I wanted for Booker. I knew I wouldn't get to have someone like him in my life. I wasn't that lucky. He was doing so much for me, though, and I wanted to repay the favor somehow. Helping him to stop pushing the people around him away was the perfect way to do that.

"Maybe you should call him."

"I'm busy."

I hummed in agreement and let him continue working, knowing I'd at least put the thought in his head.

"Can you pass me the nippers?" he asked quietly after a while, then added, "They look like big pinchers. Right-hand door." He nodded toward an honestly terrifying-looking pliers-thingy, and I cringed as I grabbed it and passed it to him.

I watched in fascination as he trimmed and shaped the hoof, switching between the two tools until suddenly he had a hoof that actually looked like a hoof again.

Booker lowered the mare's leg gently before he patted her side and stepped back. "Not bad," he said quietly.

"Are you kidding? That's incredible."

The corner of his lips ticked up, and then he grabbed his tools and started to put them away.

"Aren't you doing the back ones?" I asked in confusion.

"She's been standing for a couple of hours out here, and she's probably tired. I think we should give her a break and some feed."

"Okay, do you want her back in the stable?"

"No, she's doing okay out here. We'll monitor her and see how she does." Booker hesitated for a minute and then seemed to come to a decision. "Did you eat yet?"

I had. But I was always hungry at the moment. I'd spent too many months trying to starve myself into the perfect woman, and now I was enjoying my foodie freedom.

"I could eat."

Booker nodded and turned to the house. "Grab a hay net for her and then come and have some breakfast at the house."

He strode away before I could say anything.

I leaned back in my seat with a happy hum of contentment. Booker was an amazing cook when it came to breakfast foods.

The man in question chuckled as I patted my stomach in congratulations. Then I went to stand from the table.

"You cooked. I'll do the dishes," I said, standing and picking up my plate.

"No." Booker took the plate out of my hands and went to pick up his own.

"I think you mean thank you," I snarked, taking the plate back from him and trying to grab the serving dish from the center of the table.

"No." He hit me with his trademark glare. "I mean, sit down and rest."

"Are we back to this again?" My grip tightened on the plate as he tried to take it from me. "I'm perfectly capable of standing at a sink and washing some dishes."

Booker sighed and finally wrestled the plate from my hand. "But you don't need to."

He gathered up the dishes and carried them to the sink.

"Fine. But if you're washing, then I'm drying," I argued, grabbing a cloth from the countertop and walking to his side.

Booker sighed in exasperation. "Can you just stop trying to fight me on everything?"

"Probably not," I admitted.

He snorted in amusement. It was fast becoming my favorite sound. "Just relax, please?"

It was possibly the first please he'd ever uttered in my presence, and I should have been a better person and appreciated it for the gesture it was. Instead, a wicked grin slipped across my lips, and I pulled out a Booker classic.

"No."

I turned to the sink and waited, but he didn't start washing. Instead, he turned to face me and leaned a hip against the sink.

"You're infuriating. Did you know that?"

"Coming from you, that's an achievement."

"What's that supposed to mean?"

"You realize you're the most infuriating person to ever walk the planet, right?"

"You're the one who won't accept that you're hurt?"

"I'm not hurt!"

"If I wasn't a decent human being, I'd dig a knuckle right into your ribs," he snapped back.

"Well, I wish you weren't!"

Booker's forehead wrinkled in confusion. "What?"

"Will you just shut up and kiss me already, Booker!"

His head snapped back in surprise, and then a slow smile slid across his lips. "Thank fuck," he muttered, grabbing hold of my waist and hauling me into his body as his mouth landed on mine.

My arms wrapped around his neck as I clung to him, letting him dominate the kiss in complete contrast to how gently his hands cradled me. Booker nipped at my bottom lip, soothing the skin with his tongue, which he pushed into my mouth to stroke along mine. All the while, his hands made a slow trail down my sides until he cupped them under my ass cheeks and lifted me up, erasing the fraction of a gap between us.

I took my time, tracing my fingertips across the muscles of his back as we kissed, making him shudder beneath me.

"We should stop," Booker murmured, his mouth moving to my neck as he nipped at the skin.

"No. We definitely shouldn't stop," I gasped as he ran his tongue up my neck and sucked the lobe of my ear between his lips. "I don't want to stop."

"But you really are hurt," he whispered against my skin

as he ducked down and kissed along my chest where the neckline of my tank top lay.

"Please don't treat me like I'm broken, Booker. I want you. I want every single piece you're willing to give. It's not because I think I owe you something, and it's not because I'm trying to get something from you. You're a wonderful, beautiful man, Booker. Why wouldn't I want that in my life if I get a chance?"

Booker straightened to his full height, his hand pushing the blond hair away from my face.

"All I want to do is protect you," he told me softly. "It would kill me if I hurt you."

Booker cradled my cheeks in his hands and kissed me softly.

"You won't hurt me, Booker. I trust you."

He searched my eyes for a moment, and then he smiled that smile that made my insides set on fire.

Booker's hands wrapped around my waist, and he picked me up so my legs wrapped around his hips. "Then let me show you how true that is," he said, kissing me as he did.

Booker strode across the kitchen, sitting me down on the kitchen table, his hands coming to my jeans as he opened the fastening.

"Lift," he instructed, and I lifted my hips so he could push my jeans and panties down along with them.

Booker's lips came back to mine and smothered the groan that left my mouth as he took that opportunity to push his tongue inside my mouth.

There was no fight for dominance when it came to me and Booker. I was absolute putty in his hands. I trusted him.

My hands came to the edge of his undershirt, and I

pulled it off, breaking away from his lips so he could take it off.

Booker was the most perfect man I'd ever seen, and for a moment, I trailed my fingers across his abs. "It's not fair that you look like this," I told him. "But I'm very glad that you do."

His head fell back as he laughed, and I took the opportunity to quickly unfasten his jeans. He looked at me wryly, the corner of his lips twitching as he took over, slowly sliding the zipper down as I panted over him like a dog in heat.

But I was sadly disappointed when he stopped, leaving the jeans hanging open and not taking them off like I was desperate for him to do.

Instead, he pulled off my shirt and then ran his fingers across the edges of the lace on my bra before he pulled it down, exposing my breasts and licking his lips.

"It's not fair that you look like this," he whispered, looking back up into my eyes. "But I'm very glad that you do." His fingers gently trailed across the yellowing bruising on my ribs then, and his expression turned sad. "I hate this, though."

"I know." My hands came to his cheeks, and I kissed him gently. "But that's all in the past now."

He nodded firmly in agreement. "Lie back, baby. Let me show you how a man is supposed to treat his woman."

I laid back against the cold wood of the table. Booker gently picked up each of my ankles, putting my feet on the tabletop and spreading my legs wide.

He looked at me like a starving man facing his first-ever meal and licked his lips. His fingers trailed across my wet core and my back arched at just the slightest touch.

"I'm going to take my time with you, Reece," he told me

as he pulled up his chair and sat down. "And when I'm done, you won't even remember his name."

Booker ducked his head down and licked a line up my core. My hips shot up off the tabletop, and he gripped my hips, putting me back in place. I lifted my head off the wood and peered down my body at him, and he grinned.

"Stay still, baby. I've got work to do."

And work he did. Booker slid two fingers inside me, making me gasp as his tongue went straight to my clit, teasing that little bundle of nerves as he worked his fingers in and out of me, hooking them up to brush against that spot inside me that made my toes curl.

He brought me to the edge again and again until my head was thrashing from side to side as I whimpered and begged for him to let me come.

"Please, please, Booker. I need it. I need it."

"Patience, baby," he crooned, kissing the inside of my thigh as his thumb came to my clit and worked me up into a frenzy once more. "I've got you. I'm going to make it so good for you that you're going to fly."

"Fly? I swear if you keep teasing me, I'm going to kick you in the face," I panted.

I felt like I was vibrating. My skin was on fire, and every part of my body sang a tune that only Booker could play. I'd never experienced this before, and I was almost afraid of what would happen when he finally let me come.

"There's the fire that I want to see," he murmured before his head dropped between my legs and he sucked my clit between his lips. "Now come for me, Reece," he whispered against my core.

Booker pumped his fingers faster inside me as he worked my clit with the flat of his tongue. His free hand wrapped around my thigh as he pushed my pussy against his face and feasted.

I swear my heart stopped. It skipped a beat as I balanced on the edge of what Booker had brought to life inside me. Every muscle inside me pulled taut as the inevitable rushed toward me.

And then I snapped.

My back arched as I screamed. Pleasure flashed through every nerve of my body, setting me on fire with white-hot flames of ecstasy.

CHAPTER TWELVE

BOOKER

I was so hard I was losing circulation to parts of me I definitely wasn't willing to lose.

Even with the dark stain of her past glaring at me from that patch on her ribs, Reece was the most beautiful woman I'd ever seen.

Laid out on my kitchen table, a sheen of sweat across her skin as she tried to catch her breath. She was an absolute vision.

I wanted to go again. I wanted to hear her sweet whimpers and her whispered pleas for the thing only I could give her.

I was seconds away from beating my chest in pride. There was no greater pleasure than seeing a woman completely shattered by the pleasure you'd filled her with.

Reece weakly lifted her head from the tabletop. "Don't stop now, cowboy," she murmured, a goading grin on her face.

I shook my head, hating it when people called me that. Scooping her up into my arms, I set out for the stairs. "There are no cows here."

"True. But I do so love the hat."

I laughed then. It burst out of me with a force of joy no one else had ever brought to life inside me. No one before Reece made me feel like this. Made me want the things I shouldn't, like she could do.

She was as light as a feather in my arms as I took the stairs two at a time. I'd been so worried about taking advantage of her before that I never even considered what she wanted. Reece was a grown woman who'd gotten into a terrible situation. That didn't mean it had to rule her life, though. And she deserved the respect to decide for herself about what she was ready for. Trying to take that from her would make me just as bad as the fool who hadn't treasured her like she deserved.

I kicked open my bedroom door, striding to the bed as I gently laid her down on it. My knees came to the mattress as I held myself over her, kissing her lips because they were impossible to resist.

She looked so right lying here in bed. It was where she was meant to be, and I'd be the luckiest man alive if one day she agreed that was true.

"We can stop now," I told her, giving her a chance to back out. I might not want to decide for her anymore, but I'd also make damn sure that she didn't feel backed into a corner.

"Stop talking," she said, kissing my lips. "Get naked instead."

"Yes, ma'am."

"Mmmm," she purred. "I might like that."

"God damn."

I made quick work getting the rest of my clothes off and reached into the bedside drawer to retrieve a condom.

I was just about to ask her if she was sure she wanted to

do this when she took it out of my hands and tore open the packet with her teeth.

"Someone's impatient." I laughed as she reached for me, rolling the condom down my length and making me hiss just from that brief contact alone.

"You have no idea. But to be fair, you just spent like six hours teasing me downstairs."

"It was ten minutes."

"You're just lucky that I'm not a vindictive person," she quipped, and then she pushed me down onto the mattress, straddling my hips.

I moved my hands up her body, tracing every soft curve I could reach. "You're so beautiful," I told her honestly.

She smiled down at me, and then she raised her hips and notched the head of my cock at my core.

My breath caught in my throat as she slowly sank down onto my length. My hands gripped her hips, helping her as I fought the urge to slam myself inside her. She was tight, and her pussy gripped my shaft in a way that had me fighting to keep control.

Reece paused as she panted. "Wow, you're...that feels incredible."

"You're so tight, baby. It's...it's been a while. I don't know if I can..."

Reece leaned forward, and I groaned. She kissed me, twining her tongue with mine as she threaded her fingers through my hair. "Just feel, Booker," she whispered as she slowly lifted her hips, her lips trailing across my jaw as she did.

Reece slowly slid up and down my length, her lips kissing across my face as she set a maddening pace.

My grip on her hips tightened as I fought to keep myself under control. She needed this. She needed to be the one with all the power in this situation. I could see it in her eyes. There might also be a small amount of payback coming my way for edging her before.

"I like seeing you like this," she told me, her fingers tightening hard enough in my hair to tip my head back slightly. "I like seeing you fighting the need to snap."

"I'm all yours, baby. However you want me, whatever you need, I'll always give it to you."

Reece lowered her lips to my ear then. "Fuck me, Booker," she whispered.

And the last of my restraint was gone.

I cupped her ass in my hands as I flipped her again, holding myself over her so I wouldn't put my weight on her ribs. She hooked her thighs over my hips and grinned.

Rising onto my knees, I lifted her hips as I did and sank a fraction deeper inside her, which had us both groaning at the sensation.

The rhythm I set was fast and hard, and when Reece's hands reached for her breasts, and she started to work her nipples, I nearly lost it.

I could feel the muscles in her pussy fluttering around my cock, and I picked up the pace to an impossible speed I knew she was getting closer to a second orgasm, and I needed it more than I needed my own. I wanted to watch her expression as she fell apart beneath me, knowing that I was the one giving it to her.

My jaw clenched as I held my release back. I couldn't lose it yet, not before she did.

"Yes, Booker! Just like that. Don't stop. Don't stop," she panted.

How could I ever deny her?

I watched in fascination as Reece's lips slightly parted, her breaths coming faster as her eyelids fluttered closed. I felt the muscles in her thighs quiver, and then it was like the entire world held its breath as every muscle in her pulled tight.

Reece's beautiful pussy locked down on me as she came with a shout, and I was powerless but to follow her over the edge. I thrust home one, twice, and then lights exploded behind my eyes as it felt like a sliver of my soul broke free and joined with hers.

I sagged to the mattress, thoroughly spent, scooping Reece up in my arms to hold her while we both came back down to earth.

"That was incredible," she whispered, patting me lightly on the chest with one hand like she was congratulating me.

I huffed out a laugh, and Reece shifted slightly, making herself comfortable.

The guilt hit me then. Had I been too rough with her? Had I hurt her more than she already was?

"Are you okay?" I asked in concern, loving the way she fit so perfectly against me and hoping like hell that I deserved it. "Did I hurt you?"

Reece leaned up on one elbow and suddenly flicked my earlobe.

"Ow, what was that for?" I asked, rubbing my ear.

"I've decided every time you ask me that, I'm going to flick you," she told me seriously as she snuggled back in against my side.

"And why does my concern for you warrant this heinous assault?"

"Because I'm done being a victim, Booker. I don't want you to look at me and see some broken woman. I know I went through a horrible experience, but compared to some people, it was nothing. I was manipulated by a man, and when I tried to say no, he assaulted me. So I left. That's it. It's behind me now, and I don't want him to have the power to steal anything else away from me."

A part of me knew she was right. And if Reece had been any other person, I probably would have agreed wholeheartedly.

But she wasn't any other person.

I wanted her to be *my person.*

I wanted to push her for details. I wanted to demand that she take me to his door so I could rip out his heart and see how he liked it.

But I didn't.

I held the woman who had captured my heart so thoroughly in my arms, and I counted myself a lucky man for Reece having found her way into my life.

CHAPTER THIRTEEN

BOOKER

I stalked through the house in the worst mood I'd been in for days. I'd fucked things up so royally I was pretty sure there wasn't a way back from this.

When there was a knock on the door, I threw it open, grabbed Dex by the shirt, and hauled him inside before slamming it closed. Even his little girlish squeak of surprise wasn't enough to break through my mood.

"I fucked up," I growled as I paced the living room again.

I'd been hiding out in the house and waiting for Dex to turn up since he texted me two hours ago to say he'd be stopping by.

From the look on his face, he knew this was serious.

Dex put the boxes he was carrying down on the couch and then, like he was trying to herd a wild animal, he approached me with his hands raised.

"There's a good Booker," he murmured. "Easy, boy."

I reached out and slapped him upside the head, but the pacing at least stopped.

"Can you pretend you're a grown-ass adult for like five minutes?"

"First, ow," he said, rubbing his head and ruffling his wavy hair into an even bigger mess. "Second, what the hell is going on?"

I blinked in surprise at the annoyed tone of Dex's voice. I'd never heard him snap at me like that before, which was kind of impressive when you considered that asshole was my go-to setting.

"I. Fucked. Up!" I stressed and then stalked over to my favorite chair and sank down, running my hands through my hair as I resisted the urge to tear it out.

Dex rounded the couch and slowly sat down, looking worried.

"Look, whatever happened, I'm sure it's not that bad. Just tell me what's going on, and we'll figure it out." Dex looked at me cautiously before adding, "You're kind of freaking me out, man. I've never seen you like this before."

I hadn't considered until right now that getting help meant telling him what I'd done, and now that I was facing it down, I wasn't so sure I could do it.

Dex pulled his cell phone out of his pocket as he watched me. "Maybe I should call Trace and Xander over here."

"Absolutely not." I snatched the phone out of his hand and shoved it in my pocket. "This is humiliating enough as it is."

"Okay, humiliating is good." I looked at him like he was insane, and then he added, "Humiliating seems less like you murdered someone, and I can work with that."

I realized then how my meltdown looked from the outside and that I might be ever so slightly overreacting.

"I slept with Reece," I blurted out.

"Ooooo-kay. And she was okay with that, right?"

"Are you actually asking me that?" I shouted, shocked that he'd ever go there.

Dex lurched back, quickly covering his head with his hands as he stared at me accusingly. "Don't shout at me! I don't know what's going on right now!"

I sucked in a huge breath through my nose and then slowly blew it out. Christ, this was so fucked up.

"I did what you said. I had breakfast with Reece. It was nice. We talked, sort of. Then we argued about who was going to do the dishes. And then we had sex."

Dex nodded thoughtfully. "I'm not seeing the problem here." When he saw the look on my face, he winced. "Oh god, what did you do next?"

He sagged back on the couch with a look of utter defeat on his face.

"She fell asleep, and I went to feed the horse, but when I came back, she was gone. And then...I freaked out, because she'd woken up alone, and—"

"You've avoided her ever since," Dex finished, and I nodded once, crossing my arms over my chest as I sank a little further into the panic that was building in my chest.

"Okay." Dex sat up straighter on the couch like he was prepared to hash out a business deal rather than fix my stupid love life. "Okay, this isn't too bad. We can work with this."

"We can work with this?" I deadpanned, hoping he knew just how stupid he sounded.

"No. It's okay. This is our fault really because we gave you step one and forgot that you don't behave like a normal human being. There should have been at least twelve more steps for you to follow." Dex nodded to himself as he steepled his hands in front of his face, tapping his fingers against the tip of his nose. "This is fixable. Right?"

"Why are you asking me that? You're supposed to be telling me!"

Dex glanced at his watch. "Is it too early for beer?"

It was ten in the morning, so we both knew the answer to that.

"I'm so fucked," I moaned, dropping my head down in my hands.

I felt Dex pat me on the back, but it didn't make me feel any better. "I've never seen you like this before, Booker. You really like her, huh?"

I couldn't explain it. Reece had been in my life for a week. It shouldn't have been possible, especially for someone like me. I kept the world at arm's length, and despite my high ambitions for the ranch and what it could do for people like me, I wasn't really a people person. I was just a guy who liked horses.

"She's...incredible." I shrugged. There wasn't much else I could add. I couldn't explain it. Reece drew me in and fascinated me in a way that no other person had before.

She was strong and compassionate. Resilient and so goddamn sexy. You'd have to be a fool not to see it.

Dex sagged back on the couch, watching me carefully for a minute. "Well, this a pickle."

I raised an eyebrow, and he shrugged again before we sank into a comfortable silence that I'd always been able to find with Dex at my side.

Dex bowled into my life on the heels of my brother Xander. They met at school one day when he moved to town to live with his grandparents, and Dex had announced them as best friends as soon as they met. He came from one of those families that gave a damn about each other, and yet he'd been inseparable from me and my brothers since that very first day. I always thought that Dex saw how terrible it was at our home, the complete lack of love and caring we had as kids, and decided to step up and fill the void with his friendship. He'd become an important person for all of my brothers, me included. I never could figure out what he got in return.

"What's in these boxes that Delaney sent, anyway?" he asked after a little while, flipping the lid of the box that sat on the top.

The brown western-style hat stared at me like an accusation. An idea that had seemed like a good idea at the time. The metal badge with the word Stetson on the leather band glinted in the sun. It seemed so ridiculous now, but even now, I knew Reece would get a kick out of it. She needed something to keep the sun out of her eyes, but any old cap would have done. The other box had a pair of boots in it to hopefully make her life a bit easier out in the barn. It had driven me mad the other day, watching her sneakers slowly get wetter and wetter as we'd washed down the mare, knowing she didn't have anything else to change into.

Dex looked at me, and then a laugh burst out of him. Usually, I'd have gone on the defensive and made some cutting remark to save my hurt feelings. I didn't this time. It was ridiculous, and I deserved him telling me exactly that.

"Oh, this is amazing." Dex grinned and picked up the hat, putting it on top of his own head despite it being far too small and making him look ridiculous. "Is this how you guys feel all the time? It's so delicious I almost don't want to say it."

I cut a glare at him out the side of my eye. I hoped he was enjoying himself right now because there would be payback soon.

Dex shuffled in his seat, turning slightly so he was facing me head-on before he stretched out his arms like he was warming up for something. He cracked his head from side to side and then braced his hands on his knees. "Okay, I'm ready. Are you ready? I'm going to enjoy this more than Christmas."

I could feel the glare deepening on my face but said nothing, regretting even thinking that this doofus could be the one to help me. I should have called Delaney. At least she wouldn't have made fun of me.

Dex licked his lips and then said, "You idiot." Grinning and nodding, he added, "Yep, just as good as I thought it would be."

"What are you talking about?" I snapped, not able to take it anymore.

I snatched the hat off his head and brushed some imaginary dust off its rim, hating that Reece wasn't the first one to try it on.

"This here," Dex said, presenting the boxes with a flourish as he passed them to me. "Is the answer to all your problems."

Okay, maybe that had me intrigued. I placed the hat back in the box and then took them, staring at them but not quite seeing the point Dex was trying to get to.

"I have to do everything." He sighed, going to grab the hat again, only for me to slap his hand away. "You bought her a thoughtful gift. Go to her, give it to her, and then repeat these exact words to her. It's important you get them in the right order, so listen carefully." Dex waited a beat, and I gritted my teeth, trying to resist the urge to hit him again. "I'm. Sorry." He stressed each word as if it was actually possible I'd be able to get them wrong.

"That's it."

Dex nodded, looking far too proud of himself than he should be.

"Wait! Bearing in mind your earlier fuck up, I'm giving you some follow-up steps because we know you can't be trusted on your own. First, I'm sorry." He held up one finger, and despite the urge to snap it off, I listened. "Second, do something fun with her. Third, have a conversation. Fourth, set a date to, well, you know, have an actual date."

And that was how I found myself standing on the wooden deck outside the cottage, holding both boxes and listening to the soft sound of Reece singing inside.

This was a bad idea.

Dex had riled me up, shoved me out the door with the promise that I could do this, and then left in his truck. And now I was standing here, frozen to the spot, because I realized I didn't actually have a plan for steps two through four, and wondering if I could sneak away before she found me.

Of course, that was the exact moment Reece opened the door and then stumbled to a stop because she hadn't expected there to be someone creeping outside the door.

"Oh crap, you scared me," she said, clutching her chest and giving me flashes of her playing with her nipples as I fucked her as hard as I could.

Okay, standing here with a rock-hard erection wouldn't win me any points.

"Booker?" Reece asked, sounding concerned as I continued to stand there and not say anything.

"Right. Yes. I'm sorry." I thrust the boxes into her hands and took a step back.

Reece peered at the boxes and then leaned forward slightly, whispering, "I don't know what's happening right now."

"I didn't...but I did...and then... These are for you. And *I'm sorry*," I stressed.

This couldn't possibly be going any worse than it was right now. Dex should have given me a better plan.

"Are you having a stroke right now?" Reece asked, actually looking worried. "Does your face feel okay? Isn't there a rhyme about what you're supposed to check? Something about arms, I think. Flap them about a bit, see how they feel."

For a second, I actually lifted my arms to do as she said before I remembered I wasn't, in fact, having a stroke. I was just breaking down in the face of a beautiful woman I'd done wrong.

I cleared my throat, looking down at my boots, and shuffled awkwardly on the spot. This wasn't a good look for a man my size. I needed to pull it together.

"I'm sorry I wasn't there when you woke up yesterday," I said, mainly looking at my boots because I didn't want to see the look on her face when she told me it was a mistake.

"That's okay. I figured you had to go out to do something. I shouldn't have fallen asleep, but I think you put me into a sex coma."

I was so surprised by what she said that my head snapped up to see if she was actually being serious.

"I should have come to find you."

"Booker, seriously, it's okay. I'm a big girl. And I think we both needed to clear our heads for a bit. It was pretty intense."

"Yeah."

She took a step to the side. "Do you want to come in?"

"No."

"Right. I guess I'll see you around then." Her face furrowed in confusion, and I nearly kicked myself.

"I mean, no, I don't want to come inside because I want to do something with you," I clarified.

"Ah, see? Words can help."

She went to put the boxes back into the house when I stopped her and added, "You're going to need them."

Reece grinned and closed the door, moving to the small table on the porch to put the boxes down and look inside. Then she squealed, spinning to look at me. "Are these for me?" she asked, already putting the hat on her head and then striking a pose. "How do I look?"

"Beautiful," I told her honestly, tugging on the brim of the hat.

I wanted to kiss her, but it didn't seem right. I didn't know what she wanted out of this situation, and we needed to discuss it like adults before we got any deeper into the confusing mess we were currently in. Or I was in. Reece seemed to be acting like she was completely fine, and that was messing with my head even more.

I was almost positive I had something to apologize for here. Her not seeming to think so was worrying, to say the least.

"You didn't need to do this," Reece said, picking the boots out of the box. "I'm kind of surprised that you got my size right."

"That was all Delaney. I don't know about that sort of stuff."

Reece sat down on one of the chairs and kicked off her sneakers. I kneeled down at her feet and grabbed the boots as she watched me with a bemused expression.

I patted my bent thigh, and Reece put her foot on it. Gently holding her ankle, I slipped the boot onto her foot, tightening the laces and fastening it before checking the fit. It was perfect. Delaney had done a good job.

I repeated the process with her other foot and then peered up at Reece, watching me with an expression I couldn't figure out on her face. My thumb absentmindedly brushed along her thigh as I stared up at her, frozen to the spot.

Except it wasn't out of fear this time.

Not exactly.

Being this close to her, doing something as silly as tying her boots, I understood now that dopey expression Trace got on his face whenever he was close to Delaney.

I was starting to feel something I had no business feeling after just a week of knowing Reece.

"Come on," I said, tapping her boot and finally climbing to my feet. "I want to do something with you."

Reece stood, and we walked out to the barn together. We checked in on the mare, and she was actually doing a lot better than I would have expected her to be. I trimmed her back hooves yesterday when the temperature cooled down. When Reece hadn't come to help, I'd pretty much made up my mind that I completely messed things up with her.

If this was my second chance, I was damn well not making the same mistake again.

Doc was hanging out in the training ring on the other side of the barn. I was trying to keep the small one at the front of the house empty so we could transfer the mare to it and give her some space to move around. She couldn't go out into the pastures while we were monitoring her food so tightly, and she wasn't strong enough to be out there anywhere. Cole had taken some blood from her, and we were still waiting for the results to make sure she didn't carry anything that could pass to the other horses. Until she had the all-clear, she had to stay in isolation.

I'd tacked Doc up, intending to ride the pastures this

afternoon and check the fence lines. As seemed to be the case for the past week, I was going to push that off to Cliff or Hank for now. It wasn't like they were hugely busy at the minute anyway. They might as well do some work to earn their keep.

"This is Doc," I told Reece as I ducked through the wooden fence surrounding the training ring and patted Doc's neck. He turned his head toward me, nuzzling against my pocket to search for treats.

"He's beautiful."

"He was the first horse I bought when I got the ranch, and we've been together ever since, haven't we buddy?" Doc snorted and went to nibble at the brim of my hat, making Reece laugh. "He's getting to be an old man now."

"You ride him?" Reece asked.

"Yep, and so will you."

She looked at me with wide eyes, and I chuckled as I held out a hand, inviting her into the ring. Reece didn't look overly confident about the idea, but she ducked through the wood rails and took my hand.

"I'm not sure this is a good idea," she whispered, going to stroke Doc's muzzle, who did the same treat inspection on her as he did everyone. Reece laughed. "The only horse I've ever ridden was a pony at the county fair when I was six."

"Well, I think you'll find that Doc is the sweetest, most patient boy you'll ever meet, and if you can ride that old county pony, you can definitely sit on the back of Doc."

She looked at me like she was pretty sure I'd lost my mind, but then she shrugged and stepped to his side.

"Okay, how do I do this thing, then?"

Reece dusted off her hands and then stared at the

saddle like it was something she could figure out if she just tried hard enough.

Shaking my head at her sheer determination to do whatever she put her mind to, I came to her side. "Bend your leg," I instructed, grasping her knee in one hand when she did. "On the count of three, I'm going to give you a boost, and you're going to swing your other leg over Doc's back and sit in the saddle. Grab the front of the saddle with your left hand and then grab it with your other hand when you're on the way up."

Reece peered over her shoulder at me, and I could see the doubt in her eyes. "I got you," I reassured. "On three, remember? One... two... three."

Reece jumped, and I pushed her up, completely underestimating how light she actually was, and she shot up into the air with a squeak of surprise. Thankfully, I still had hold of her leg, so instead of firing her over Doc's back, I pulled her back down into the saddle instead.

She landed with an oomph, and when she'd recovered enough to loosen her iron grip on the saddle, she scowled down at me.

Doc gave him his due and didn't even move a step.

"Sorry about that." I grinned up at her, and she instantly relaxed. "I forgot you were a skinny thing."

Reece cocked her head to the side as she thought. "I'm going to just believe that was a compliment and move past it," she quipped.

"I promise you're going to have fun," I said, grabbing the reins and passing them to her.

I had no idea if that was actually true, but hopefully, this would be a solid step two.

CHAPTER FOURTEEN

REECE

I had no idea if what I was doing was right. All I'd really learned from this experience was that having a distractingly hot cowboy walking next to you while trying to concentrate on balancing on the back of a horse was a terrible idea.

And damn, if Booker wasn't the most distracting man I'd ever laid eyes on.

I couldn't remember the last time someone had gone out of their way to get me something I needed.

It didn't matter that he'd needed help. I wouldn't have a clue what size boots he needed, let alone if hats even came in different sizes.

He'd seen something I needed, and he'd just done it because it was a nice thing to do. It shouldn't have made me want to cry as much as it did.

"I can see why you like this," I said, even if it was just because I wanted something to say.

Booker hummed in agreement. "I always knew this was where I was supposed to be."

I watched how Booker walked by Doc's head, his hand

resting lightly on his neck, more out of companionship than to guide him. But I could see the way his shoulders seemed less tense. The way that he walked had less of a grumpy storming from one point to another kind of attitude to it.

"What was your grandfather like?"

Booker glanced over his shoulder at the question, but he had a soft smile on his face as he did. "He was everything my parents weren't. He came from money, but he didn't particularly like it. He loved this place, working the ranch, being outside. Gramps wasn't afraid of an honest day's work. Even though we only lived on the other side of town, we spent nearly the entire summer here. I'd have stayed forever if my parents would have let me. He taught me how to ride, to fish. We went camping, hunting. He was a busy man, but he always had time for his grandsons."

I could hear the hint of sadness in his voice for the grandfather he'd lost. Life was cruel that way. No matter how hard you loved someone, you always lost them in the end. And the more you loved them, the worse it hurt.

"I never really had anything like that. My dad passed when I was young, and I don't really remember what it was like when he was around. My mom did her best. She worked hard to pay the bills, but she wasn't really all that interested in me. At a certain point she decided she wanted to find someone else, have a second chance at love, and then it was like she forgot about me altogether."

"She still around?" Booker asked.

"No. She passed about five years ago. I didn't find out until about six months later. Her new family didn't invite me to the funeral. It didn't really matter, though. I think, in some ways, I lost her the day I lost my father."

Booker fell back a step, so he was walking beside me

His hand rubbed against my calf as we did another lap in silence, both of us lost in thoughts of the past.

"My parents always had this vision of what life was supposed to be like. They wanted the money, the status, and their sons were a way to build even more of it. My father went into property development, and he was good at it. Hell, he owns half the town now. And my mother lives for that shit. She loves walking around, thinking that everything and everyone belongs to her. I hated it all. The parties, the boasting, the expectations. All I wanted was to be outside, riding a horse, and working the land. As you can imagine, that didn't go down well in the museum they called a home."

"They wanted you to work with your dad?" I asked.

"Yeah. What's the point of having millions if you can't turn it into billions, right? It probably sounds like such rich kid problems. The funny thing is, for all their pushing, all their lectures, none of us have ended up where they wanted us. Trace worked with Dad for a while, but then when everything came out about what our mother did to Delaney, he left and never looked back. They were so caught up in everyone thinking we were the perfect family that they destroyed the whole thing."

"People are allowed to have problems, Booker. It doesn't matter how much money they have." I could see how much he hated complaining, how much he thought he didn't deserve to say that he was in pain.

"It's strange now, looking back at it. They wanted us to be so much like them, but they were never around. We barely ever saw them. Once a week, we'd have family dinner, and our mother would make us report our progress. If it wasn't good enough, then she'd sit there and lay out every single flaw she saw in us. And there were a lot."

"That's...so cruel." I couldn't believe someone would treat a child like that.

Booker looked up at me with a wry smile. "Yeah, it wasn't fun."

"So your grandfather gave you this place so you could get away? That must have made your brothers angry."

"Nah, he split everything between the four of us. My parents were the ones who were pissed because they were cut out of the will. The ranch was part of my inheritance, but the others got a bigger share of the rest of it. I didn't care. This place was all I ever wanted, and I still had enough to live off for the rest of my life."

"So you're like super rich, then?" I asked, only realizing how it sounded after the words blurted out of my mouth.

Booker laughed but didn't answer. He didn't really have to. I could tell by the way he was trying to shrug it off that not only did he have more than enough, but he also kind of hated it.

"Is that why you want to use the ranch to help people?" I asked carefully.

"It helped me. I think it could do some real good for other people, too."

"You're a good person, Booker."

He shrugged again, uncomfortable with the comment. There was something that was bothering me, though.

"You shouldn't put everything on the line for this, though, Booker. You've got a business plan, right?"

He looked over his shoulder then with a grin, bringing Doc to a stop before he reached up for me. "You worried about me, Reece?"

"Apparently."

I slid off Doc's back, and Booker gently lowered me to the ground. I bit my lip as my mouth drew level with his.

The need to kiss him was almost overwhelming, but after the awkward post-sex situation, I didn't know if it was the right thing to do.

"I have investors," Booker said, his voice gravelly as he continued to grip my hips, holding me against his body.

"Investors?" My brain was mush with the tension that lingered in the air, and all I could focus on was Booker's lips.

"For the ranch plans." Booker's lips twitched with a smile. "I have a solid business plan and backers. I haven't put everything on the line. I would if that was what it took. My father apparently imparted some wisdom somewhere along the line, though."

Even as he spoke, his hands roamed my sides, and I sighed softly at the feel of his touch.

Booker's head dipped down, his lips grazing against mine as he whispered. "Go out on a date with me."

"A date?" I leaned back in surprise, even though it was the last thing I wanted to do.

"Yeah. Dinner or something?"

"You want to go out on a date with me?"

"I think we've established that already."

"Well, I don't know," I said, stepping back and tapping a finger against my lips. "I have a very busy social calendar, you know."

"The busiest," Booker agreed, stepping forward and trapping me against the side of Doc.

"But I could maybe squeeze you in." I shrugged and leaned up on my tiptoes, grazing my lips across his.

Booker's arm wrapped around me as he kissed me back, his lips fiercely pressing against my own as he groaned. One hand cradled my cheek, the fingertips grazing my neck and making me shudder.

When he pulled back, neither of us moved away. I stared into his eyes, seeing an emotion growing there that he'd no doubt see mirrored in mine.

It scared me.

Not because I didn't want to feel it.

But because I didn't want to risk losing everything I'd found here if I messed this up, just like everything else.

"Booker," I started.

But then his finger pressed against my lips to stop me.

"I know. Let's just agree to try. To see where it goes and just have fun. We don't have to put a label on anything until we're ready to do that."

I nodded, a wave of relief flowing through me that just made me feel guilty. I couldn't start anything with Booker without telling him my story. Not the part about my lonely childhood, the part that I ran from.

I could see myself building a life in Willowbrook. The cute small town in the middle of nowhere had a charm that made me never want to leave. And so what if Booker stood beside me in that picture? The guy I'd only met a week ago with a heart of gold he didn't want anyone to know he had.

CHAPTER FIFTEEN

BOOKER

I would never hear the end of it from Dex that his advice about Reece had actually worked. The weirdest thing was that I didn't even care. I'd live a life of his incessant teasing if it kept Reece by my side.

I saw the doubt in her eyes when I asked her out. It wasn't that she didn't want me. She was afraid. And I couldn't blame her. It was hard enough to put your heart out there, and doubly so when someone had already abused it.

But I was okay with slow. Not that we'd really followed that advice up until now.

This thing between us burned with a fire I'd never experienced before.

That was how I knew. How I knew she was the one I wanted to fight for. The one that was worth the dance.

But right now, none of that helped me. Because here I was, sitting in my truck outside of my parents' house, trying to work up the courage to go inside.

I hated this place. I rarely, if ever, came back if I could

help it. In fact, I rarely, if ever, saw my parents, and they were just as okay with that as I was.

They had such high hopes for their eldest, and once I'd failed every single one of them, they'd cast me aside. It was possibly the nicest thing they'd ever done for me.

Now, we all did our best to pretend the other didn't exist, and my parents tried their damndest to make sure no one else knew about it. I didn't really give a damn about what the town thought. As long as they left me alone, and I could live my life however I wanted, I didn't really care about any of it anymore.

Dex: The parts are here. Reece's car will be done in a couple of days.

Me: You already told me that.

Dex: I know. I just wanted an excuse to text you so I could pretend I hadn't been wondering all day if you asked Reece out.

Xander: Wait, you're asking Reece out? When did this happen?

Trace: Damn, now I owe Delaney twenty bucks.

Xander: Do we like Reece?

Me: You don't have to like her at all. I'm the one who's going out with her.

Xander: Hey, I'm in this family too. I just want to know if she's good enough for my big brother.

Trace: According to Delaney, she's amazing and exactly what he needs.

Me: Why does that sound so insulting?

Trace: They're all too good for us.

Me: I can't think about Reece right now.

Dex: Oh, man. She said no?

Me: Of course she didn't say no.

Dex: Then what's wrong, big bear?

Me: I'm at the parents' house.

Xander: Why?

Me: Someone needs to get the info on Gage.

Dex: And you volunteered as tribute? Shit, Booker, you should have let me come with you.

It should help that they knew why I didn't want to do this and fully supported me not being around those people.

Except it didn't.

Someone had to do it, and I wasn't about to let Trace or Xander walk into that place. Not when they were finally free.

That was why I'd driven my ass here this morning. I was the black sheep child that they didn't want around. Yes, I'd be subject to the worst of our mother's criticism, but she wouldn't try to suck me back into her plans. I was the last person on earth she wanted in them.

Trace and Xander couldn't say the same.

I'd failed Gage. I hadn't been there when he needed me. Hell, I hadn't even known he needed me. And, as a consequence, he'd fled in the middle of the night, leaving only a brief note, and I'd never seen my brother again.

I wouldn't fail my other brothers.

Me: It needs doing, and it might as well be me.

Dex: Do you think they'll actually give it to you?

Me: I'm not leaving without it.

Trace: I'm leaving now. Wait for me.

Me: No fucking way, brother. I'll be done by the time you get here anyway.

Damn it.

I shoved my cell into my pocket and climbed out of the car. I wouldn't let Trace ride in here thinking he was acting the hero and getting sucked back into this bullshit.

At least I'd gotten my motivation to get this done.

I wasn't surprised when the door swung open as I approached. They'd have known the minute I drove through the gates that I was here.

That it was my father standing in the doorway and not Emmie, the housekeeper, was a surprise, though.

"I need to speak with you," I said, avoiding any of the usual formalities.

He was so used to how I felt about this place that he didn't even flinch anymore. Only my mother would have had some kind of cutting remark about how I'd lost my manners in the gutter or some other such bullshit. Jasper was used to my disdain by now.

The brief flash of sadness that crossed his eyes was new, though. Not that I'd let it suck me in. It was probably just his latest manipulation tactic. The only surprising thing about it was that he'd try to waste it on me.

"We can talk in the study," he offered, holding out a hand to point the way as if I'd have forgotten.

I shoved my hands in my pockets and walked through the ostentatious hallway to the oak-lined study my father had always closed himself inside when we were kids. There was a time when I'd thought he didn't know what our mother did to us. That he was so busy it had completely passed him by.

Now that I was an adult, I saw the truth of it, though. Of course, he'd known. He just liked to pretend that he didn't.

I came to a stop in the middle of the room. There was no way I was sitting down and drawing this out any longer than it needed to be.

"I'm here for the details on Gage," I told him. "I know you kept track of him."

My father rounded his desk, sitting in his seat with a sigh before opening the top drawer of his desk. He drew out a manilla file and dropped it onto his desk. It baffled me how a man who had been so successful in life could still live in an analog age. Or maybe it was just his dirty secrets that he preferred to hide away in his paper files.

"I have my man looking for him..."

"Don't bother. We'll do it ourselves."

Gage would never come home if our parents were the ones making the offer. He needed to know that his brothers wanted him. That we didn't blame him for the things our mother had dragged him into as a child.

My father sighed, leaning back in his chair. I could almost see the gears spinning as he tried to figure out how to use this to his advantage.

"Okay." He held out the file for me, and I cautiously took it.

"Okay?" There was no way it would be this easy.

"Yes. I know I've been a terrible father. That I turned a blind eye to things that shouldn't have happened. I should have been more present. I should have been stronger for you boys. I failed you."

"Terrible things? The nights when she locked us in the stables for failing to achieve her impossible standards. The staff she fired for sneaking us food when she'd decreed that hunger would make our minds sharper. Are these the terrible things you're only now regretting?"

My father went pale. There was no way he hadn't known, even if that was the impression he wanted to give. He couldn't have been so blind that he didn't know what was happening in his own house.

"I've made so many mistakes that I don't know how to make up for it," he admitted.

"Sometimes there is no making up for the things you did in the past. Sometimes you just have to live with the consequences."

I turned around to storm out of the house only to find my mother standing in the doorway, glaring at me like I was something that had been dragged in on the sole of a shoe—not one of hers, of course. She'd never stoop so low as to have that happen.

"Why are you here?"

"I'm saving my brothers from having to come to this place. But don't worry, I'm leaving now."

She didn't move. Even at her barely five feet in height, she just stood there and looked down on me. I wasn't above pushing past her, but there was a sick part of me that wanted to hear what she had to say. To hear the cutting remark she'd spit at me to prove that I'd done the right thing.

"Regina, everything he said..."

"I did to make them *stronger*," she spat at my father. "Someone had to. We all knew you were too busy."

I looked back at my father over my shoulder. He'd surged out of his seat and was bracing his hands on his desk. The glare he leveled at my mother actually made me frown.

There was no possible way he hadn't known it all. Was there?

"Booker, we need to talk," my father called after me as I took another step forward to leave.

My mother sneered at me. I knew I was her greatest disappointment, but I didn't know when she'd started to hate me this much.

"Let him go," she scoffed. "We don't need his kind around here. Think of the property value, Jasper." Then she laughed like it was the funniest thing she'd ever heard.

"Regina, for god's sake," my father snapped.

"There's a reason why people take out the trash, dear. All it does if you keep it around is stink up the place."

"Shut. Up!" My father bellowed so loudly that my mother's mouth actually snapped shut with a click of her teeth.

Spinning on the spot, she stormed out of the room, leaving behind a cloud of Chanel that caught in the back of my throat, making me want to gag.

I was a step behind her, ready to put this place and the people in it behind me for as long as I could get away with.

"Booker, wait!" my father called after me. I heard his footsteps clacking on the marble floor behind me. I just didn't want to stop and talk to him.

I had what I needed. There was nothing else left here for me.

"Please," he said as he followed me down the steps.

I hesitated at the truck, turning back to him in a moment of weakness. "What?" I snapped.

"I didn't..." His voice broke, and he turned to look off into the distance, clearing his throat before he could meet my gaze again. "If there's anything I can do to help you locate Gage, let me know."

"There's nothing I need you for anymore."

And I got into my truck and drove away, those words ringing through my head as I drove away.

I pulled the truck to a stop at the gate, pulling my cell from my pocket to fire off a text before I turned out onto the main road, swearing this was the last time.

Me: It's done. I have the file.

CHAPTER SIXTEEN

REECE

I was getting ready to feed the mare again when I heard the tires of Booker's truck come to a skidding stop on the gravel.

I'd never heard him rush anywhere, and knowing he'd gone to his parents' house this morning, I had a terrible feeling that it hadn't gone well.

There was a part of me that felt like I shouldn't get involved. Booker had touched on his childhood the other day when he was teaching me to ride. I knew he hadn't told me the full story. I could understand needing to keep parts to yourself private until you'd processed them. Even then, sometimes your sad stories were such a big part of you that you weren't ready to let them go.

I came out of the barn at the same time that he was slamming the door of his truck closed. It almost seemed like a black cloud hung over him as he dragged one hand through his hair and then put his hat back on his head.

A moment of doubt hit my mind, but I shook it off. Holding back now wasn't what Booker needed. That was what everyone in his life had done, and I wanted to show him that there was a different way.

So before I could second guess myself, I strode out of the barn toward him. He caught sight of me as I approached, and I saw his lips twitch with happiness, even if it didn't fully make it to the surface.

That was okay. These were baby steps we were taking

I leaned up on my tiptoes and wrapped my arms around Booker. It was like he didn't quite know what to do at first, but then his arms slowly came around me, and his face burrowed against my neck.

We stood like that for a moment, Booker soaking up the affection he needed.

I needed it too. Maybe it was a selfish gesture, but there was so much I felt when Booker held me in his arms. Feelings I didn't think I'd feel for another person for a very long time.

"Thank you," he said as he pulled back.

I smiled. There was no need for thanks. I'd spend all day curled up on his lap if he wanted me to.

"Did you get the information you needed?"

Booker held up the file between us. "Come on. Let's go get something to eat, and we can look at this."

I hesitated for a second, not sure if this was something I should get involved with. It seemed really personal, and I didn't want to insert myself where I didn't belong. This thing between me and Booker was so new. We weren't even at the stage of putting a label on it, and we'd only just decided that we wanted to see where it goes.

Booker glanced over his shoulder and hit me with one of his smiles. "Come on. I'm not making lunch all by myself."

I shook my head and followed as my stomach growled loudly, transforming Booker's smile into a full-on grin.

"Hungry?"

I looked him up and down, appreciating the way the denim cupped his ass. "You could say that."

He laughed, jogging up the porch steps. "Be careful what you ask for," he warned.

"Just so we're clear, I'm definitely asking for wild, hot sex."

Booker stumbled a step and then spun around, walking backward further into the house. "I'd better get you fueled up and ready for a workout then."

Oh damn, today was going to be so much more fun than I'd woken up thinking it would be.

Why did sandwiches always taste so much better when someone else made them?

I tore another bite out of the club sandwich Booker had made and groaned in delight.

"What did you put in this?" I asked around a mouthful.

Booker sniggered. "Have you not eaten today or something?"

I raised an eyebrow, trying to look annoyed by the implication. "You've got a bit of mayo here," Booker joked, swiping at the corner of my mouth with his thumb.

Well, that didn't quite work as planned.

"I can't help it. This is fantastic. You have a bright future as a sandwich artist." I waved the last of my sandwich at him to prove my point before ungracefully shoving it into my mouth.

"I'll write it on my resume in case the whole ranch thing fails," Booker answered wryly, picking up his own sandwich and taking a bite that looked almost delicate compared to mine.

Then he did the one thing that could possibly make me fall in love with him. He lifted his plate and offered me the other half of his sandwich.

"This is the nicest thing anyone has ever done for me," I whispered, staring at my prize and licking my lips.

"That's the saddest thing I ever heard."

"Eh, it is what it is." I shrugged, nodding over at the file that sat on the corner of the table. "So did you look inside?"

Booker looked at the file and then sneered as if the thing had insulted him. "Nope."

"Are you...going to look at it?" I asked carefully.

"I suppose." Booker leaned back in his chair and continued to glare at the file.

I'd honestly seen nothing like it. It looked like something you saw old-school PI movies using. Who had actual paper files anymore? Well, obviously, Booker's dad, but for a guy who was apparently worth millions, he really needed to embrace the digital age.

"Do you want me to do it?" I asked.

When Booker picked it up and gave it to me, I was genuinely surprised. I hadn't actually thought he'd want me to. I was banking on it prompting him to flip it open and look himself.

Now that it was in my hand, I didn't really want to open it either.

"See," he said smugly. "It's not that easy, is it?"

Luckily for Booker, my stubbornness kicked in, and I laid the file between us, flipping it open, and reading the first page as if I was trying to prove a point. But once I looked, it was like I couldn't look away.

Booker stood from the table, gathering our dishes and heading to the sink. I knew he needed space from the information we had, and I pulled the file in front of me as I sunk into the details.

"Can I use your laptop again?" I asked, not taking my eyes off the file as I flicked through the pages.

I heard him leave the room and then return before Booker set the laptop down next to me.

Glancing up at him, I found him watching me curiously. "It's not that bad," I said softly. "Do you want me to stop?"

He thought for a moment, his eyes moving to the two pages that were currently laid out in front of me.

"No." Then Booker braced one hand on the back of my chair and the other on the table as he leaned over me and finally looked at the information his father had given him. "Does it say where he is?"

"It says where he was." I flipped the pages back to the beginning, which contained a summary. "He moves around a lot. It looks like he spends a year at most in one place before he travels around for a couple of weeks and then settles into one location for an extended period. Probably because he got a job there. You said your grandfather left you all money. I'm assuming he gave Gage a share, too."

Booker nodded. "As far as I know, it's still sitting in trust for him. He'd already left by the time he passed, and he never came back to claim it."

"It's strange that your father didn't have his PI approach him about it. Isn't he legally required to do that or something?" I asked.

Booker shrugged. "He wasn't the executor of the will. My grandfather's lawyer took care of that. I guess, legally, that gives him an out. It won't win him any favors when Gage comes home and finds out, though."

I hummed in agreement. Part of me didn't want to get involved with the drama surrounding Booker's family, but I could see how much he needed someone to talk to about it.

"Do you think your parents regret what they did?" I asked as I pulled up the usual social media accounts and logged in.

Booker watched in interest before finally grabbing a chair and pulling it up to see what I was doing.

"I doubt it. My mother would never admit that she was wrong. My father? Maybe. He seems to be going for the 'I had no idea this was happening' route. I'm not sure if that makes it worse or not."

My hand moved to Booker's knee, and he just smiled at me sadly.

It made my earlier idea seem even better than it had before. The only parts of Booker's family that he wanted had fractured under the weight of their past and ran as far and as fast as they could. But now, they were starting to slowly return, and even if it took me years, I'd find a way to bring them all back together. I'd make sure that Booker got all his brothers back. They could build the family they always wanted between them. They didn't need their parents in their lives to have something beautiful.

I checked down the list of places where Gage had spent a longer length of time and picked one at random before googling it. As I pulled some general images from the internet, I set about changing my social media accounts to show me in the same location.

"This feels an awful lot like trying to catfish your brother," I murmured, and Booker looked at me strangely. "And you don't know what that is." I realized.

Booker shrugged, picked up the file, and flicked through to the end. "He was last in Oregon, but that was nearly a year ago. It seems like he dropped off the grid for a while."

I posted a couple of the pictures, sending friend requests to some people Gage was linked to in the area. Mostly guys, because I knew they'd accept without even thinking about it. The aim was to make it seem like I was where Gage had been, so he'd accept a friend request, and then maybe I'd be able to spark up a conversation with him. It didn't hurt that it made me seem like I was a lot further away from my ex than I really was.

By the time I was done, Booker looked completely defeated. "I wouldn't come back if I was him," he finally said. "Look at this life he's had. He travels through all these places, doing these incredible jobs."

"It must be lonely, though." Booker looked confused, so I explained. "He never stays anywhere, so he never makes any connections with anyone strong enough to make him *want* to stay."

It wasn't the right thing to say.

Booker looked completely defeated.

"I failed him. I'm his big brother. He should have known he could come to me."

"Booker, you were all kids. None of you are to blame for your parents' actions."

He shook his head, either not ready to hear it or just not believing that it was true.

"What can I do?" I asked, desperately wanting to make this better for him.

Booker wrapped an arm around my shoulders and drew me into his side. "Tell me about this." He nodded at the computer, and after a brief explanation of what I was doing, he looked at me in surprise. "How did you get so good at this stuff?"

"Well, it used to be my job. Not catfishing people. I think that might be illegal. But social media promotion for businesses and organic content campaigns." I could see I was already losing him. "I ran social media accounts for businesses so they could reach their customers in ways that didn't involve paid advertising."

Booker squinted in suspicion. "And why are you working in my barn?"

"Because you offered me a job doing that?"

"I mean, why aren't you doing that job for me? There are a lot of businesses in town that could benefit from that too. Delaney would probably bite your hand off if she knew you could do that for her company."

The more Booker spoke, the more excited he seemed to get.

I'd never hated my job. If anything, it was actually pretty fun. And I missed it at times. But I loved working in that barn. I loved spending time with the little mare I hadn't thought of a name for yet.

"What's wrong?" Booker asked when he saw the look on my face.

"I like it here," I whispered. "I enjoy doing this."

He squeezed me tighter and then huffed in annoyance before he scooped me out of my chair and deposited me in his lap instead. "That's better," he grumbled. "You don't have to do your old job if you don't want to. I'd love the help, but I'm sure you could point me in the right direction of someone else if you didn't want to do it. I just don't want you to waste your time feeding horses when you're clearly qualified enough to do something better."

I leaned my head against Booker's shoulder, trying to figure out how to say what I wanted without upsetting him. But then I realized Booker was the last person I needed to worry about explaining this to. Because he'd already told me he felt exactly the same way. It was the whole reason he'd walked away from the life his parents had wanted for him.

"There's just something about this place, Booker. It's special. I honestly haven't been as excited to get out of bed and go to work as I have been since I've been here. But if you promise I can keep doing what I'm already doing, I'd be happy to help you out with the other stuff. I think sharing this with the rest of the world and giving people a chance to find out how special this place is would be a really amazing thing to do."

He kissed me then. "You're amazing, you know that?" he whispered before he kissed me again.

"I'm not sure I did anything to deserve the compliment, but I'll take it, anyway."

Booker's head threw back as he laughed and then we were on the move again as he cradled me in his arms and suddenly stood up.

"Where are we going?" I squeaked, clinging to him a little tighter.

"Someone mentioned something about wild, hot sex, and I think you deserve a reward." His eyes glinted with amusement as he looked down at me, and I swallowed hard with the emotional whiplash.

Not that I wasn't completely for this course of action.

In fact, there'd been little I'd thought of since the first time Booker had taken me to bed.

Booker took the stairs quickly, striding into his room as he kissed me again. He twisted in the air as he fell back on the bed, maneuvering me so that I was straddling him. My hands came to his shoulders as I plundered his mouth, my hips twitching in anticipation.

This was exactly what we needed.

A chance to get lost in each other and forget about the rest of the world for a while.

CHAPTER SEVENTEEN

BOOKER

Reece was all soft curves and beautiful whimpers as I ran my hands up the back of her shirt, feeling her silky skin beneath.

Obviously, I'd been with women before her, but I always got out of town when I needed a night with someone else. One-night stands with anonymous women were easier. There was no baggage, no constant reminders of expectations of more when you ran into them every day.

But it was different with Reece.

I wanted to learn every inch of her body. To find out the things that made her breath catch, the ways to make her writhe in pleasure.

I might be obsessed with the feel of her body against mine, and I doubted I'd ever be able to get enough.

She sat up, straddling my thighs as she grasped the hem of her shirt and tore it over her head. I couldn't stop myself from tracing the edges of the lace that covered her breasts. Watching the way her back arched slightly into my touch and her nipples pebbled, begging for attention.

"Tell me what you need," Reece whispered, leaning back down to kiss me again.

"You. Only you."

My hand threaded into her hair as I deepened the kiss, the other brushing down her body until I cupped her ass and pressed her harder against me.

How had I lived so long without her?

As we sank into the rhythm of our lips brushing against each other, the sweet bites along her jaw that I trailed my tongue over as I made my way to her neck.

I wanted to taste every inch of her body. I could spend days lying here, learning the map of freckles painted across her skin.

I rolled us both to press Reece back into the mattress, needing to reach all the parts of her I couldn't before.

As my tongue trailed along the edge of her lace bra, she brushed the hair back from my face, watching as I sucked her nipple into my mouth, teasing the tip with my teeth.

She groaned, her hips twitching at the sensation, and I reached down to quickly unfasten her jeans and strip them down her legs.

I found myself standing at the end of the bed, staring down at Reece in her white lacy underwear and licking my lips.

"The things I want to do you," I murmured, pulling off my shirt.

Reece smiled, leaning up on her elbows as she slowly spread her legs. "Hmmm, well, get over here and come and do them then."

She didn't need to ask me twice, and I crawled up the bed as I held myself over her. Her fingers ran across the muscles of my stomach before they moved to my shoulders and down my arms.

I loved the feel of her gentle touch, but there was something I wanted more.

I slowly lowered myself down, touching her with just my lips as I moved them down her body, licking and kissing across her skin. I watched in fascination as the muscles in her stomach fluttered beneath my touch, and I added my fingers to the mix, tracing the contours of her body toward the dip of her belly button.

"Booker," she whined. "You're always such a tease."

I smiled against her skin, my fingers brushing along the edges of her panties as her hips kicked up in anticipation once more.

"It'll be worth the wait," I told her, letting my lips move across the lace between her legs.

Reece groaned again, but it definitely sounded more like impatience than anything else, and I couldn't leave my lady wanting. So I gave her what she wanted.

My fingers wrapped around the edges of her panties, and I tugged them down, swiping my tongue across her core as I did.

Reece sighed, lifting her shoulders off the bed as she quickly pulled off her bra. Her breasts were impossible to resist, and I kissed the soft mounds as her hands quickly went to my waist, and she pushed the rest of my clothes free.

Moving away from her was near torture, so I quickly found a condom in the bedside drawer and dropped it onto the bed. It wasn't easy to search through a drawer when you had a minx in your bed trying to distract you with her lips.

Reece made a grab for the condom, but I tsked, batting her hand away.

"Not yet. Come and sit on my face first," I told her,

lying back and licking my lips at the thought. "I want to taste you."

She groaned in delight but wasted no time in crawling up my body. I loved that she wasn't one of those women who tried to make excuses to not do the things they really wanted to do.

I was just about to grab her hips and claim my prize when she surprised me and spun around, angling herself down my body instead as her knees came to either side of my shoulders.

"I'm not so sure that's a good idea if you want this to last longer than—"

The words froze in my throat as she licked up the length of my cock, circling her tongue around the tip before she wrapped those beautiful lips around me and gently sucked.

My hands tightened on her hips as I closed my eyes and gave myself a moment to just feel. Stars burst behind my eyelids as Reece moved up and down my length, licking my cock like a lollipop before starting the whole thing again.

It took all of my restraint to hold still, to not thrust up into her mouth and push further into her throat.

So I grabbed onto the only distraction I had, the one I'd wanted all along, and I pulled her down to my mouth and showed her just how appreciative I was.

Reece gasped as I worked her clit with my tongue, pushing a finger inside her beautiful wet pussy as I held her to my face. I felt her try to pull away as she suddenly released her mouth from my cock with a gasp.

She wasn't going anywhere. Not until she'd come all over my face.

Her hips twitched as her forehead dropped to rest against my thigh, and I could feel her breath ghosting across my cock and making it twitch at the sensation.

"Ride my face, baby," I murmured as I pressed another finger inside her. "Take what you need."

She groaned at my words, but as I went back to work on her clit, she didn't hesitate, and her hips started to slowly grind against my fingers inside her.

"Oh god, Booker. That feels incredible."

I could hear the desperation in her voice, and as much as I'd like to tease her until she begged me to come, I also couldn't wait to finally sink my length inside her.

Reece groaned again as I picked up the pace, sucking her clit between my lips as I did. My fingers moved quicker, and Reece's hips kept moving in time.

I was in heaven.

I could feel the quiver building in her thighs, and I knew she was close.

Reece whimpered and panted, her hands clutching at my thighs as she crept closer to the edge of orgasm.

With shaky hands, I felt her roll the condom down my length. Just feeling her delicate fingers sliding down me had me wanting to come. But there was no way I was letting this end that quickly. Not before I'd heard her cry out my name.

But before I could get her there, before I got to hear those sweet cries I craved, Reece slipped from my grasp and moved down my body before she impaled herself on my cock.

"Fuck!" I yelled as my cock slipped inside her, and Reece's pussy immediately clamped down on me as she quickly came.

Reece's head tipped back, and her beautiful blonde hair cascaded down her back as she arched, gripping her breasts with both hands as she ground down hard on me.

I sat up, wrapping my arms around her as I gritted my

teeth and used every ounce of my control not to come inside her.

"Minx," I groaned as I held her tightly against my chest, and Reece laughed.

"You can't be the boss all the time," she purred.

"That just sounds like a challenge to me."

"Really?" She glanced back at me over her shoulder, and the sassy smirk on her face had me grinning in response.

She had no idea what she was asking for.

"You're not healed enough for that just yet," I told her, kissing her creamy white shoulder and trailing my fingertips up her sides.

Reece sucked in a breath at the sensation, and her nipples pebbled into tight points as I let my hands gently caress over her breaths. She tipped her head to the side with a sigh.

"That shouldn't feel as good as it does," she murmured, her hips slowly circling as she did.

I could tell she was ready for more, and as her shoulder tipped back so her head lay against my shoulder, I dragged that gentle touch slowly up her throat, before pinching her chin and turning her head to kiss her lips.

"Every time someone touches you, it should feel nothing less than incredible," I told her. "And I'm going to prove that to you for as long as you'll let me."

Her eyes darted back and forth as she searched my gaze, and then a soft smile touched her lips like she'd found the truth there. She said nothing. Instead she slowly rose and started to lazily ride my length.

It was slower than the things I wanted to do to her, but Reece had enough of men trying to impose their will on her for a lifetime. Plus, there was something about this slow, lazy pace that had me clinging to her even tighter.

It filled me with a need to have her in my arms forever.

To cherish her like she deserved.

Like no one had ever done before.

My lips peppered kisses along her jaw and down her neck, crossing her shoulder. She sighed dreamily, keeping up that maddening pace as she rolled her hips and rose onto her knees.

My hands came back to her waist, helping her keep the pace. In this position, it was all I could do to help her. I couldn't thrust up into her without losing the connection of her leaning against my front, and I wasn't prepared to let that go.

"Booker," she whispered.

Her hand came up to wrap around the back of my neck like she was trying to draw me closer. Then she took one of my hands from her waist and moved it down between her legs.

My fingers came to her clit, and she gasped as I gently brushed across that tight, oversensitive bundle of nerves.

"Yesss," she hissed. "Come with me, Booker. I need you to come with me."

Damn this woman. As if I could ever tell her no?

"I've got you, baby."

Reece picked up her pace. The lazy roll of her hips took on an edge of desperation as she chased the next orgasm she was already so close to catching.

We were both covered in a sheen of sweat as we moved together. Nothing but a wave of carnal motion. My heart pounded in my chest so hard that I was sure she must have been able to hear it. To hear how it beat only for her.

A thought surged to the front of my mind, a declaration

I had no business in making. Not yet. Not now. Reece and I had barely gotten to know each other, and I'd be out of my mind to blurt out those three little words right now.

Three little words I'd never said to anyone before.

There'd never been any other person who had gotten anywhere close to my heart before.

Not like she had.

The impossible girl I'd saved on the side of the road.

But there was no time to say any whispered words as we both careened over the edge, crying out each other's names as we clung together tightly.

I watched in fascination, cataloging all the changes in her expression as she gave herself over to the euphoria sweeping through her body. And then, when I couldn't take it anymore, my eyes closed, and I swept right along with her.

It was almost more pleasure than my body could handle, and it changed something inside. Something essential. Something primal.

I didn't think I'd ever be able to let Reece go now.

CHAPTER EIGHTEEN

REECE

The food smelled incredible, but it did nothing to stop that nervous need to pace the kitchen or maybe throw up a bit.

Nope, I was not going to sit down to dinner with Booker and his family with the smell of puke on my breath.

Ugh, why did that make me want to throw up even more?

I looked up and caught sight of Booker leaning against the kitchen door frame, watching me with a soft smile on his face.

"You're cute when you're panicking," he said.

"I'm not sure that's the compliment you think it is. In fact, some people might even think it was a bit of a red flag." I tossed the dishcloth I'd been twisting into knots into the sink and tried to look far more confident than I felt.

If there was one thing I knew about Booker, it was that he didn't even remotely resemble a red flag. He might be the kindest and most honorable man I'd ever met.

And I wasn't entirely sure what that said about my life choices up until this point. Not to downplay how amazing the man in front of me was. But really, why hadn't I allowed myself to be surrounded by good people before? Why did I put up with people who were content to make me feel less about myself?

Yikes, this really wasn't where I needed my mind to be going when I was about to stand in front of Booker's family and friends as his...girlfriend? Were we even ready to put a label like that on this?

Oh hell, now I'd gone and given myself a whole other thing to freak out about.

The sensation of Booker gently pinched my chin as he tipped back my head brought me back to my senses, and I stared up into his beautiful eyes.

There was nothing about this man that didn't mesmerize me.

"Stop it. You're perfect, and they'll love you. You've met most of them already, anyway. You have nothing to worry about. If this is because you're not ready to be around so many people, we can cancel. No one will mind."

I leaned into his solid chest, taking a moment to soak in the feeling of safety that Booker's presence seemed to give me now. He wrapped his arms around me and tucked my head under his chin.

Damn, he gave the best hugs.

"I know what you're doing," I whispered. "And you're not using me as an excuse to get out of this."

I felt his chuckle of laughter against my hair as he squeezed me tighter for a second before leaning back so he could look into my eyes.

"What is family dinner, anyway? And why do we need to do it? They can feed themselves. They've been doing it for years. I don't see why there's a sudden need for me to do it."

"Well, considering that I did all the cooking, I don't think you need to worry in that department," I teased gently.

Frankly, I was grateful he didn't point out the fact that I'd chased him out of his own kitchen this morning and refused his numerous offers of help.

The sound of the gravel driveway crunching under a car's tires helped, as well as Booker's head turning to see who was coming.

"Well, at least it's solved one problem," he said cryptically, and when I looked around him and saw it was my car driving closer, I gasped in surprise.

"What? Is that...?" And then I slipped out of Booker's arms and ran for the door.

"Hey, I was enjoying that," he grumbled, and I shook my head at the impossible man.

I was already jogging down the porch steps when my car pulled up in front of the house, and a guy I'd never met stepped out. He looked like a giant stepping out of a clown car as he unfolded himself from the driver's seat of my old Honda. Not that he seemed to care, as he smiled at me happily. His red hair caught the sun as he pulled off a baseball cap and ran his fingers through the unruly lengths before he tugged it back on again.

"You must be Reece," he said, closing the door and walking closer with his hand held out.

We shook hands, and then he jingled the keys in front of me.

"She's all ready for you. Not quite as good as new, but damn close."

I quickly grabbed the keys, practically jumping for joy.

"Thank you so much!" I called out as I darted to the car, opening the door and nearly crying from the new car smell that should have been impossible for this former piece of crap car.

I hadn't realized I was as attached to this old thing until I'd seen it driving down the driveway. I'd kind of always taken it for granted as it sat in the parking garage, barely being used. It didn't fit the image I was supposed to be showing to the world, not that I really had anywhere to drive back then.

I sighed at how naïve I'd been, feeling a wave of disbelief that I'd allowed myself to be maneuvered into that situation in the first place.

This car had taken me away from that place. It was the piece of freedom that wasn't stolen from me, and it had saved me from something I doubted I'd ever be really ready to think about.

"Well, you could feed me whatever it is that smells so delicious and then pretend to listen while I explain to you what an oil change is and why you need to do them," he quipped.

"Awww, you were doing so well."

My hands came to my hips, and I glared at him playfully.

"Personally, I think you're giving him more credit than he deserves," Booker called out from the porch, where I hadn't noticed him.

"I don't know. He fixed my car, which was on fire at one point." The guy pointed toward me, frantically nodding his head like I was making an excellent point. "And you should smell it! I'm pretty sure this car has smelled vaguely like cheese ever since I bought it."

At that point, his eyes widened in alarm. "Please tell me you didn't buy a car that smelled like cheese."

"Well, I needed something cheap, and I got him to knock a hundred bucks off it because of..."

I could tell by the way he was staring at me like I was insane that there was nothing I could say that was going to make me look any better. The truth was, I had no idea about cars or what to look for when I bought one. As long as it ran and I could afford it, I didn't really care.

Honestly, it was just a car, but I didn't think that would win me any points with this guy either.

"She made lasagna, Dex," Booker called out again. I could already see where this was going. "From scratch," he added.

Dex took a moment to think about it, but I could see the smile he was trying to hide. "How about you still let me eat some of that lasagna, and I won't tell you why the car smelled like cheese?"

My eyes widened in alarm, and my mind screamed that I really didn't want to know that under any circumstances.

"Deal!" I declared. "I'll even throw in some garlic bread and not make a fuss when you don't eat your salad."

We both headed to the house laughing, and as we passed Booker, I heard him whisper, "You're going to tell me, right?"

Dex just laughed and playfully shoved his shoulder. I didn't know him well enough to know if that was a yes, but I had a feeling that if it was, Booker would have the perfect ammunition to tease me with.

"Oh my god, I think I'm going to explode," Blake declared, rubbing her stomach as she groaned. "If you decide that you can't put up with Booker, please, for all that is holy, come and move in with me."

"Wait, wait, wait." Delaney waved her arms in front of her. "Let's at least consider all the options. I could convert a barn into a kick-ass cottage for you, and I'll even throw in a monthly supply of cider. Besides, she still hasn't moved out yet."

"Stop trying to bribe the woman," Blake gasped.

"I'll be your best friend too," Cade chimed in, swirling a piece of garlic bread through the meat sauce left on his plate.

"Betrayer!" Blake gasped dramatically. "Et tu, Brute?"

Cade squinted in confusion, not getting the reference, and then turned to me to give me the biggest smile.

"Wow, so it's like that. Just, wow." Blake crossed her arms but then darted a hand out to snag another piece of garlic bread.

Even though she seemed absolutely devastated, I could see how close they all really were. Even Booker was smiling at their antics, not that he'd ever admit it. This was exactly what he needed.

Booker might have moaned and pretended to be annoyed as his friends and family had turned up at his door. But sitting at this table now, surrounded by people who actually cared about each other, I could see just how happy it made him.

Looking around this table, I saw a group of people who had become the family they always wanted for themselves. A part of me was almost envious of Booker. There were a lot of people out in the world who were still trying to find something like this.

Delaney and Trace gave each other a dreamy look over the top of their son's head, and he reached around to run his hand over her back as he smiled at her. They were the picture of domestic bliss, and from what Delaney had told me of their story, they absolutely deserved it.

This was the family Booker didn't realize he had. The one that was slowly pulling back together after what their parents had put them through. One that was built on a foundation of respect and caring.

Yet Booker wasn't the one who I was worried about right now. Even if that was a bit strange, considering that I'd never really met Xander before unless you counted my slight freak out when he drove to the ranch the other day.

"Can I get anyone anything to drink?" I asked, giving Xander a smile and hoping it wasn't creepy.

Everyone declined, and when I looked back at Xander, he just shook his head silently.

He looked so uncomfortable, and I had no idea what to do to stop that, or why no one else seemed to have noticed. He'd barely said anything, choosing instead to sit back and watch the conversation unfold in front of him. At least he seemed to enjoy the food, even if he had been nursing the same glass of water since he arrived.

Maybe it was me? Maybe I freaked him out with the way I acted when he turned up the other day.

Did he hate me?

It couldn't have looked good that his own brother had seemed ready to set his dog on him because of some random woman he'd never even heard of.

Maybe I should just try to talk to him. Let him see I wasn't a massive weirdo who was out to take advantage of his brother. Yeah, that was probably a good idea.

"So, Xander, Booker mentioned you were a doctor in the city. What type of medicine is it you practice?" I asked politely

"Primary care," he answered and then added absolutely nothing else.

Okay, so maybe that wasn't the best tactic to win him over to my side.

Blake glanced at him out of the side of her eye and then over at me. She reached for her wine and sat back for a minute, and I tensed, waiting for her to say something that would make the situation a million times more awkward. If there was anyone in the room who would call it like it was, I could already tell it was her.

"Are we all excited about the carnival?" Blake asked, and I almost sighed in relief.

She gave me a quick wink, and I resisted the urge to leap out of my chair and hug her for breaking the strange tension that was closing in around us.

I heard Booker grumble something under his breath, and Xander cut a glare at his brother, not saying a word.

"Yes!" Cade cheered. "I'm going on all the rides and doing all the games, and Dad is going on the Ferris wheel with me!"

Trace looked like he went a slight shade of green, and Delaney chuckled at his discomfort.

"You know, if you ask, they sometimes stop it when you're at the top," Blake said, sniggering as Trace groaned at the suggestion.

"Not a fan of heights?" I asked.

"Not a fan of carnival rides that have traveled down the highway and then suspend me two hundred feet in the air," he grumbled.

"That's a big Ferris wheel," I quipped before realizing what I'd said, and Delaney snorted in amusement. "Do you have a carnival in Willowbrook often?"

I was really hoping they were going to say yes because

this was the sort of small-town life I could get on board with. Plus, I'd give anything to go on a Ferris wheel finally.

"No, actually, this is only the second time," Delaney said, and I saw Blake look just as disappointed as I was. "But it's hopefully going to be an annual thing now."

A grin slipped across my face and when I looked at Booker, he was giving me a curious look, like he was trying to figure me out.

Wait, please tell me he wasn't a carnival hater!

"We need this one to be a success first," Trace said ruefully.

"It will be. You know it will be."

"I don't. I don't have access to any local business information anymore."

I looked around the table at the people present. There was clearly something more to this that I didn't understand. Blake, thankfully, took pity on me.

"Trace used to work with his father at The Farrington Group, which basically had its fingers in all the town pies. They're trying to get some increased tourism into the town, boost the economy, blah blah blah. Trace is freaking out because he doesn't work there anymore, so he doesn't have all his behind-the-scenes access anymore."

"Oooh, okay. But all the businesses are still individually owned, right?"

"Yeah, we were more of an investment group," Trace agreed.

"And a way to exert your mother's dictator-like control over people," Delaney muttered.

Blake snorted at the comment, but no one disagreed.

"So you could just have a town meeting then," I suggested. "Get all the business owners together, see where you stand, who needs what, brainstorm together."

Trace's spine seemed to snap straight, and he looked at me with wide eyes. "Why aren't we doing that?"

"Erm, are you asking me, or is this one of those rhetorical things?"

He finally seemed to exhale before turning to Delaney, who was already pulling her phone out of her pocket. "I'll start a group chat with whoever I have numbers for and see if we can get a time and a venue decided in the next few days."

They quickly fired off questions and details between themselves like the rest of the room had faded away.

"They do this a lot," Blake said, and Cade nodded, rolling his eyes.

Dex pulled out his phone and sighed dramatically. "I guess I don't count as a local business owner, then. Rude. Not even added to the group chat. It's like I'm not even here!"

Booker apparently decided this was a good time to join in the conversation. He dramatically pulled out his own phone and showed the screen to Dex, who sighed loudly again. "It's just the two of us against the town, Book. Two stallions put out to pasture, no longer useful to society..."

"Hey, no one's putting me out to pasture," Booker quickly added. "I'm in my prime."

In a total un-Booker-like move, he gave me a cheeky wink, and I felt the blush rush to my cheeks. He was getting absolutely no arguments from me in that department.

"Ewwww," Delaney said dramatically.

"I don't get it," Cade suddenly said, and I looked at him in alarm.

Oh dang, I'd have to get used to having a kid around.

"Well, it's like this..." Blake started.

"Uncle Booker is just worried that Dex thinks he's old

and we're all laughing because he is," Delaney quickly interrupted.

"Hey!" Booker objected. "I'm not old."

"If the shoe fits, brother," Dex quipped.

My gaze quickly bounced to Xander who just sat watching the situation unfold in front of him in interest. At least he looked slightly less miserable as everyone made fun of his older brother.

"Who wants dessert?" I offered, quickly getting a grateful look from Booker.

"Me!" Blake and Cade both shouted at the same time.

As I got up to fetch the three desserts I'd made, because I was having a meltdown about people who might not like cheesecake, I couldn't help but smile. Booker might be slightly upset about being called old, but he was happy.

There was a time when I'd decided this would be how I'd repay Booker for helping me when most people wouldn't have. But now there was a part of me that really wanted to have something like this for myself.

I'd never really considered myself lonely before I came here. I thought I was progressing through life like I was supposed to. I had a job I'd worked hard for, a man who I stupidly thought cared about me. At some point, there probably would have been some kids. I'd thought that would make all the doubts and the questions disappear. That the only reason it didn't feel right was because I wasn't trying hard enough. I wasn't fulfilling some hidden need.

And I couldn't have been more wrong.

Because having people around you that cared about you wasn't about trying to change yourself to make them happy, it was about being happy because of exactly who you already were.

CHAPTER NINETEEN

BOOKER

I hadn't believed her when she said a family dinner would be a great idea. If I was completely honest with myself, the only reason I went through with it was because Reece seemed to really want to do it.

I hadn't even considered that I really had a family. And that thought made me feel like an absolute ass right about now.

It wasn't that I didn't think of Trace as family. Of course, I did. He was my brother, and I might not say it out loud, but I loved him. I guessed I'd just never really considered that we met the criteria of what a family was supposed to be. And that wasn't even taking into account Xander. We'd grown apart over the years, but that didn't mean I didn't care about him either. We'd just gotten too caught up in our own lives that it was easy to forget about the other, which made me feel like an even bigger ass than before.

Looking around at the people gathered in my home, I could see how mistaken I'd been.

They'd been here this whole time. I'd just been taking

them for granted and not giving them the credit and respect they deserved.

Even poor Dex. He'd been our friend since childhood, and he was always there whenever we needed him. Hell, he'd fixed up Reece's car, and I know for a fact that there was no way he'd charged me for all the work he'd done on it.

Over the years, I'd closed myself off. I'd shut myself away on this ranch, convincing myself that it was for the best. That I was protecting myself. All I'd done was deprive myself of the life I'd always dreamed of. I pushed away not just the people who hurt me but those who genuinely cared about me as well. And I wasn't the only Farrington brother who'd done that. Pushed and pushed at the cost of not just themselves but the people around them.

That was going to change.

Because Reece was right, and I was absolutely telling her that when we were finally alone again.

But first, there was something more serious I needed to deal with.

"Come on," I said, pushing Xander's feet off my coffee table as I stood up. "You can help me with some last things around the ranch for the night."

He looked up at me in alarm and then down at his fancy slacks. "What? I'm working for my supper now, am I?"

"Damn straight. Now, move your ass."

I strode through the kitchen and headed out the back door, Val running around me before she fell into step at my side. This was her favorite part of the day and even the promise of belly scratches from Cade wouldn't keep her from the ranch chores.

If only everyone else had the same attitude. Well, minus the belly scratches. I had my limits, except for Reece.

I could hear Xander's footsteps as he jogged down the

steps behind me, and I gritted my teeth as I pushed my feelings down.

He was my brother, and that won him a certain amount of understanding. But I wasn't living my life the way we had in the past. I wasn't shutting up and watching anyone treat the people I cared about like shit.

"Val, come," I snapped, immediately feeling bad as she looked up at me from my side. "Sorry, girl." I ducked down and ruffled the hair at the back of her neck, keeping pace until he reached the barn.

Unfortunately for Xander, the closer we got to the door, the more my frustration built.

Three steps inside and I was spinning on the spot, grabbing my brother by his starched shirt collar and tossing him against a stall door.

"What the fuck!" he gasped as he bounced off the wood, and I pushed him back to pin him in place.

"What the fuck? Damn straight, what the fuck, Xander! What do you think you're doing?"

His brow furrowed in confusion, but he didn't push me away from him. He hung there looking almost resigned and waiting for what came next.

It made me pause, and my gaze moved over my brother as I really looked at him for the first time since he'd arrived in town.

With a sigh, I stepped back. "What's going on, Xander?" I asked, slightly calmer than before.

He brushed his hands over his shirt like he was trying to straighten out the non-existent wrinkles. It was a tick he'd had since he was a kid. It came from the impossible standards our parents had held us to and Xander's constant pursuit of them.

Until he stopped.

And he went off to college, barely ever returning to town again.

Xander's eyes moved to his shoes, and then he went to move past me. "What did you need help with?" he said as he tried to walk away.

I didn't push him back this time, even if the anger inside me really wanted to. My hand came to his shoulder, and I stopped him in his tracks.

"Don't do that. Don't ignore whatever it is you need to talk about."

He glanced at me over his shoulder. "You're not exactly one to talk. A minute ago, you were throwing me across the barn, and now you want to hold hands and talk about our feelings?"

"I'm not holding your fucking hand. Now tell me what's going on?"

Xander sighed. He moved back to the stall door and leaned against it of his own volition this time, but his eyes stayed on the ground as he tried to find the words for whatever it was he was struggling to say.

"I messed up, Book," he finally said. When Xander looked up and finally met my eyes, I almost didn't recognize my brother. "I really messed up."

My hand moved back to his shoulder, but instead of shoving him away from me, this time I pulled him closer and hugged him tight. I stepped back from a bewildered-looking Xander.

"It won't be as bad as it seems. We'll fix it, but you're done being rude to Reece. Whatever stick you shoved up your ass before you came here, you need to pull it out. And you owe her a damn apology."

Xander's eyes widened almost comically. "I wasn't. ." Then he sighed. "I'll apologize. I'm sorry, Book. I didn't mean...Hell, I'm too lost in my head. I don't know what I'm doing half the time."

"It's never as bad as it seems," I repeated and then nodded toward the back of the barn where the little unnamed mare was still stabled. Xander followed as I headed to the hay storage. Val pushed her way between us and then moved closer to Xander like she always did when someone was hurting.

"I'm an alcoholic." Xander laughed wryly, and my shoulders tensed at the impact of his statement. "I've never admitted that to someone I know before."

"Okay, well..."

"And I lost my medical practice."

"What!"

Shit, that wasn't the right reaction, but hell, you didn't just casually drop a statement like that and expect a person to shrug it off.

"Yep, everything caught up with me, and my partners didn't want to deal with the fallout, so they strongly suggested that I let them buy me out, and then casually threatened they'd report me to the medical board if I didn't."

"Whoa, whoa, back up a bit. I'm still digesting this."

Xander glanced at me out of the side of his eye and then made his way over to where the hay bales were stacked in the corner before dropping onto one. "There's nothing to digest, Book. It's a done deal. I took the deal, and they bought me out ten months ago."

"Ten months?"

"Yeah. I may have sat and wallowed for a while after."

I took a seat on the hay next to him, trying to think about what to say next. Xander had worked so hard to get to where he was. It was practically unheard of for someone at his age. I had a feeling that our parents had a hand in it, but if they did, they never told him or anyone else. Which was most definitely unlike them.

I couldn't see how he could be so laid back about this whole thing, but I guess he'd had a lot longer to come to terms with it.

"So what's the plan now?" I asked.

"Finish up my treatment and then figure out how to salvage my career."

"You're in treatment then."

"Working the steps. Got a sponsor and everything. He keeps telling me I can go back to work, but I just...I don't know. I need some time. I want to get a year under my belt. I want to prove that I can do it. Not to mention that I've got absolutely no clue what to do next."

"Doc Matthews closed up the practice in town," I told him. "Willowbrook is crying out for a primary care physician."

"Yeah, because running back to the root of all my problems is just what I need right now."

He wasn't wrong. Our parents were the root of most of our problems. It was the curse of the Farrington family that our mother could never accept. In her eyes, she could never be the problem. Regina Farrington existed in a world of absolute superiority over those around her. It couldn't last though, and I was sitting back, waiting to watch the fallout. As long as it didn't hurt any of my brothers, it would be the best damn time of my life.

"I wondered why you were back in town."

"Trace told me about Cade, and I wanted to meet him. Plus, we all need to talk about Gage. We're bringing him home, right?" Xander looked around the barn and sighed. "Not that 'home' is really where any of us want to be."

I knew what he meant. Our parents' house had never really been a home. We'd all gotten out of there as fast as we could and never looked back. Maybe dragging Gage back to all this was cruel. He was free of it all. Living life the way he wanted. Wasn't that what we'd all dreamed of back then?

"I don't know about bringing him back. That's a choice for him. But he needs to know that we know the truth now, and it shouldn't be something that keeps him away. Reece has tried to get in contact with him through his social media accounts, so I guess we'll see if he bites."

Xander looked at me in question. "Reece?"

"She did some social media job before all this. I don't know anything about that stuff. Besides, he's more likely to respond to a beautiful woman than any of us," I said, waving my hand around.

"You're not wrong there."

Xander sighed and leaned back. Val put her head on his lap, and he absently played with her ears while he thought. I didn't think I'd ever done this before. Just sat in silence with Xander and existed in the same place without any kind of expectation.

"I'm sorry," I finally said, breaking through the silence. "I should have been there more for you when we were growing up."

He shrugged. "It is what it is, Book. None of us had it any easier than the rest. We're lucky that Gramps gave us the means to do whatever we wanted and get the hell out of that place. There are a lot of kids worse off than we were."

He was right, but it didn't make me feel any better. It didn't make the situation any easier.

I wanted to be the guy that had moved past all this. The one who didn't let the past affect his present so much, but how was that ever going to be possible when they still lived so close by? When heading into town came with the constant risk of seeing my mother around every corner.

My grandfather had saved me for a brief moment when he'd left me the ranch, but he also chained me to this town and my parents in a way I'd never realized before. I could never leave the ranch. I could never leave the potential of everything I was building here. It could do so much good for so many lives.

And because of that, I now saw that I'd never truly be free.

I couldn't bring Gage back into this. He shouldn't have to live his life surrounded by his biggest regret. The kindest thing was to let him keep having the life we all wished we could have had as well.

"How has it been so many years and it still feels like such a mess?" I mused.

Val lifted her head from Xander's lap and looked at me, a soft whine escaping her until I laid my hand on her back.

Suddenly, Xander started laughing. It was the deep belly laugh of hysteria and damn if it wasn't contagious. The moment he locked eyes with me, it came bursting out of my mouth as I threw back my head and laughed along with him.

Poor Val just sat between us, looking confused until she jumped off the hay bale and trotted away, clearly done with our antics.

"Have you ever seen such a sorry pair?" Xander asked. "A drunk and an asshole."

"Hey! I've been nothing but nice to you."

Xander looked at me wryly. "I have to admit you are weirdly nicer now that you've got Reece in your life. I just can't decide if that's a good thing or a bad thing."

"Is that why you've been so rude to her all night? You

think she's some kind of devil woman out to corrupt my soul?"

"Don't flatter yourself." Xander pushed me gently and huffed out a laugh. "Your soul was lost years ago. I'm more worried that you're trying to lure her in by being someone you're not. The poor woman might need an escape route, and I'm such a nice guy that I'd have to go completely out of my way to provide her with one. It's going to be a massive inconvenience considering that I live in the city."

"Yeah, ever the nice guy," I quipped.

"Out of all of us, I'm definitely the nice one."

I was pretty sure the look I gave him following that comment said it all.

"Does Trace know?" I asked, not sure how I felt about that.

Xander nodded. "It's hard to hide when you've been staying with someone for a while."

I guess that made sense. It didn't take the sting out of him not feeling like he could come to me sooner. I was the eldest. I was supposed to be the one that protected them all.

"I'm turning the ranch into a therapy center," I blurted out.

Xander raised his eyebrows in surprise, and I stood from the hay bale, walking over to the stable for the little mare and leaning on the door. When Xander joined me, I continued. "Healing horses has always been something I've been passionate about, but I want to expand on that. I want to help people as well."

I could almost feel the look of surprise on Xander's face at that statement but chose not to take it personally.

"This place has done so much for me. I know it can help others too. Plus, with the funding I could raise, it gives me the means to bring in more staff, expand our rescue numbers."

"You've really thought about this," Xander said.

"You could say that. I have my investors lined up, and I've already started work on putting in some cottages on the property for people to stay in."

"That's really impressive, Book." Xander sounded impressed, and even if it warmed a corner of my heart I didn't want to admit to, I didn't know if he'd feel the same way after what I planned to say next.

"I need a doctor in town, Xander." I turned to look at him to gauge his reaction. It was actually the one part of my business plan that I hadn't been able to square down. I needed an on-call medical presence in case something went wrong.

Xander sighed, his head falling forward as his shoulders slumped. It was the reaction I'd been expecting.

Here I was thinking about how Gage deserved to live his life on his own terms, and yet, the first chance I had, I was reeling Xander back in.

Being on his own hadn't been the answer for Xander though. We'd all seen him partying in high school, and obviously, that continued in college. But if it had reached a level after that to put his entire career in jeopardy, then maybe distance wasn't what Xander needed.

Our parents were an issue we all needed to deal with. But we had support and family in each other. Reece was right. We should be building on that. We should let the people who cared about us take some of the load.

Hell, maybe we could even figure out a way to free ourselves of the parental curse if we worked together. Take back the town for ourselves and everyone who lived in it.

Okay, that sounded a bit too murderous for real life, but

consequences could be a bitch, and it was time the eldest Farrington generation started facing them.

The little mare shuffled forward a step, and we both paused, practically holding our breath as she slowly, cautiously, moved closer. When she stretched her neck and her soft muzzle brushed across Xander's hand, I knew I had him from the cautious smile that slowly came to his lips.

Xander slowly turned his hand, and the mare pressed her nose against his palm, huffing out a breath when she realized there wasn't one of the treats there that Reece had been sneaking to her. He gently ran his hand over her muzzle, and the mare moved closer instead of cautiously stretching out to test the person in front of her.

Xander sighed again. "Tell me more about this plan of yours."

CHAPTER TWENTY

REECE

I stared at my phone screen and sighed. It had been three days now, and there was still no response from Gage. I'd really thought it could work, but he didn't seem active on any of his accounts. Maybe he'd abandoned them for new ones.

Feeling disillusioned that I couldn't do this one thing for Booker, I shoved the phone into my pocket and looked up at the little mare in the stall in front of me.

She moved forward, sniffing at my outstretched hand, and then gave me a look I always interpreted as complete disbelief that I'd dare to come around without an apple slice or two for her.

"You know I wouldn't forget," I said, taking the Ziplock out of my pocket and laughing as she shuffled closer in anticipation.

"She really trusts you," a voice came from behind me as the little mare happily chomped down on her favorite snack.

I glanced over my shoulder to see Cole approaching, carrying his bag of supplies.

"I didn't realize she was due for another check-up today." I racked my brain, wondering if I had my dates wrong, as Cole shook his head.

"I was just driving past, so I thought I'd come visit my favorite patient. Don't tell Booker, but this is honestly the best part of my day. It does me good to spend time with the success cases. Helps balance out the sadness with the others."

Cole came and leaned against the stall door next to me, his gaze moving over the mare as he cataloged the changes in her.

"She's moving well, and she's definitely getting some weight on. Has Booker tried her out of the stall yet?"

"We're all scheduled for tomorrow. I think he's going to see if she will walk around the training ring first. He wants to see how well she's moving."

Cole nodded. "They can get some pretty severe muscle wasting in cases of neglect like this. Giving them too much space to move about can do them more harm than good sometimes. Booker's definitely one of the best at rehabilitating these horses, though. He seems to have a never-ending supply of patience for them. People, not so much," he added wryly.

I grinned happily. Everyone seemed to say this about Booker, and yet I'd barely ever seen that side of him.

To me, he was the man who took a chance on a woman on the side of the road. A man who protected what was his and stood up for what was right.

I might even say he was perfect. Not that Booker would ever accept such a label.

"I think you're selling him short there. Look at what he's doing here."

"You're right." Cole nodded. "It's hard to see people

differently when you've spent your entire life growing up alongside them. The stories I could tell you. It's the small-town curse, you know. Everyone knows everything, and it's hard to prove them wrong."

"I've never really had that many people in my life that gave enough of a crap to get to know me that well. It might not be as much of a curse as you think it is."

"I never thought of it that way," Cole conceded. "Don't get me wrong. I love this place more than is probably healthy. I couldn't imagine being anywhere else in the world."

I looked around the dusty barn that I spent far too much time in and knew exactly what he meant.

"Do you think it will feel different with more people coming into town?" I asked.

It was the goal at the end of the day, but maybe the charm of Willowbrook was that it was this sleepy little town nestled among the rolling green fields. You didn't have to fight through the crowds to get where you needed to be. You couldn't get lost in the anonymity that a city provided. Which probably sounded like a nightmare to some people, but not to me. Not when I'd only just escaped the isolation and the dangers that hid inside it.

"Nah. Willowbrook has this special quality that will always be there, no matter how many come to enjoy it. It's not just in the place. It's in the people, and I think the world could benefit from having more people touched by that who then take it home with them."

"Awww, that's really poetic."

Cole was good-looking, rocking those country boy muscles every girl dreamed of, and a goddamn vet to boot. He had to have the ladies beating down his door for a date.

"Yikes, don't tell anyone. It will ruin this bad boy image

I have going on for myself." And then he hit me with the cutest silly grin that made me cackle.

"Yeah, I can see how well that's going for you."

He laughed, shaking his head as he ducked down to grab a stethoscope from his bag. "I might as well check over my favorite patient while I'm here if you don't mind me barging in on your time together."

"Go ahead." I grimaced down at my watch. "I need to run back to the house to check the pie I have in the oven, anyway. Do you need anything while I'm up there?"

"No, I'm good. I'll only be two minutes, anyway."

I waved goodbye and set off for the little cottage that was starting to feel like home. I'd spent my time between there and Booker's place, but there was something about having a space that was my own that settled a part of me. Being around Booker was amazing, especially the nights and the little amount of sleep we ended up having. But there was something about the quiet here that felt comforting. Not like there was something hiding in the shadows, but rather that the world was holding its breath and letting me have time to think. Giving me that much-needed moment to breathe.

It had been so long since I'd felt like I could pause and just breathe. I'd forgotten the sense of peace it brought with it.

I smiled as I approached the cute little cottage and jogged up the step onto the porch. My coffee cup from this morning was still sitting on the table, so I quickly grabbed it as I knocked the dust off my boots.

The smell of sweet caramel apples flooded my senses, and my mouth watered in response. It didn't even register with me about why I could smell it already as I reached for the door handle.

And then my hand paused midair as I stared at the shadowy line of the door standing slightly ajar.

I pulled my hand back like something had burned me and then took a cautious step back. I could have sworn I'd closed the door this morning. I hadn't locked it because why would I? There hardly seemed a need to all the way out here with the illusion of safety of Booker's house standing right next to mine.

Shaking my head, I pushed open the door, cautiously looked inside, and then laughed at how ridiculous I was being. I must have just not closed the door properly this morning, and it was probably pushed open by the wind. All those years of being on edge, in fear of doing the wrong thing, had gotten to me.

I was free of that place now, and yeah, it might take a while for my mind to catch up, but I'd get there eventually. I couldn't expect it to happen overnight.

I rinsed the mug and sat it in the sink to wash later. Grabbing some oven mitts, I turned...and then my entire world came to a crashing halt.

There on the counter sat the steaming pie with a slice cut out and a plate covered in crumbs at its side. At the same time, a door slammed shut somewhere inside the cottage. The loud, jarring sound finally kicked some sense into me, and I turned and sprinted out of the cottage. I'd barely made it two steps out the door when I collided with another body.

My hands instinctively came up to cover my face, and I cowered back, waiting for the blow to follow. Every muscle in my body tensed, preparing for the inevitable pain.

But nothing came.

The sound of a soothing voice floated around me, but my brain wasn't online enough to really register it. It was only when hands gently gripped my wrists and pulled my hands away from my face that I realized it was Cole I stood in front of, not the man who stalked my nightmares.

Embarrassment flooded me hot and ladened with an unhealthy dose of shame.

Not again.

I couldn't believe I was humiliating myself in front of someone else.

"Reece? Reece, are you with me?" Cole said, stepping back away from me and giving me space as soon as I wasn't freaking out.

"There...there was someone in the house."

Cole didn't hesitate. He ran past me and straight into the cottage. I could hear him moving through the rooms, opening and closing the doors as he checked the place over. By the time he came back out the front door, I'd nearly convinced myself that I was hearing things.

"Your clothes are thrown all over the bedroom, and the window is open," he said, pulling his phone out of his pocket and putting it to his ear as he came to stand beside me. "Booker, you need to come back to the ranch. Someone was in the cottage. Reece is fine. She's here with me, and I'll wait with her until you can get back."

I zoned out then.

Someone was in the cottage.

Someone had pulled all my clothes out of the closet and trashed the bedroom.

"They stole my pie," I whispered.

Cole looked like he didn't know what to say. I couldn't blame him. I wouldn't know what to do with someone I barely knew having some kind of mental breakdown in front of me either.

"Let's get you inside Booker's place," Cole opted for. His hands came to my shoulders, and he steered me toward Booker's house.

We climbed the back porch steps and walked into the kitchen, and then I ran into Cole's back for the second time.

He looked around the kitchen cautiously, and it took me a moment to realize that it was because he was wondering if whoever had been in the cottage was now inside the house.

Cole's arm came back, and he reached for my hand as he backed up, pushing us back toward the door without taking his eyes off the house.

"Cole?"

"I think we should wait in my truck," he said slowly as we reached the door, and he went to back outside. "I don't want to leave you alone while I check through the entire house."

Because he thought whoever had broken into the cottage had come here to hurt me. Or had Booker said something to him on the phone?

"What did you see in my bedroom?" I asked, my feet planting on the ground before he could back me out of the doorway.

For some reason, the fear inside me was dissipating, and in its place was a whole other emotion rising to the surface.

I'd come here for a fresh start. All I had was what little I could pack into my car from my old life, the one I'd had before it all went to hell.

And now someone thought they got to take that away from me.

They thought they had a right to take away the feeling of safety I was only just getting back.

For god's sake, they stole my goddamned pie!

"Everyone knows the first slice is the best," I suddenly shouted, outrage flooding through me as I pushed past Cole and strode back into Booker's kitchen. "Are you in here, you damn pie-thieving miscreant?"

I was about to charge through the house on a quest for justice against the pie-based crime when Cole's hand tightly gripped the top of my arm.

"Are you out of your mind?" I didn't miss the crooked smile on his face or the fact that he was barely holding back his laughter.

"They stole my pie!" I repeated in outrage.

"I got that. I was more worried about them stealing your life, though."

"Yellow-bellied, pie-thieving piece of trash," I muttered, trying to storm into the house again, forgetting that Cole's grip had me locked in place.

I shot him the look I saved for people who abandoned their shopping carts in the parking lot, and he quickly raised his hands in surrender.

"Okay, look. Let's be honest. If I let you storm into the house to seek revenge for your pie, Booker is going to kick my ass. I am actually begging you right now to take pity on me and wait for him to...oh thank god."

Cole physically sagged in relief as Booker's truck tore down the driveway and came to a skidding stop on the gravel outside. It barely seemed to be stationary by the time he was leaping out and charging into the cottage. A few moments later, he came out and tore into the kitchen. Cole darted out of his way as Booker hauled me into his arms and gripped me tightly to his chest.

"What happened?" he asked Cole over my head.

"We were in the barn talking, and Reece went to do something at the house. I checked the mare and the foal's heartbeat and was coming to find her when she suddenly came tearing out of the cottage, looking like she'd seen a ghost. There was no one inside when I checked, but I didn't want to go too far into the house in case they'd come in here."

"Val, with me," Booker barked and then physically passed me to Cole, who looked like he'd just been passed a bomb. Cole uneasily held me at arm's length as Booker took off and started tearing through the house.

"He does realize I'm standing here and capable of speaking for myself, right?"

"Right now, Booker is in full-on protection mode. He's not going to be able to even think about anything else until he knows no one is waiting in here for you." Cole looked down at me with that boyish smile again and added, "Or your pie."

"Stole my damn pie," I muttered in outrage, not caring that Cole was actually making fun of me.

The nerve of some people.

"There's no one here," Booker announced as he strode back into the kitchen with Val at his side.

The dog clearly knew something was wrong because the fur down her spine was bristled and at full attention, and she seemed on full alert. Val probably loved pie, too.

Cole gave me a slight shove, and I was suddenly back in Booker's arms.

"Am I allowed to speak now, or are we still in full caveman mode?" I snapped.

"And on that note, I'm going to head out," Cole said, backing toward the door. "You know where I am if you need anything. I'll be by in a few days to check on the foal again. I'm surprised and pleased by her progress."

Cole darted out the back door before either of us could

say anything, and I pried myself out of Booker's arms long enough to open the door and shout thank you. Cole waved a hand over his head in acknowledgment and then jumped into his truck to leave.

I tried to turn around and head back inside, but before I knew what was happening, my feet had left the floor, and Booker was carrying me into the family room. My mouth opened to object, but then I caught sight of the look on his face.

Booker was scared.

I immediately deflated. He'd done so much for me, and here I was only thinking about myself.

As Booker dropped onto the couch, he held me firmly in his lap, leaning back with a sigh as he stared up at the ceiling. It was like I could visibly see him pulling himself back together.

"Are you okay?" I whispered after the tension seemed to have left his body.

He nodded and then looked at me. "You're staying here tonight," he told me. "If you want the guest room, that's fine, but Val is going in with you. Tomorrow we're getting the locks changed and looking into getting security cameras."

"Booker, you don't need to do all this for me. It was just someone messing about, it's—"

"It absolutely wasn't," Booker said sternly. "You don't do that in someone's bedroom unless it's personal."

"It could have just been kids," I suggested lamely, not really wanting to think about the alternative.

"I'm going to call Xander and see if he can stay at the ranch for a few days. He could take the cottage, and you move in here. Just until we have the cameras in place."

"I'm sure Xander has better things to be doing."

"He doesn't."

Booker wouldn't take no as an answer here, and it occurred to me that while I could fight him on this, it wouldn't cost me anything to let him have this. I wasn't the only person here who'd had their personal space invaded today. If putting up some cameras and having his brother stay for a few days would make him feel better, there was no reason not to do it.

"Okay," I conceded. "On one condition."

Booker raised an eyebrow, and I could see he was getting ready to fight whatever I was about to say. "You need to run me into town in the morning so I can get the ingredients to make a new pie for you."

"You were making a pie for me?"

"Caramel apple. But it's been defiled by the intruder."

Booker opened his mouth to ask a question and then seemed to think twice about it and closed his mouth again. I could practically see the thoughts flying through his mind until he asked, "I'm going to need you to explain the defiling."

I smiled, sinking back into his chest as I got myself comfortable. "They stole the first slice and ate it! And I made that pie as a surprise for you."

Booker chuckled and held me tightly. "Of all the crimes that have been committed here today, that has to be the worst."

Finally! Someone understood where I was coming from.

But then he ruined it and added, "No one eats my baby's pie, but me."

Heat blossomed low in my stomach as Booker tilted my head back and kissed me. I had a terrible feeling that whatever had happened here today was just the beginning, but I pushed that thought to the back of my mind. All I wanted to do now was feel safe in Booker's arms.

He twisted on the couch, gently laying me back against the cushions as he held himself above me.

"If you want me to stop, if you need time to process what's happened..."

"Don't stop, Booker. When it comes to you, I never want it to stop."

CHAPTER TWENTY-ONE

BOOKER

My gaze kept moving to the woman sleeping at my side, and no matter how hard I tried not to creep on Reece, I couldn't help it.

I'd never been as terrified as I was yesterday. Not in all my life. Knowing that there was someone at the ranch and she was in danger had my instincts going into overdrive. I owed Cole a drink, or a horse, or something because I had no idea what I would have done if he hadn't been there with her.

After she fell asleep last night, I slipped out of bed and made some calls. Xander was packing his stuff up before I'd even finished explaining what had happened. I didn't even have to ask him to come and stay for a few days. He offered without hesitation. It actually surprised me. After all those years of distance, he was still the brother I remembered him to be.

Willowbrook might have been the place where all his troubles began, but he looked good being back here. I could cut him in on the business plan for the ranch. Give him a reason to stay here with us. The practice in town would have been enough to keep him busy, but there was something about the idea of another practice that didn't seem to excite him like it used to. There wasn't that spark in his eyes that he usually got when he talked about his career. But Xander had listened to every word of my business plan for the ranch. He made some suggestions I hadn't even considered, which was saying a lot as I'd been dreaming of this for years before I worked up the courage to actually make it happen.

I talked Xander down from jumping in his car and driving here late last night. It felt good to have someone who was so ready to do that for me, especially considering the rocky start he seemed to have with Reece. I hadn't told her about his drinking. It didn't seem like the sort of thing to talk about behind his back. But I didn't want her to think that Xander hated her, and from the way he was acting at dinner, she couldn't be blamed if she did.

Damn, it was nice to have family around me again, but it came with an annoying set of complications.

The call I had with Ethan hadn't gone quite as well. The police chief had told me, realistically, there was little he could do. Resources in Willowbrook weren't like the big cities, and even then, they wouldn't do much either. He made some recommendations about security cameras though, and I already had emails out to get some installed. If we could catch this guy on tape, Ethan had said it would be a whole different story.

My gaze moved back to Reece, only this time she wasn't asleep, and her sleepy brown eyes were looking back at me.

She rolled and snuggled into my chest as I tried to ignore how my heart started pounding at her touch.

We'd known each other for such a relatively short amount of time, and I had no idea how she'd become this important to me. There was nothing I wouldn't do for this woman.

"Good morning," she said, holding a hand over her mouth and making me smile.

I worked on a ranch with sweaty ranch hands. There was no way her morning breath could compete with that.

I pulled her hand away from her face and kissed her. Reece hummed happily, her leg hitching over my hip as she did. It took no effort at all to roll onto my back and pull her on top of me as I did.

"Didn't you have enough fun last night?" she whispered against my lips and kissed me again before I could respond.

I could spend a year in bed with Reece, and it still wouldn't be enough.

I trailed my fingertips up the outside of her silky thighs, bunching up the shirt of mine that she'd slept in as I went. There was something primal about seeing a beautiful woman sleeping in your clothes, but it was nothing compared to the feeling of her—

"Booker!" Xander shouted up the stairs. "Are you up there?"

Reece yipped in surprise and darted out of my lap, pulling the covers up to her chest as she stared at the door with wide eyes.

"What are you doing?" I laughed, reaching out for her.

"I don't want him to walk in and see us...you know!"

"Why would he walk in here? Come back here, and let me do all the filthy things I've been thinking about for the past hour while I watched you sleep."

"Awww. You watched me sleep like a cute little stalker."

"First things first, there's nothing little about me, woman," I said, reaching out to pull her closer to me again. "And second, let's not crack any stalker jokes until I can get over what happened yesterday. Otherwise, I'll have you tied to my side and never let you out of my sight for the next five years, minimum."

Reece tipped her head to the side and smiled. I could see the sympathy in her eyes, and strangely, it didn't bother me. There was a time when I would have hated that look. But it didn't come across as mocking when it came from her. This was a woman who cared about me and was concerned about my feelings.

"I'm sorry," she started, and when I went to object how none of it was her fault, Reece laid her fingers over my lips to stop me. "I'm sorry that I didn't check in with you last night about how you were feeling about this whole thing."

Reece slowly moved her fingers away, and I grabbed her wrist, pulling her hand back and kissing those beautiful, concerned fingers before I let her go.

"I don't think I've ever been through something like this. I've never cared enough about someone to invite something like this into my life before."

My head was all over the place right now. All I could think was protect, protect, protect. I knew it was the worst thing I could ever do for Reece. She'd just escaped some douche who had tried to take her freedom. The last thing she needed was for me to do the same even if it was for entirely different reasons.

But I couldn't do *nothing*. I couldn't sit by when there were people out there that could hurt her.

"I care about you too," she whispered, her fingers coming to my jaw as she brushed her thumb across my cheek. "We'll figure this out, Booker."

"I think I'm supposed to be the one saying that to you," I told her wryly.

"I know, but I can see how worried you are."

"Reece, do you think this could be your ex?"

I asked the question that had been burning inside me since I'd received the call from Cole. Part of me hoped it was him. What I wouldn't give to feel my knuckles collide with his nose. The ranch was a big place. There were places around here where no one would ever find him.

"I doubt it. He doesn't know where I am. I have no links to Willowbrook that would make him think to come looking for me here. I just don't see how it could be." She looked confused, and my heart broke for her.

This was the last thing Reece needed. She should live a carefree life, doing what she wanted, whenever she wanted, and I hoped like hell there was room for me in there somewhere.

"I've got an idea," I said, throwing back the covers and slapping her delicious ass before climbing out of the bed. "Get dressed. I'm going to take you somewhere."

"Erm, okay." Reece looked around the bedroom and then turned back to me. "I don't exactly have any clothes, though."

I was already at the dresser, pulling out my clothes when her voice cut through the air, and I turned slowly around.

"Damn, I didn't think about that."

"Could you grab me something from the cottage?" she asked.

I winced. I hadn't let Reece out of my sight, and what had started on the couch had made its way to the bedroom before she'd passed out from exhaustion, so I knew she didn't have time to sneak out there.

Reece had no idea what someone had done in her bedroom.

I walked back over to the bed, sitting on the edge, and her face fell.

"I don't think I want to know," she said, turning to get out of the bed, but my hand whipped out to grab her wrist and stop her.

She paused, staring at the ground for a moment before she slowly turned to face me. Reece looked so sad, and I hated everything about what was happening to her.

"Whoever broke into the cottage pulled your clothes out of the closet and tore them apart," I told her gently. "It's all destroyed."

Her face fell, and I linked my fingers with hers, holding her hand as she worked through her emotions.

"Everything?" she asked quietly.

"Yeah, baby."

"Why would someone do that?"

"I don't know. I called the sheriff last night, and he's coming to the ranch today to have a look around. I didn't see the point in him coming yesterday, not when it was already getting dark and whoever had been here was long gone."

Reece slowly nodded. Her face seemed to wrinkle with fear.

"The sheriff?" She sounded so worried.

"Xander will deal with it. Ethan won't need to speak to you, and if he does, he can swing by later. This is more important."

"What's more important?" Reece asked, looking genuinely confused.

"You." I leaned forward and kissed her lips because they were impossible to resist. "Now get a shower, and I'll see if Delaney or Blake have some clothes you can borrow for a couple of days."

I saw her getting ready to argue, but then a strange look

crossed her face, and she nodded, getting up and heading into the bathroom.

I couldn't lie. I was transfixed by the sway of her beautiful ass right up until she closed the door.

"I'm not so sure about this, Booker," Reece said nervously, and I fought back the laugh that I desperately wanted to set free.

This woman. She was ready to face down an intruder over the supposed insult of eating the first slice of her pie, but put her on the back of Doc outside of the training ring, and she looked like she was going to throw up.

"Doc won't do you wrong," I told her, trotting to her side and reaching across to adjust her hands on the reins. "Hold them like this, and use one hand on the pommel to steady yourself if you need to. I promise you we won't go fast enough to shake something loose."

Reece glared at me, and I stood in my stirrups, leaned across, and kissed her.

"Or if you prefer, you could sit that sweet little ass in my lap, and I'll keep you safe."

I could see her actually thinking about it, and I steered my horse away from her to resist the urge to pull her out of her saddle right then and there.

If I had Reece in the saddle with me, we wouldn't make it further than the crest of the first hill. But at least that was far enough for me to spread out a blanket and have my filthy way with her without any nosey ranch hands interrupting our fun.

But that wasn't the point of today.

Well, that mostly wasn't the point.

I was taking us up into the forest on my favorite trail to show her the view over Willowbrook. Much to Xander's amusement, I even had a small picnic for us in my saddlebags.

I swear if he tried to feel my temperature one more time, I was going to throw his ass down into the dust.

"I can do it!" Reece objected, even if she didn't sound so sure of herself. "Just know that if I fall off and break my ass, you're going to be my nursemaid and slave for at least a month."

"Baby, don't threaten me with a good time. I'd gladly press my lips to every curve of your beautiful ass."

She blushed the prettiest pink and shook her head.

It didn't take long for Reece to settle into the slow rhythm of Doc's gait as we headed across the pastures toward the tree line.

"How long have you had the ranch now?" she asked suddenly.

"Eight years. It was bittersweet when it finally became mine. I love this place. Every inch of this ranch, every tree and blade of grass, it's ingrained in me. I'm pretty sure my blood runs with more ranch dust than anything else. I would have camped out in the pastures if my parents would have let me. But the ranch becoming mine meant I lost my grandfather, and, at the time, he felt like the only person who was ever really on my side."

Reece listened quietly, but the silence didn't have that edge to it that it normally did. It didn't slice at my mind, making me want to flee a situation where someone expected me to fill it. To spill a part of myself that they'd get to claim for themselves.

She radiated nothing but peace and understanding.

And for the first time in my life, I actually wanted to talk.

"The Farrington land used to run down this whole side of the town. My grandfather let my father portion of a section at the far end, and he had a house built there for my mother. She wanted to be as far away from this place as she could get. There was nothing about a ranch that fitted the image she wanted for the Farrington name. Maybe that's why I always loved this place so much. It was exactly what she didn't want, and that made it even more special."

Reece hummed in agreement. "This was your escape. A place where you could be yourself."

"If it hadn't been for my brothers, I think my grandfather would have let me stay, and I probably would have accepted. I couldn't leave them in that house alone, though."

"Is that why you stayed so long?"

"Yeah. I was the eldest. I still don't think I did enough, but I wasn't about to go off to college and leave them with that woman. So I went to the local community college and got an agricultural and business degree. That outraged her enough to take the heat off them for a good while." I laughed at that point because the ridiculousness of it all wasn't lost on me.

Regina hated that we were a small-town family and that she couldn't tear my father from this town or me from the ranch. And that was where all the money had come from. If there was one thing she didn't hate, it was the money.

"They were lucky to have you," Reece said.

She looked at me like I'd done something impressive, and it made me shift uncomfortably in my saddle.

"It was nothing. I'm supposed to look after them. I'm the eldest. And I didn't exactly do a very good job of it.

Anyway, I didn't need some big fancy degree to run the ranch."

Reece's eyes darted back and forth, and I knew she was searching my gaze to try to figure out how serious I was being.

But that was the thing. I was deadly serious.

It didn't cost me anything to do what I had for my brothers. And yet, it hadn't been enough. It hadn't saved Gage from feeling like he could never face us again, and it hadn't saved Xander from drowning his feelings in a bottle for most of his life. I hadn't even been able to stop Trace from losing Delaney and Cade for ten years. It had all been for nothing.

Thankfully, before Reece could say anything else, the tree line came into view, and we were going to have to take the trail one at a time for the first stretch.

"Do you want me to lead the way or are you happy for Doc to? He knows where we're going, and you can just sit there and enjoy the ride."

Reece didn't say anything at first. Judging by the cute little pout on her lips, she wasn't impressed by the sudden change of subject. In the end, she sighed. "You go first, and we'll follow," she said, letting me pretend I was getting away with dodging the conversation.

This was where I got uncomfortable. I didn't need a pat on the back or a damn certificate. It shouldn't be so surprising when someone does the right thing. It should be the default setting.

We carried on a little way in silence until the trail turned into a slight incline. I turned in my saddle to check on Reece, and she happily looked at the scenery, her reins held relaxed in her hands as she let Doc lead the way. He preferred it that way, anyway.

Reece had naturally leaned forward slightly to account

for the incline, but I still felt like I should point it out to her, so she didn't panic when she realized we'd started heading up a hill.

"The incline gets a little steeper for the next couple of minutes, but nothing Doc can't handle. Lean forward in your saddle to keep your balance."

Reece made eye contact with me and smiled. All thoughts of our earlier conversation and the events of yesterday seemed to have slipped away. "Sure thing. I can see why you love it here so much." She looked around again, taking in the trees as we slowly passed them by. "It's so peaceful."

"Yeah, this is my favorite place on the whole ranch. I'm honestly thinking of being selfish and not including this trail on any of the tours. We should keep it just for us."

I glanced over my shoulder at a happy, blushing Reece and vowed there and then that this was what I wanted for the rest of my life. Every single moment would be dedicated to making this woman smile.

CHAPTER TWENTY-TWO

REECE

Today should have been terrible. I was wearing someone else's clothes because all of mine had been destroyed by some weirdo who went on a slashing spree in my home. The sheriff needed to talk to me, and I didn't even get to have a slice of my pie.

Yet, here I was sitting on top of the sweetest horse, unable to contain my smile because the man in front truly couldn't see exactly how incredible he was.

Booker sat on his horse, reins in one hand, looking like he was ready to conquer the West. The ends of his dirty-blond hair licked out from beneath his cowboy hat and cast a seductive shadow across his steely eyes. I was transfixed by his denim-clad thighs and the taut muscles on his forearms where he'd rolled up the sleeves of his red flannel shirt.

If Booker didn't realize he was putting on a show for me right now, then I wouldn't be the one to tell him. I could bask in this secret obsession every day for the rest of my life as my own private fantasy.

And that was when I realized it.

I was happy. Deliriously happy.

And the fact that I didn't think I'd ever felt this way in my life didn't make me sad, because it felt so right now. It felt like all these years I'd been waiting for Booker to find me on the side of the road.

I'd disappeared in my old life. Faded into the background and been hidden away like a possession that was coveted and hoarded. But Booker saw me. He let me stand in the light and shine any way I wanted. He didn't try to steal that light just for himself. He stood in the glow and let me illuminate all the dark parts of him that he didn't want anyone else to see. Even if it did seem like it was getting harder and harder for him to hide them away now.

I hadn't even realized we'd come to a stop until Booker was standing at my side, taking the reins, and then reaching out to help me down. The way he let my body slide down his front set me on fire. My fingers trailed along his jawline, and he gave me that smile I could have basked in for days.

"Close your eyes," he whispered, and I did without any hesitation. "It's just a few steps this way."

Booker gently tugged the brim of my hat down over my eyes, and his hands came to my shoulders as he steered me around the horses.

At least the hat and boots that Booker had bought me were saved from the stranger's rampage because I'd had them on at the time. I'd have been devastated to have lost them. Part of me felt like I should have been more devastated about the loss of my other clothes, but there was a tiny voice in the back of my head telling me they were the last parts of my old life and maybe it felt right to finally let it go.

My wallet, on the other hand, wasn't as optimistic. And now that I was in a relationship with Booker, I didn't know how I felt about taking his money.

Booker drew me to a stop, and I felt his body press

against my back as he turned me slightly to face whatever he wanted to show me. I leaned back into his comforting presence as he pulled the hat from my head.

I blinked. The bright light of the sun blurred my vision with tears. Then, as I focused on the scene before me, I gasped.

"Booker! This is beautiful!"

We'd somehow made our way up a hill that placed us above the ranch. The trail had ended at a small clearing on the crest of the hill, which the trees didn't quite cover. Before us, you could see the ranch and the surrounding pastures, Booker's house, and the little cottage that would forever hold a place in my heart. Beyond that, the town of Willowbrook covered the gentle dips and hills, surrounded by farmland and patches of trees.

"Which is Delaney's farm?" I asked, tipping my head back to look at the man behind me.

Booker pointed out Delaney's house, which you could just see peeking out from behind a hill. The ever-expanding rows of what I now knew were apple trees should have given it away. There was even a cute little pond sitting behind it that looked like heaven.

Then my gaze found the imposing modern mansion sitting on the other side of town, just beyond Delaney's farm. It was obvious who it belonged to. It looked so cold and isolated, sitting there with its manicured gardens that didn't match the rest of town.

Some people might dream of having a house like that but knowing what Booker had been through cast it in a whole different light for me. It was so impersonal and not a place I'd ever want my children to grow up in.

Booker moved back to the horses, and I watched as he opened up his saddlebags, pulling out a blanket and some containers of food. If there was anything sexier on this planet than a man pulling out a picnic, I challenged you to find it.

Because damn!

When he turned around, he must have seen the look on his face.

"What?" Booker asked cautiously as he shook out the blanket and laid it on the ground where we'd get the best view.

Booker reached for my hand and then pulled me down onto the blanket, opening a container and passing it to me.

"This is really impressive, Booker," I said, staring down at the sandwich, chips, and a bottle of water that he'd tucked inside.

"It's just lunch." He shrugged.

I looked up in surprise. Did he really not know how special this was?

"That's a shame," I said, opening my chips and popping one in my mouth, crunching it slowly as he looked at me in confusion. "People usually get rewarded for doing something nice."

As expected, that definitely had Booker's attention.

His tongue darted out to swipe along his bottom lip as he carefully took off his hat and laid it on the blanket beside him. As he leaned back, stretching out that muscled frame before me, I swear I was ready to jump him.

Thankfully, there was absolutely no reason I shouldn't.

The corner of Booker's lips ticked up in a smile as I climbed into his lap, and his hands came to my waist as that smile turned into his sexy smirk.

"And just what kind of reward did you have in mind?" he asked.

"Well, there *was* a particular something I had in mind

this morning before we were disturbed," I whispered, leaning forward to kiss his lips. Pulling away a fraction, I added, "And just an FYI, Booker. When you send me into the shower, I expect you to follow me."

Booker groaned and then his hands tangled in my hair as he pulled me back to his lips and deepened the kiss.

My hips rolled, and I felt Booker instantly grow hard beneath me.

There was something about Booker's kiss that felt protective and possessive all in one. And I couldn't get enough. It should scare me. Hell, it should probably terrify me. But I wanted him just as much as he wanted me, and when that need was mutual, there was nothing oppressive about it.

Booker suddenly wrapped his hands around my ass and raised up on his knees, taking me with him. I yipped in surprise before he smoothly laid me down on the blanket, holding himself above me as he brushed the hair away from my face.

"You're so beautiful," he murmured, his fingertips trailing across my jaw.

I felt the blush rise to my cheeks.

I knew I wasn't unattractive, but I wasn't used to hearing someone say it aloud. It made me immediately want to deny it, to tell him he was wrong. But the serious look on Booker's face left no doubt in mind that he'd never agree with me.

"Will you come with me to the carnival?" he asked. "Like a date."

He suddenly looked nervous. Did Booker not know how I felt about him? Or did he just not think that he deserved it?

"There's nothing I'd like more," I told him, hoping he

could hear just how much I meant it. "I like you a whole hell of a lot, Booker. I hope you know that."

Booker kissed me gently. His hand ran down my side as he seemed to map my curves, staring deep into my eyes as he did. I knew he was looking for something. Some kind of confirmation and it killed me he'd gotten this far in life without being able to take someone at their word for something so simple as how they felt about him.

It was one of the most vulnerable moments I'd ever seen him in, and I knew it wasn't a side of him he'd show to many.

Whatever it was he was searching for, Booker must have found it, because he leaned down and devoured my lips with his kiss. His hand reached my knee, and he pulled my leg over his hip, grinding himself against my core and leaving me breathless and desperate for more.

"Just how private is this trail?" I asked when he pulled back for air.

"Do you really care?" The smirk was back on his lips, and I shrugged.

"I mean, I'd maybe have suggested you hang a sock on a tree branch or something. Give a hiker a warning about what they're about to walk in on."

Booker shook his head, and when he didn't, in fact, get up to hang socks around the clearing, I had to admit I was slightly relieved.

Relieved enough that I wiggled free of Booker and quickly pulled off my top as proof.

He wasted no time in leaning forward and pressing kisses over the mounds of my breasts before slipping his fingers into the lace and tugging the cups down out of his way.

The way his teeth grazed teasingly over my nipple

before he moved to the other side, repeating the action, had my head tipping back on a moan.

My fingers ran through Booker's hair, and I pulled him closer, loving how his hands wrapped around my waist as if he wanted to hold me in place.

But then he was pulling away. I automatically reached out to try to pull him back until I realized Booker was heading south. I leaned up on my elbows and watched as he made his way down my body, that sexy smirk on his lips as he did.

Except he just kept going down...until he reached my feet and picked one up, pulling off my boot, then my sock, before he kissed the top of my foot and placed it back on the ground.

Then he picked up the other foot and repeated the process.

"Why is this so sexy?" I asked, watching in fascination as Booker stripped the boot from my foot.

"Maybe you've got an unexplored foot fetish?" He shrugged but grinned that sexy smirk at the same time.

Damn this man.

I tried to think of something smart to say, but I had nothing, and as soon as Booker's gaze met mine we both laughed. It cemented those feelings that were creeping in firmly in the center of my mind.

Leaning forward, I gripped the hem of Booker's shirt and pulled it over his head so I didn't have to deal with the buttons. He tossed it to the ground beside him, and before he had time to do anything else, I struck.

And licked a long line up the center of his chest.

There was nothing sexy about it.

Booker looked wryly down at the damp trail on his skin and then at me, his eyebrow ticking up in question.

"Is this another weird fetish?"

"Nope, but it's official now. I licked you, so you're mine."

He shook his head, unable to keep the smile from his lips. "You're too damn cute."

"It's a burden, honestly, but someone has to carry it." I shrugged nonchalantly, but it might have been ruined because I couldn't take my eyes away from the man kneeling in front of me.

"The world doesn't know how lucky it is to have you in it."

Booker's eyes almost twinkled as he spoke like he was laughing, but he looked so serious that it felt like this could be the beginning of a conversation I didn't think either of us was ready for.

I shook the feeling off. It was probably in my head anyway, and I wanted nothing to ruin this perfect moment we were having. So rather than getting lost in a conversation, I kissed him instead.

And the moment my lips touched his, everything changed.

My hands moved to the waistband of his jeans as our lips moved together. I fumbled with the button, and Booker quickly helped me as we stripped the clothes from each other.

Then we paused. The chill of the air brushed across my skin, and I felt a rush of heat sweep over me.

It was different this time. The urgency we always had between us had bled away into something new. Something almost reverent as Booker cupped my face in his hands and lowered his lips to mine.

I could feel the heat coming off his skin as his body pressed against mine. It was impossible not to run my hands up his chest, letting my fingers trail across his skin as our lips moved together.

When I couldn't take the fraction of distance between us any longer, I pressed Booker back onto the blanket, sliding one leg across his body as I straddled him. Our lips didn't part for a second, and Booker's hands tangled in my hair to keep me exactly where he needed me. In the one place I'd never be able to leave even if I wanted to.

His hard cock pressed against my already slick entrance, and I felt Booker lift his hips, pushing just the tip inside.

My mouth opened with a gasp, and his tongue slid into my mouth, twisting with my own. This kiss deepened to the point where I didn't want it to end.

Booker's hands trailed up my spine, and I felt his fingertips flex as he tried to hold himself back from pushing into my body like I knew he wanted.

I could feel the quiver of restraint in his muscles as I slowly pushed myself down, sheathing him inside me at a maddeningly slow pace.

Part of me wanted to rush. We both wanted it. We both needed that feeling of completeness that came from finally coming together in this way.

But there was something about the anticipation that made every fraction of an inch feel so much better than the last. That pinch of pain as my body stretched to accommodate his size and how Booker's breathing picked up its pace as I slowly gave him the thing he craved most.

Me.

When my hips were finally pressed tight against his, Booker sat up, clasping my body in his arms as he pulled my knees around him. His hands trailed up my thighs, gently brushing up the sides of my body until I seemed to lean back without even meaning to, just to have the feel of his thumbs brush across my stiff nipples.

"Reece," Booker whispered in awe, his gaze moving down the front of my body, which had been revealed to him.

There was an emotion hanging in the air between us that I was afraid to acknowledge. It was too soon. Saying those words now could burst this bubble we'd found ourselves in. I couldn't ruin it. I wanted to stay in this one perfect moment forever.

I slowly rose on my knees, watching how it made Booker's lips part as he hauled in a breath. His eyes roamed across my body before he slipped a hand between us, his thumb brushing against that bundle of nerves that made my body suddenly set on fire.

Even though a sense of urgency ran through my body, I set a slow pace. Luxuriating in the feel of Booker's body beneath me. Watching the slow bunch and flow of his muscles as he worked my clit in time with my movements.

I leaned forward again, finding it impossible not to taste his lips once more.

"Booker?" I whimpered, as the feeling of pleasure started building higher inside my body.

It shouldn't have been possible with the slow way we were moving. But as the muscles inside me clenched and fluttered, the orgasm that was building inside felt like it had the power to devastate me absolutely.

And I needed it more than anything else I'd ever needed before.

"I know, baby," Booker murmured, his free hand coming to my hip as he helped to guide my movements. "I feel it too."

I pressed my forehead to his, my motion slowly building as I breathed in every breath that flowed through his lips.

It was sensual, erotic, and my head felt light as the building pleasure clouded my mind.

Booker's lips parted like he was about to say something, but the words never came. In its place was the crest of pleasure we were both chasing. I locked onto the look in his eyes as we both slipped into oblivion and came together.

He felt this unnamed emotion just as much as I did, and it wouldn't be long before it changed everything.

CHAPTER TWENTY-THREE

BOOKER

The downside of having Xander at the ranch was that he was here to see the dopey look on my face when I came back from the ride with Reece. From the grin on his face, he was definitely storing this information for future taunting.

And I didn't care.

I was happy. I'd reached a point in my life where I woke up with a smile on my face.

A goddamn smile.

It wasn't that I hated my life before. It just was what it was. I woke up. I got to work. There was a plan, a set of tasks that needed to be done, and I took comfort in doing them.

It was only now that I realized I wasn't happy, though.

I was going through the motions.

It wasn't a terrible life, but it was just existing.

There was nothing.

I'd never gone out in search of anything more because happiness wasn't something I'd ever seen in my life before.

Happiness definitely wasn't something that had existed at home when we were kids. Even the people around me hadn't really had it until recently. Dex was the same perpetual bachelor that I'd been, and there was nothing in Trace's previous marriage that would have made anyone happy.

But Trace had been the first domino to fall. Seeing him with Delaney was like watching the Nature channel. It all looked so similar to the world we knew, and yet everything about it was different at the same time.

And now, I had it in my life.

It came with the terrible realization that I had no idea what I was doing, and this thing that made me so happy could be lost just as easily as it had been found.

The horse beneath me danced to the side, his ears twitching back in agitation as I realized that my grip on the reins had tightened too much.

"Steady, Bullet," I murmured, running a hand across his neck as I loosened my grip. "Sorry about that, buddy. My head got carried away there for a minute."

He snorted in agitation, but at least he didn't tear ass down the field like he usually did when something annoyed him.

After taking Reece back down the trail to the house, I left her and Doc by the training ring while I rode out to bring in the other horses for their evening feed. It was probably time to push it later into the evenings now that the days were getting longer, but as I was already on Bullet, there was no point in putting it off.

Part of me hadn't wanted to leave her, and that wasn't just the part that wanted to carry her upstairs and continue where we'd left off.

And then there was what had happened last night. Ethan would come by soon, but he'd already warned me it was unlikely he'd be able to do much. It was a glaring reality check for me and the security measures that I needed to get in place around here.

This whole thing would have been solved if I'd had the forethought to put up some damn cameras. This cozy little town had made me forget what the real world was like and just how close to home we didn't like to believe it was.

For now, Xander would have to do. It also gave me a chance to make him sit down and actually talk to me about what was happening in his life. If he'd come up with a plan. Xander had always been the brother that we looked at as the one who would make it. The one who had it all together, escaped this tiny town and went and made something of himself.

I could see the pressure that must have been on him now. A pressure that probably pushed him to the alcohol that had become the problem.

I was so lost in my thoughts that I didn't realize I'd ridden the full length of the fields and straight past the horses I was supposed to be driving back down to the ranch.

Bullet's ears twitched, and when I swung him around, clicking my tongue to urge him on, I felt him stretch out his stride as he let loose. Bullet was one of those horses that when he wanted to run, it felt like he actually flew. I didn't ride him often because he was a favorite with the ranch hands, but if Reece was going to be riding Doc, maybe Bullet and I could become a team.

Or I could buy her a little filly of her own.

That might be getting ahead of myself.

She'd look so good on a palomino mare, though.

With thoughts of her filling my head, it felt like it took no time at all to have the rest of the horses heading back to the ranch. They knew it was time to come in to eat. This was the easiest part of the day.

I took a few moments to assess each horse and make sure they were all running easily without any sign of injury, and then my gaze was fixed straight ahead, waiting to round that last bend when the ranch would come into view.

My heartbeat kicked up a notch at the thought of seeing her again, and when the yard finally came into view, and I saw the sun bouncing off her golden hair, I was grinning like a schoolboy at the thought of having her back in my arms.

I could see Reece standing just outside of the fence, talking to Xander. She glanced up with a dazzling smile as she saw the horses galloping toward the feed but then Xander said something that drew her attention away.

Seeing her happy with my brother meant more than I ever would have imagined, and yet I could feel a sense of panic rising at the scene in front of me.

My eyes darted along the yard, an impending sense of danger setting me on edge.

Something was wrong. Something was different. And after what had happened yesterday, just one slight difference had my subconscious screaming in alarm.

Bullet sensed the tension in his reins again, his ears flicking back as he stretched out his neck, picking up speed.

We pushed into the herd of horses in front of us. It wasn't something I'd ever do normally. It was stupid, and it was dangerous.

But not as dangerous as Xander and Reece standing in front of the galloping herd with the gate completely wide open. The horses were going to charge straight through. They wouldn't stop at the fence line, not when there was an opening in sight. That wasn't how animals like this worked.

One mare slammed into the side of Bullet, and my ankle screamed in pain as I hunched into my saddle, leaning into the gallop that Bullet had started, urging him to go faster.

Even as he veered to the side from the impact, I could see the next horse coming. We were in too close quarters now. There was no avoiding them.

And I had no intention to.

All I needed to do was stay in the saddle and push through to the front of the herd.

Maybe I could reach the gate first, maybe I could...

My senses finally returned to me as the fact that it was impossible slammed into my mind.

There'd be no closing the gate. That was why I always made sure it was secured before I rode out to bring the herd in.

I was so sure I'd done it this time, too. I always did. I... was completely loved up and distracted by Reece.

Fucking hell, had I done this?

Two of the herd closed in on either side of Bullet, pinning him between them, and he thrashed his head, turning to bite the one that was pissing him off the most.

I got one foot on the horse's flank and pushed it back to give us some space, but Bullet had already slowed down.

His ears were pinned flat to his head now, and I knew he was about to throw a Bullet-sized tantrum that would most likely end up with me on the ground if I didn't get him under control. The ground was a place I definitely didn't want to be right now.

But then I heard Xander screaming my name, and I looked up as the relief felt almost overwhelming.

"What the hell are you doing?" Xander screamed.

Reece had her hands covering her mouth, and I could see her eyes wide with fear as she watched another horse slam into Bullet, who stumbled and nearly went down.

The entire herd was panicking now. They didn't understand why Bullet and I were diverting from the norm, and my panic was probably flowing through the herd as well.

"The gate!" I screamed, standing up in my saddle and madly waving my arm in its direction.

Bullet slowed down, and I let him. I wouldn't be able to reach it and close the damn thing. I needed to get him to the back of the herd and then find a way to slow him down before we reached the yard, which was just meters away now.

Xander sprinted for the gate, and I felt a tear prick my eyes as my gaze locked with Reece. She looked so scared, but not for herself. I didn't even know if she'd realized what was happening yet.

Everything seemed to move in slow motion then. A horse slammed into Bullet's side, snapping at his neck in agitation, and he reared up, suddenly twisting to the side. Reece's hands reached out as if she thought she could catch me. Her mouth opened, and I watched her lips form my name.

And then I was falling.

My eyes stayed on her for as long as I could. I didn't want it to end this way, but at least, for a moment, I'd been happy.

I'd had her.

As she disappeared from view, my shoulder slammed into the hard dirt ground, and Bullet came down practically right on top of me. Every part of my body screamed in pain, as I felt like I took a hit from every side.

Then everything went black.

I didn't want to leave. I wanted to be with the woman who had captivated me from the first moment I laid eyes on her. But no matter how hard I fought, the pain was too much, and my consciousness floated away, leaving me with nothing but my regrets in a sea of black.

CHAPTER TWENTY-FOUR

REECE

"NO!"

I went to sprint for Booker but found a pair of arms banded around my chest, holding me in place.

Running into the herd would be the stupidest thing I'd ever done, but that didn't mean I wouldn't.

I thrashed and screeched, fighting with everything I had. All I knew was that I needed to get to Booker. I needed to help him.

If we could get there soon enough, if I could figure out how to...

But reality reminded me of my limitations, and I sagged in defeat.

My eyes never left the spot where Booker and his horse had gone down.

"He's fine. He's going to be fine," I muttered, shaking my head in denial of the thought that wouldn't leave me alone. "He doesn't get to go out like this."

The arms that were banded around me gently squeezed and then released me.

"What the hell just happened?" a gruff voice asked. "Booker knows better than to ride in among the herd."

When I turned around, I saw the ranch hand who had brought the little mare to the ranch already running for the gate where Xander was watching anxiously, trying to catch sight of his brother.

"He was driving the herd in, but the gate was open, and we were standing in the yard. They would have...He was trying to save us." Xander's head was shaking in denial, but he was already climbing the gate as Hank's hand banded around his bicep.

"You can't go in yet." He looked distraught at even saying it. "You need to wait for the herd to settle. Whipping them up and getting them more agitated will just have them stampeding back to the fields and right back over him again."

The tears were streaming down my face now. He was near the back. I'd seen him pulling back when he saw Xander had the gate. But now that we were waiting, the restless agitation of having to stand here and not help started itching at my mind. I couldn't recall just how close to the back of the herd he'd been.

"He was pulling back," Xander said, staying on the gate, ready to jump over as soon as he could. "He was moving to the back."

"I saw him go down," Hank said grimly. "You're the doctor, right?"

Xander nodded, and then slowly all the emotion leached from his face. A mask of professionalism slid over his face, and I could see him working through the steps in his mind about how he was going to save his brother.

"Hank, call an ambulance. I know Booker has a medical kit. I'm going to need it all. He might not have time to wait for the ambulance. We need to give him what medical attention we can as quickly as possible." He paused as he fished in his pocket, and then he tossed me some keys. "Reece, there's a first aid kit in the trunk of my car. Get it and the blanket out. He'll be going into shock, and we need to keep him warm."

I snatched the keys out of the air and was running before he'd even finished speaking.

"The emergency kit is in the barn," I heard Hank say. "Don't you dare go over that gate until I get back."

The sound of his running had me assuming that Xander had agreed, but I doubted he was telling the truth. There was no way I'd be able to stand there waiting if Booker even remotely came back into view.

I fumbled with the key fob in my hands as I skidded on the gravel next to Xander's car. The damn fancy thing was all buttons, and I had no idea what any of them did, so I just pressed them frantically until the trunk popped open.

I grabbed the red first aid kit and bundled the blanket under one arm. I was just about to run back to Xander when I saw the water bottles and grabbed two, thinking we might need them.

It took me less than two minutes, but when I turned back to the horse yard, Xander was nowhere in sight, and I knew he was already making his way to his brother.

Some horses had stopped to eat the feed Booker had placed around the yard, but others were still prancing in the middle, their eyes wide in fear as they seemed unable to settle.

I knew little about horses, but even I could tell the situation was still balanced on a knife's edge.

"Goddamned it," Hank swore as he emerged from the

barn with an even bigger kit than the one I was carrying. "I told him to wait."

I got to the gate moments before he did. I glanced over my shoulder at Hank and saw the annoyance cross his features as he realized what I was about to do.

"Don't you dare," Hank warned me. But I was already climbing the iron bars of the gate before he could utter the words. "Wait for me, at least."

I paused at the top of the gate, and it took every single ounce of willpower that I possessed.

There were still a few scared horses in the yard, even if more of them had been lured across to the food. I knew I wouldn't stand a chance if they turned and ran, and I didn't have enough experience to know what to do if I ended up in a situation that could mean trying to save myself as well.

The last thing we needed was more people injured. It would take the precious few resources we had away from Booker, and I wouldn't risk him any more than he'd already risked himself.

Idiot.

He knew better than that. I knew he did. He should have trusted Xander and me to see what was happening and get ourselves out of there in time. When was Booker going to learn that the entire world wasn't waiting for him to save it?

The problem with sitting at the top of the gate waiting for Hank was that it gave me a completely uninterrupted view of Xander as he ran around the horse that was lying on the ground. It lifted its head slightly, giving a soft whinny before it dropped back to the ground.

"Come on, sweetheart," Hank murmured as he reached my side. "Stay at my side and keep me between you and the horses. Booker will have my ass if you get hurt."

I nodded numbly as I watched Xander drop to his knees behind the horse. Part of me was too afraid to move, but then Xander looked up, his gaze locked with mine, and he nodded.

The relief surging through my heart spurred me into motion as I jumped from the gate and jogged across the yard at Hank's side.

"Easy, Bullet," Hank murmured as we approached the injured horse. "Easy, boy."

At first, I was confused about what he was doing, but then my eyes finally found Booker, and I saw how he was lying on the ground between the horse's legs. I saw the danger he could be in if Bullet tried to get up.

"He's unconscious, but he's breathing. I can't assess him properly like this. Hank, I need you to help me pull him clear of the horse." Xander sounded so calm as he spoke that the whole situation didn't seem real.

"Don't move him," I suddenly snapped out, looking at Xander in alarm. "We're not supposed to move him, right?"

My hands stretched out like I was going to make a grab for one of them, but I had no idea what to do in this situation. I had no idea how to help.

"We need to get him clear of the horse, Reece," Xander said calmly. "He's at less risk if we move him carefully than if he stays where he is."

I nodded numbly as Hank gently patted my shoulder before moving to Xander's side. They each put a hand under one of Booker's shoulders and then did their best to steady his head as they counted to three.

I held my breath as they quickly moved Booker, my gaze moving across every part of him trying to see where he was hurt.

He was so still when they gently rolled him onto his

back, and the tears broke free of my eyes when I saw the blood staining his face.

This couldn't be happening. It didn't feel real. What had seemed like the perfect day had turned into a nightmare.

Xander was already checking him over, his practiced hands examining his brother as Hank opened up both medical kits within reach. He checked Booker's pulse, his pupils, his neck and then moved down his body, continuing his assessment.

Xander moved back to Booker's head, parting his hair to see where the bleeding was coming from as he pulled a dressing from the bag and had Hank hold it in place.

"He's got a broken right arm, a nasty cut on his head, and a whole hell of a lot of bruises. I need to get him an MRI to be sure, but—"

"Will you stop breathing in my face," Booker mumbled.

A sob of relief burst out of me just at the sound of his voice.

"I swear to god if you try to give me mouth-to-mouth, I'm kicking your ass." Then Booker groaned in pain.

Xander dropped back onto his ass in surprise as Hank laughed, shaking his head.

"You ain't kicking anyone's ass for a while, boss. I think I'm holding your brain in my hand."

"Please! You haven't got hands big enough."

Booker tried to sit up, and Xander came back to his senses, pushing on his brother's shoulders to keep him on the ground.

"Did you not hear what I said?" he chastised.

"No, I was too busy trying not to smell your breath."

"Ass. You just had a herd of horses stampede over you, and you think now is the time to be difficult. I always knew you were like this because you got kicked in the head by a horse as a kid."

Booker tried to push Xander to the side and only then seemed to realize that he did, in fact, have a broken arm and swore at the pain it no doubt caused.

"Where's Reece?"

"I'm here." I cautiously moved to Booker's side, not quite believing that it was possible for him to be moving around already. I reached out to touch him but then was afraid I'd just hurt him more.

When I went to pull back, Booker's other hand grabbed mine.

"Are you okay?" he asked.

A hysterical laugh bubbled out of me, and I shook my head as the tears continued to pour down my cheeks. "Am I okay? Booker, you could have died!"

He hissed out a breath as Xander tore open his sleeve and checked over his broken arm.

"I'm a little beat up, I'll give you that. But Bullet took the worst, and his body sheltered me. It would be a lot worse than this if he hadn't gone down with me."

Booker's eyes found Hank, and he knew what he was asking him as he got up and moved to Bullet's side. The horse hadn't made a sound since we'd been at Booker's side, and I didn't need Hank to say aloud what we all already knew to be true.

"I'll call Cole," Hank said grimly.

I listened to his quiet, murmuring words of comfort to the horse as Xander finished checking over Booker.

"It shouldn't be possible, but I think you're going to be fine. When the ambulance gets here, you're getting in with no argument and having an MRI," Xander told him.

I saw Booker open his mouth to protest and quickly added, "Please, Booker."

When he turned to look at me in response, Booker's eyes seemed to take in my expression, and he finally nodded once, wincing as he did.

We hadn't all been lucky today, and poor Bullet was going to pay the price for what had happened here. But as we waited for the ambulance to arrive, I wondered just how much was down to luck.

Because I'd watched Booker close that gate after he laid out the feed. I'd leaned against it, daydreaming as I watched him climb back into Bullet's saddle, and I had no idea how it could have possibly been opened by the time he came back.

CHAPTER TWENTY-FIVE

REECE

Why did time move so much slower in a hospital than anywhere else on the planet?

I'd come in the ambulance with Booker, Xander following behind us in his car. Hank stayed to help Cole with Bullet, who'd arrived just as we were getting ready to pull out.

I knew what was going to happen to Bullet, and I was glad I didn't have to be there when it happened. It felt so wrong when he'd saved Booker that we couldn't do more to save him, too.

The doctors had taken Booker through some double doors, and Xander and I had been pacing a waiting room ever since. Even Delaney and Trace turning up barely registered for me as I watched those doors, waiting for the news that Booker would be okay.

The paramedics had called it a miracle on the way here, shaking their heads as they did their own examination. I'd kept my eyes on the heart monitor for the entire ride, not quite ready to believe that everything would be okay.

I needed tests and results. I needed proof.

I couldn't let myself relax until there was absolutely no doubt, and only then would I even let myself consider how we'd gotten into this situation to start with.

"I'm not waiting out here," Xander finally said when he couldn't take it any longer, striding for the doors with a purpose that only a medical professional could have in a setting like this.

He'd made it three steps before they burst open, and we all seemed to hold our breath looking at the grim-faced doctor who walked toward us.

"The Farrington family?" he asked.

Trace and Xander moved forward as I stood there, wondering if I really had a right to be here right now.

"He's a lucky man," the doctor said as Delaney came and wrapped an arm around my shoulders. "Nasty break in the right arm, which is going to take some time to heal. But apart from the head lac and some bruising to his shoulder and side, he's going to be fine. He'll probably need some physical therapy on the arm, but I can't see it giving him any long-term problems. He's young, he's healthy, he'll be back on his feet in no time."

"Thank god," Trace sighed, turned around, and then strode to me and Delaney and wrapped his arms around us both.

This was the strangest situation I'd ever been in. Not just because of Booker being hurt, but because these people seemed to have accepted me as one of them so quickly.

Trace leaned back and gave me a smile. "He's going to want to see you first."

My eyes widened in surprise, and when I looked at the doctor about to ask if that was okay, he just nodded. "I take it you're Reece?"

"Yes."

"He's asking for you. Perhaps you can persuade him to stay overnight at the very least. He seems to think that because he's not dead he's invulnerable, and I need him to at least pretend he needs my help, even if just for my ego."

Xander barked out an unexpected laugh, and we all looked at him in surprise. "Good luck with that," he said with a shrug.

My first instinct was to jump to Booker's defense, but even in the short time I'd known him, I knew they weren't exaggerating.

"I'm not sure even my powers of persuasion are that good," I told them both.

"Oh, I've got an idea," Delaney suddenly piped up, but then Trace's hand slapped over her mouth before she could say another word.

"Let's save it for ourselves," he murmured, quickly kissing her on the cheek and then making a face, pulling his hand back in disgust. "Did you just lick me?"

I left them bickering in the waiting room and followed the doctor through the doors that apparently held no special powers and just led up to some examination bays. In fact, the other side of them was just anticlimactically an ordinary hospital suite.

"I kind of thought there'd be something else back here," I mumbled, looking around.

"Nah, we keep the really cool stuff in the back," the doctor quipped before he showed me to a curtained-off bay.

I could hear Booker's irritated sigh before I'd even reached to pull it back.

"Don't even think about sticking me with that needle," he snapped. "I told you I don't want the damn painkillers."

"Mr. Farrington, please. It will just take the edge off

while we get your cast on. You'll heal better if you don't move around too much."

"And you won't let me leave tonight if I'm flying high on whatever's in there," he countered.

I saw the guilty look on the nurse's face before she looked at me beseechingly. "Maybe you can talk some sense into him," she mumbled.

Booker's gaze moved to me then, and the annoyance instantly melted off his face. "Come here."

I moved like I was in a dream, needing him as much as he seemed to need me. As my hand slipped into his, I felt my heart settle. Seeing him sitting up and bitching out a nurse was a surprisingly reassuring sight. But touching him and knowing it was all real was even better.

"I might be slightly angry with you," I told him, my head tipped to the side as the relief cleared my mind enough for me to realize just how true that was. "What did you think you were doing?"

"I was riding to your rescue like a goddamned knight. You're welcome, by the way."

"It was pretty brave," I conceded. "I was so scared for you, Booker."

"Not half as scared as I was for you, baby," Booker said, pulling me closer and then wrapping his arm around my waist as he drew me into his side. He kissed the top of my head lightly before he rested his forehead against mine. "I'm so sorry, Reece. I should have made sure the gate was closed. I can't believe I was so stupid to leave the damned thing open. If you'd been hurt, I don't know what I would have done."

My head reared back in surprise. "You didn't leave it open, Booker."

He shook his head, almost like he didn't believe me.

"Trust me. I remember you closing it. I remember leaning on the gate and staring at your ass as you got on Bullet."

The nurse snorted out a laugh, reminding me she was still there and had apparently gotten to work wrapping Booker's arm up while I had him distracted.

"Sorry," she apologized, continuing with her work.

"Did you open it?" Booker asked, and for an impossible moment, I'd actually forgotten what we were talking about.

"No. When you rode down to the fields, I went to the house to find Val, but she wasn't in the kitchen. I came out to check the barn, and then I saw Xander getting out of his car. We started talking just as the horses came in from the field."

Booker's eyes squinted, moving side to side as he was deep in thought. "Val didn't come out when you were in the yard?"

"No, I don't remember seeing her."

"That's...not right. She would have come into the yard if she heard people talking."

"I'll get Xander to check around for her," I told him quickly, not wanting him to get worked up. "She probably got stuck in a stable or something. Or maybe she'd been out with Hank. He turned up just as you fell."

"I need to get back to the ranch," Booker suddenly said, trying to sit up only to find me and the nurse pushing him back down.

"If you want to use this arm again, young man, you will stay where you are, and you will quit moving," she snapped.

That she had to be about ten years younger than Booker should have made the whole situation funny.

Except it didn't.

Because now that Booker had raised it, I was worrying about Val, too. The whole situation was off somehow.

Booker sighed, but it came out as more of a reluctant hiss than anything else.

"I'll take that as a yes ma'am," the nurse quipped and went back to her work. "This is just a temporary cast. You'll have an appointment with orthopedics tomorrow to get fitted with something else. Be grateful you don't need surgery. If you can hold still for five more minutes, I can get this done. You're supposed to wait at least an hour to have this checked over, but I'm guessing that's going to be no from you."

Booker nodded, and she rolled her eyes.

"Your brother is a doctor, right?"

"Yes," Booker rushed out. "He's staying at the ranch with us."

"I might persuade the doctor to discharge you into his care, but I'm going to need a hand on your heart, solemn vow that you'll be back at this hospital tomorrow for your appointment."

Booker nodded, giving her one of those rare Booker smiles that had her looking as swoony as I no doubt did when he did it. "It's a deal. But my hands are currently engaged right now."

Booker hugged me tighter, and the nurse tsked but got back to her work, and true to her word, she finished quickly.

"Wait here, and I'll go find the doctor. Do you want me to tell the rest of your family that they can come through?" she asked.

"That would be great. Thanks."

She slipped away, drawing the curtain back around the bay as she went, and we were suddenly alone.

"I wonder how long we've got?" Booker asked, the corner of his lips ticking up as he looked at me.

"Really? I have never been so scared in my whole damn life. I don't know how you can even think about that right now."

"It's hard not to when I'm with you," Booker said, kissing my cheek sweetly. "I was scared too, sweetheart. I just want to get home, figure out what the hell is going on, and then fall asleep with you in my arms."

As nice as that thought was, I couldn't bring myself to think about it right now. Because there was another in my head that I didn't want to taint it.

"Do you think..."

"That the guy who trashed the cottage is still hanging around?" Booker asked grimly.

I nodded somberly.

What had happened today had been dangerous on so many levels. We could have all been hurt. Hell, someone could have been killed. This was beyond tearing up someone's clothes, and I couldn't even bring myself to be slightly outraged about my pie when I was facing the reality that Booker could have died today.

"It's time to tell you my entire story, isn't it?"

"Yeah, baby, it is. But it can wait until we get home. Just you and me, okay?"

Booker's arm tightened around me, and I was opening my mouth to tell him I just wanted to get it over with and tell him everything now, but then the curtain was pulled back, and his worried family walked in.

I could wait.

Booker's eyes found mine as the others started fussing around him, and I could see his understanding in them. He knew there were parts of the story I hadn't wanted to tell him. In reality, he knew most of it already. The only question left about the whole thing was *who*.

Only Camden Carter.

And all the ways he could ruin our lives.

CHAPTER TWENTY-SIX

BOOKER

Someone had rung my bell harder than it had ever been done before. Yet it was nothing compared to the pain in my heart when I saw the scared reluctance on Reece's face about facing her past.

Whoever this guy was, she was scared of him. But it seemed like something so much more than I'd thought before. I'd assumed he was just a guy who got off on breaking women, not that that wasn't bad enough. From the look on Reece's face back at the hospital, she seemed to think there was something so much worse.

I climbed out of the back of Trace's truck as Delaney and Reece fussed around me. It should have been pissing me off, but there was something nice about knowing someone cared that much about you. As nice as it was, though, I was reaching my limit. But I gritted my teeth and tried not to come across like a completely ungrateful bastard.

"Okay, now one step at a time," Trace said as we approached the front porch. "Hold on to the railing. Better yet, wrap your arm around me."

"Nope, that's it! I can't take it anymore!"

Trace started laughing, and I glared at my brother and the amused look on Delaney's face. That Reece looked thoroughly confused was the only thing that saved her. That and the fact that I was now absolutely certain I was madly in love with the woman.

"Twenty bucks for me!" Trace crowed.

"Damned it! You play dirty, Trace," Delaney said, waving a finger at him.

"What can I say? I have more years of experience at poking the bear than you give me credit for."

"I hate you both," I snapped as I stomped up the steps, followed by their laughter and a confused-looking Reece.

Damn, I needed that, though. I needed a dose of normalcy to scare the worry away from my mind. If that bastard had done something to Val, I was ripping his legs off.

I stormed into the dining room we rarely used, checking under the table before heading into the kitchen to look for her. It wasn't like Val not to come out if someone turned up at the ranch. She wasn't one of those dogs who would sleep in her basket all day.

I laid my hand on the cushion of the basket and found it cold.

When I turned around, scowling in thought, trying to think of where to look next, I found Reece standing in front of me with a sad look on her face.

Trace and Delaney were looking around, confused, but Trace seemed to figure it out first.

"Where's Val?" he asked.

"We haven't seen her since before the...accident?" Reece looked confused by the word, and I couldn't blame her.

We were the only two who suspected the truth at the moment. I knew she was feeling bad enough about the whole thing. I didn't want her to have to face answering everyone else's questions until I could persuade her that none of this was her fault.

Xander walked into the house at that point, storming into the kitchen with a scowl on his face that rivaled even mine. "Now I remember specifically telling you that you were going straight to bed. What I'm confused about is what you think you heard me say."

He crossed his arms, staring me down.

"Val—"

"Is a dog. Get your ass up the stairs."

We glared at each other across the kitchen, and I was about ready to see how hard I could bounce this cast off his skull.

"How about we look for Val?" Delaney said calmly, walking between Xander and me as she tried to break the stare down. "Reece can get you settled upstairs."

They were clearly forgetting that not only was I a grown man who could do whatever the hell he wanted to do, but there was also a door behind me I fully intended to escape through.

Before I could turn and storm away, Reece's hand slipped into mine.

"We can check the barn together," she said gently, not even trying to tell me I had to wait behind. "But your family is trying to tell you they're worried about you, Booker. They just need some reassurance."

I saw Xander's expression crumble at that moment. I'd never seen him look like this before.

"I was so scared, Booker." Xander shook his head as he spoke. "I thought we'd lost you. All these years I've spent sulking at the bottom of a bottle, and now I'm finally getting my life together, I lose you. We're supposed to be rebuilding something here. We can't do that without you."

I strode across the room to my brother and pulled him into a hug. Xander clung to me, and I felt his shoulders shaking as he let his emotions go.

It was selfish of me not to even consider what they were going through right now.

But this was Val. She'd been by my side for years. There were days when the only time I spoke was to Val. It might be stupid to admit, but she was my best friend. I couldn't rest if she was out there somewhere hurting.

"I'm right here. I'm fine, Xan." When I leaned back to look at him, he quickly swiped the tears from his cheeks and gave me a weak smile. "I'm sorry for scaring you."

"Let's check out the barn," he said, rolling his eyes. "I know there's no persuading you once you've made up your mind."

We didn't even make it a step because Trace was suddenly there, throwing his arms around us both as well.

"I'm not missing out on the Farrington bro hug," he said, pressing his face against my back. "Let's maybe just get together for things like dinner and carnivals in the future, though, yeah? I'm not sure my old heart can take emergency calls to the ER anymore."

The girls joined us then, joining in the hug on each side, and I suddenly found myself in the middle smothered by people who cared about me. Even the dull ache in my arm and the throbbing in my head couldn't take away how much this moment meant to even a grumpy ass like me.

A noise came from behind me as someone cleared their throat uncomfortably.

Hank stood by the door looking awkward at having interrupted our strange scene.

"Erm, good to see you on your feet, boss." He gave me a lopsided grin as he pulled the hat off his head. "Cole is out in the barn with Bullet. He wanted to know if you wanted an update before he left."

"Bullet?"

"Yeah. He thinks he can save him. He had a dislocated front leg that he reset and a couple of broken ribs, but he can pull him through if you want him to. I wasn't sure. Given everything that happened, I thought maybe you'd want..."

"Whatever he needs. Cost isn't an issue," I said in relief.

I'd seen poor Bullet as they loaded me onto the stretcher, and I'd been around horses for long enough that I knew Cole was coming for one reason only. Most vets would have just shot him and called it a day. The fact that Cole was even willing to try meant I'd made the right move in picking him to work with the ranch. He was a good man, and he cared about the horses nearly as much as I did.

"Oh thank god," Reece rushed out a sigh.

I was surprised to see her tucked under Xander's arm when I looked at her, but I was just glad that Xander had finally pulled his head out of his ass for long enough to see how good of a person she was.

He gave me a slight shrug when he saw me looking at him, and I turned back to Hank.

"As long as my doctor doesn't mind, I'll come out and talk to Cole myself."

I heard Xander's scoff because I didn't even wait for his response before I was heading for the door. Reece laughed softly, and I heard them all follow.

Bullet deserved a medal for everything he'd been

through. And he was about to have a whole crowd of people ready to do whatever it took to get him back on his feet.

As we made our way to the barn, my eyes went to every bush, every shadow, looking for Val. The wave of relief when we went inside the barn and found her sitting in the corner of Bullet's stall genuinely made me think I was about to cry.

"Val!" Reece rushed out, making the dog leap to its feet and rush to her feet. "Where have you been?"

Reece dropped to her knees to fuss over Val, who immediately rolled onto her back, whimpering and crying in a way that I'd never seen before.

"I checked her over quickly," Cole said, prepping a syringe of something. "She's fine. A bit shaken up I think, nothing else. Hank found her locked inside one of the stalls when we were bringing Bullet in."

My forehead creased in a frown, and I moved to my best friend, dropping to my knees as I ran my fingers through her soft fur. "What did you get yourself into, girl?"

She whimpered and wriggled closer to me, shoving her cold nose into my hand, which was partially covered by the cast, and sniffing it.

If Val hadn't been shut inside the stable, I dreaded to think what would have happened to her when I came off Bullet in the herd. She would have tried to reach me. I know she would have. And she would have been hurt. Whoever had shut her in there didn't do it for noble reasons, but it had most likely saved her life.

Cole finished giving Bullet the shot and then started packing up his bag. "I've done all I can," Cole said, his gaze roaming over Bullet as he spoke like he was checking to make sure that he hadn't missed anything. "I think he should pull through fine. Once we reset the leg, we were able to get him up on his feet. He's not putting any weight on the injured leg for now, but that's to be expected. I've given him painkillers, antibiotics, and something to bring the swelling down. There's nothing to do but wait and see for now. I'll come by and check on him in the morning. If he lies down, let him. There's no point stressing him by trying to keep him on his feet. But I have to warn you. If he goes down and we can't get him back up again...Well, you know the rest."

I nodded, moving to Bullet's side and laying my forehead against his neck. "Thank you," I whispered, running my hand across his neck.

I had no idea how we'd both made it out of this. We might be hurting, but there was no way I was losing Bullet now. I meant it when I said whatever it took.

Cole ran through the care routine for Bullet with Hank and Reece. I'd be relying on the ranch hands even more over the next couple of months while the cast was on. Maybe now was the time to bring on some more help. We could ramp up the renovation plans and get some movement on the project while I had time to concentrate on it.

But first, I needed to get Reece alone and have a long overdue conversation.

Someone was on the ranch. Whoever had broken into the cottage hadn't left like we'd assumed.

It was time to show them what happened to people who thought they could put the people I cared about at risk.

CHAPTER TWENTY-SEVEN

REECE

The house felt too quiet once everyone had left. Xander was staying in the cottage and had taken Val with him. I had a feeling he and Booker were hoping whoever had broken in would do it again. But just the thought alone was making me want to throw up.

This had all gone too far.

The more I thought about it, the more convinced I was that Camden had done this. He loved messing with people. He liked to mess with the stuff people loved and then laugh it off, like ruining their dreams wasn't a big deal. How I'd fallen for him completely evaded me now. He was an ass, he'd always been an ass, and honestly, I was embarrassed that it had taken me so long to walk away.

I just didn't understand how he'd found me. There was nothing at Willowbrook that tied me here, no connections from before I'd met him. I wasn't registered anywhere that would show up. I didn't have a bank account, and I hadn't even been anywhere that would have kept any record of me.

Booker walked into his room and found me sitting on the edge of his bed.

"I'm exhausted," he admitted as he came to sit next to me.

He wrapped one arm around my shoulders and laid the other gently across his lap. I reached out and ran my fingers along the cast. This was my fault. He was hurt because of me.

"I'm sorry, Booker. I've brought all this trouble to your door when all you ever did was help me."

"You don't know that it's him."

I loved that he was the type of person who would try to reassure me this wasn't my fault. Even when we both knew it wasn't true.

"Who else could it be?" I sighed. "I...Fuck! This is such a mess."

I pushed my hair back from my face, my fingers raking through the lengths in desperation. A sensible person would leave. They'd take their troubles with them and get the hell out of town.

As I looked up into Booker's understanding eyes, I knew that was the last thing I wanted to do. I loved him so much. Leaving him would be worse than anything else I'd been through. But Booker was hurt because I'd blown into his life and turned everything upside down. I couldn't let that happen again.

"You're not going anywhere," he told me sternly, his eyes darting side to side as he searched my gaze. "This isn't your fault, Reece. We'll deal with it. *I'll* deal with it. And then we'll go on and live our lives together. Happy, like you were always supposed to be."

I reached up for his cheek, brushing my fingers across his face, trying to find the words to tell him everything I was feeling.

"Just tell me his name," Booker whispered. "Start with that, and we'll figure it out."

"Camden Carter," I whispered.

It was so much easier than I'd thought it would be. Looking into Booker's eyes, I doubted I'd ever be able to find something to be afraid of. My fingers trailed up to his hair, and I made sure to stay away from the stitches that started just inside his hairline. It hurt to look at his injuries, to see the deep color of the bruise that was starting to cover his cheek, extending to his jaw and disappearing into his beard. Under his shirt was probably even worse, and I didn't know if I could face them. Face seeing the evidence of what I'd caused.

"Why are you scared of him?" he asked quietly.

"Because he's untouchable," I admitted. My voice sounded flat and expressionless, but I kept staring into Booker's eyes, soaking in the safety that I found there. I could get through anything if I let myself get lost in those beautiful eyes.

"No one's untouchable," Booker said confidently.

"Yes, they are. And it's not what you think. He's not part of some crime family or anything. It's worse than that."

"He's rich," Booker said, like the whole thing was so obvious. I supposed it was for him. It was the reason his own family had fallen apart.

Money. It never changed people for the better.

Unless you were someone like Booker.

"It's not just that," I told him. "His father is the governor. He can do anything. No one will stop him. They don't want to end up on the wrong side of his father's politics. I've seen it happen, Booker. The police won't touch him. It's not worth the trouble. It's why I left and never reported anything. It wouldn't have gained me anything, and he'd have just known I was leaving. The only option I had was to leave quietly and hope I could get far enough before he knew I was gone. Except I didn't get very far. Still, I don't know how he found me."

"Maybe he hired someone to track you down." Booker shrugged. "Maybe it's for the best. I don't give a fuck who his father is, and I think me and Camden Carter are long overdue for a conversation."

I could see the fury brewing in his eyes, and with my fingers, I smoothed out the frown lines on his forehead.

"I should leave," I whispered, hating the words as they slipped through my lips. "If I go, he'll follow me. I can disappear..."

"No."

His abrupt denial made me smile. It brought back memories of our early days together.

"We can have tonight," I told him sadly. "Tomorrow, I have to leave."

I leaned in to kiss him. Booker had to see that this was for the best. I couldn't bring this kind of trouble to his door. Maybe, one day, I could come back. Governors didn't stay in power forever, and Camden wasn't going to chase me all over the country. He'd get bored after a while and move on to some other poor girl.

"I'll give you tonight," Booker said, his lips brushing across mine. "But then I want the next night and every night that comes after it. You're not going anywhere, Reece. I love you. I'm not letting you go just because this douchebag thinks he has some kind of right over you. If you can tell me you don't feel the same way, if you can look me in the eye and tell me you really want to leave, then I'll let you go. I won't hold you here against your will. But I know you, Reece. I know your heart, and I know it beats in time with mine."

My eyelashes fluttered as I tried to hold back the tears.

"How did the man who used to only say no to every one of my questions suddenly learn how to say something so beautiful?" I asked, sighing as he gently kissed me.

"I've heard being kicked in the head by a horse can cause brain damage," he murmured cheekily.

"I love you, Booker."

"I love you more."

Booker moved back, pulling me onto the mattress as he leaned over me, his good hand brushing the hair from my face.

"You're the most beautiful woman I've ever met. You're kind, generous, and you'd do anything to help the people around you. You got my busted-up old heart to beat again. Stay with me, baby. Let me try to earn a place by your side. If you really want to go, if you really can't bear to stay, I'll sell it all. I'll give it all away if I have to and come with you."

Booker kissed me again, and I felt him pour every ounce of emotion into that kiss. His thumb brushed against my jaw, and I had to remind myself that he was hurt as every part of me wanted to jump the man confessing his feelings for me.

"I'd never make you leave this place, Booker."

He shook his head, and I could see him getting ready to tell me it didn't matter. That he didn't care. I could see the lie forming on his lips. We both knew it wasn't true. The ranch was special, and it would be wrong not to share it with the world when Booker had finally figured out a way to do that.

But it was more than that.

I loved this place nearly as much as I loved the man himself. I'd found a place here. Not just with Booker, but in the beginning of a family I wanted to build, friendships I wanted to make, and a purpose that made it worthwhile to get out of bed in the morning.

This was the life I'd chosen for myself, and I wouldn't let a man like Camden Carter take that away from me.

"If you really think we can deal with this together, then of course I never want to leave."

Booker laughed for joy, peppering my face with kisses.

"Tell me again," he whispered against my lips.

I could have pretended that I didn't know what he was talking about. I could have teased him until he persuaded me with gentle kisses to whisper the words he wanted to hear. But I was done holding them back. Now that I'd admitted my feelings, it was impossible to hold it inside.

"I love you, Booker. I love you so much."

"I'd get kicked in the head by a horse any day for you," he said, kissing me one more time.

"And they say romance is dead."

He laughed and shook his head while I dreamed of how this could be every night for me. Of how I'd slowly help Booker out of his clothes as I laid gentle kisses on his forming bruises. We'd slide between the sheets and sleep would be the last thing on our minds.

We should have been tangling ourselves in those sheets, whispering words of love as we came together in gentle movements and soft caresses.

This wasn't how the night you first confessed your feelings was supposed to go, but as I laid my head on the pillow and looked at the man I loved, I knew in the grand scheme of life it didn't matter.

Camden Carter was a temporary problem, and together, we'd deal with him.

Then we'd have a lifetime of nights to get lost in each other.

CHAPTER TWENTY-EIGHT

REECE

Booker had been stomping around the ranch all day, and it was actually pretty cute, not that I'd admit it to his face.

I could tell he was hurting, but he was being stubborn and refusing to take any painkillers. Xander was just about ready to throttle him and was currently trying to threaten him into going back to bed for a nap before he took him to the hospital for his next appointment.

So I'd been hiding in the living room pretending to read a book as an excuse to stay out of both of their ways.

I heard the kitchen door slam, and then Xander appeared in the living room doorway wearing exactly the same expression that Booker normally did when things weren't going his way.

They were so alike it was funny. The fact they clearly didn't think they were made it even funnier still.

"I give up on him. His arm can drop off for all I care." Xander huffed as he dropped into the armchair and put his feet on the coffee table, crossing his arms as he sulked.

I shoved the bookmark between the pages of my book and put it on the arm of the couch.

"Did you really think a nap was going to work?"

"He needs to rest." Xander was practically pouting now, then he squinted at me with a calculating look on his face. "You could persuade him to go to bed."

"Are you trying to use me as sexual bait, Xander Farrington?"

"You wouldn't have to actually sleep with him." He sighed dramatically. "I wouldn't force that on anyone."

"That's big of you. I doubt even I could...No, I definitely could. I'm just not going to. If you want him to stop stomping about the ranch, you need to offer him something he's not going to refuse."

"I tried, but you won't cooperate with me!"

I knew he was teasing me. Apparently, trauma really did bond people because Xander and I had gone from slightly frosty acquaintances to co-conspirators in the space of twelve hours.

"Trace and Delaney are coming over," I told him, deciding not to engage with his earlier plan. Honestly, I was saving that one for this evening. "And Cade will be here. And Booker loves his nephew, who I happen to know is coming with a stack of Pokémon cards and apparently a burning desire to tell Booker about each and every one of them."

"I want him to rest, Reece, not to torture the poor guy."

I swiveled on the couch, curling my feet beneath me so I could look at Xander properly. "Did he tell you?" I asked.

Xander didn't even pretend not to know what I was talking about. "He did."

"You know he's just using the horses as an excuse to

check the barn, the cottage, and everything in between them. He's not really doing any work."

"And what do you think he's going to do if he actually finds this guy lurking in the shadows somewhere?"

I sighed and flopped back against the couch. He had a point. I guess I'd just assumed that Camden wouldn't be stupid enough to still be hanging out around here, but he'd proved me wrong on that already with the whole gate incident.

As I stared up at the ceiling, I found the courage to say what I was really thinking.

"Is it wrong that I kind of hope he punches him in the face and then somehow reverses a truck over him?"

"Not in the slightest...as long as he remembers to use his good hand."

I snorted out an unladylike laugh, then, with a sigh, stood up. "I'll check on him."

As I went to walk past Xander, his hand gently wrapped around my wrist, and I looked down at him in surprise.

"We won't let this guy anywhere near you, Reece."

My eyes must have widened comically because Xander hit me with a boyish smile that I'd never seen on his face before.

"You're good for him," he said with a shrug. "I can see the difference from the guy I saw three years ago who communicated in mostly grunts and growls. He's happy finally, and it's about time that Booker had someone looking out for him as much as he looks out for the rest of us."

I moved to perch my butt on the arm of the couch and bit my lip nervously. "Will you stay?" I asked him, my eyes nervously glancing toward the door to check that Booker hadn't come back inside.

I knew he wanted his brother here. He just didn't know how to ask him.

Xander rubbed the back of his neck as he half shrugged. "I don't know. This place has never been good for me, Reece. I don't know what I have to keep me here. I'd do better finding somewhere to start over. Somewhere without all the memories that want to drive me back into the closest bottle."

I understood where he was coming from, but it shocked me he thought he didn't have anything in Willowbrook to stay for.

The front door flew open, and Trace, Delaney, and Cade came tumbling inside. Cade was standing on Trace's shoes as he did a strange waddling walk, walking them both inside, and Delaney laughed at their antics.

"Where's Uncle Booker?" Cade shouted, jumping off Trace's feet, much to the relief of his father, who shook out a foot with a grimace.

"He's out by the barn," I told him, smiling as he charged through the house.

"Come on, Dad! We need to show Uncle Booker my cards, and I want to sign his cast!"

"Wait up!" Trace called out as he ran after his son, laughing. "He's getting it changed today, anyway."

"I'll sign that one too," Cade shouted, his voice disappearing out the door.

Delaney stood in the doorway, watching the two of them with a soft smile on her face. Then she glanced at us with a wry smile. "Sorry about that..." she started, only to be interrupted by the sound of a crash outside. "Oh hell!"

And then she was running for the door next.

I turned to Xander with a smile on my face as he

watched on in horror at the chaos that had just blown through the front door.

"Them, Xander. You have a *family* to stay for."

The look of genuine surprise on his face was a little sad, and I cursed his parents for all the things they'd done to their sons so they couldn't see a chance of happiness when it was right in front of them.

I stood from the couch again, giving Xander's shoulder a squeeze as I walked past him, leaving him to his thoughts of the future and how he wanted that to look.

He had so many opportunities in front of him. He just needed to open his eyes and recognize them for what they were.

"This damn thing itches," Booker grumbled as he tried to stick a finger inside his new cast.

"Will you leave that alone? It's supposed to be helping you heal. Poking and prodding at it is just going to make this take longer," I warned him.

The petulant look I got from him made me laugh, and I quickly kissed his lips to stop him from being annoyed with me. It must have worked because he wrapped an arm around me and pulled me closer.

The town meeting still hadn't started, even though it was scheduled to begin nearly half an hour earlier. It seemed like people were still arriving, and honestly, the people of Willowbrook were so busy catching up with each other and being excited about the fact that they were having a town meeting to begin with for anything to happen.

"It's barely broken," Booker said, rolling his eyes

dramatically. He'd tried this with the doctor earlier when he was trying to persuade him he'd be fine with just a brace.

"Booker Farrington, there is currently a bone in your arm that is in three pieces instead of one. Do not make me pull up the picture of your x-ray on my phone again," I snapped.

I knew taking that picture was a good idea.

He leaned closer, his face coming level with mine. "It's kinda hot when you get all schoolteacher snippy like that." Then he quickly pecked my lips before pulling back with a smile.

"Aww, Booky bear, I love seeing you all loved up and gooey like this," Blake gushed as she slipped into the seat on the other side of him and wrapped her arms around his good arm, clinging to him.

She caught my eye and grinned at me before she looked up at Booker with big Bambi eyes. "Did you get a boo-boo, Booky bear?"

The laugh burst out of me in the loudest snort that I swear echoed around the suddenly silent room. Everyone turned to look at me, but thankfully, maybe, Blake drew the attention away from me as she leaped from her chair.

"No, Booker, spank Reece. She'll enjoy it more than me!" she squealed as she ran off.

"She's like a four-year-old on crack who was the result of some kind of deal with the devil," Booker grumbled.

At least most of the town turned to watch Blake run away cackling rather than me, until an elderly lady in the corner joined in.

"I'd be down for a spanking," she loudly told her friend, who nodded in agreement.

Booker turned to me with a look of absolute horror on

his face. "If you fake a medical emergency right now so I can carry you out of here, I'll pay you a thousand dollars."

"Booky bear, if you think scooping me up in your big manly arms is going to help in this situation, then you haven't read far enough into that romance novel of yours."

For a split second, he looked annoyed at my adopted use of Blake's pet name for him. Then what I'd said seemed to register, and the blood drained from his face.

"I don't know what you're talking about," he mumbled, turning to face the front of the room as he tried to cross his arms over his chest, and then scowled at the cast impeding his progress.

I leaned over and whispered in his ear. "The one you keep under the couch cushion."

Every muscle in his body tensed as he stared at me out of the corner of his eye. "Tell me you didn't show Xander."

"Would I betray you like that?" I gasped. Then I leaned closer, pressing my breasts against his arm as I licked my lips and whispered, "But maybe skip ahead to page 187, and we can give it a try tomorrow night."

"Minx," he grumbled as Trace stood at the front of the meeting and called for everyone to take their seats so they could get started.

I caught the twitch of Booker's lips and laid my head against his shoulder to hide the smile on my face.

It should be illegal to be this happy.

I guess the meeting was going as well as expected. The people were scared and honestly pissed that no one had told them earlier the direction the town was heading. One thing

I hadn't anticipated was the town looking for someone to blame.

"But why was this kept a secret for so long?" a woman asked to the agreement of the crowd.

"So the Farrington's could come in and buy up everything cheap. You know they were going to put a golf course on the Barrett land? That's all they want, to run the rest of us out of town and bring in their rich friends," a man added.

The crowd was getting whipped up, and we weren't reaching any kind of conclusion. The plan that Trace and Delaney had been talking about made sense. Investing in the town and the businesses that were already here was smart. I really liked the idea of starting seasonal events to display local goods and bring in visitors. But as soon as they started talking about investing, a lot of people had shut down. Some didn't even want to open the town up to draw in more tourists. They liked Willowbrook how it was, and I couldn't blame them.

Finally, Booker surged to his feet. "Look, I get that you're angry. You should be. A lot has been done around here, and whether it was done with good intentions is hard to say. What I can tell you is that Trace is trying to help you. If you would just see what they have planned at their farm, you'd see what it could do for the town." He looked down at me, and I nodded.

"I'm going to be expanding the business at the ranch," he announced, and a murmur ran through the crowd. "You all know that I've been bringing in horses for rehab. Well, I want to keep doing that and open up the ranch for people to come and find some peace, too. Work with the horses if they want. Find a quiet place to help them heal. It might not bring a lot of people into town, but they'll be people who will shop at our businesses. Who will see Willowbrook for the peaceful and beautiful community that it is. We need families, we need revenue, and why not share what we have with new folks? Sometimes you find they're exactly what you need."

Booker looked at me with a soft smile and then awkwardly took his seat as his cheeks flushed.

"Stealing our men more likely," the old lady who apparently liked spanking mumbled.

"Oh, please, June. A woman like you would have broken the poor boy anyway," her friend added, and Booker looked like he was praying for a heart attack to take him away.

Dex stood up next. From the look on his face, I was sure he was about to say something that Booker would hate, and I braced myself for the explosion that would no doubt follow.

"Look, I know we don't all talk about stuff like this. We have our heads in the sand because we want everything to stay the same. But the garage has nine months tops before we're out of business. There just aren't enough of us to keep the small businesses afloat much longer. This *has* to happen. Small towns die every day, and if it's a choice between Willowbrook disappearing for good and suffering through a boom in the economy from tourism, well, I know what I'm hoping for."

Booker looked at his friend with concern as he took his seat and people talked among themselves. Trace let them talk. It was important people came to their own conclusions, and at least there was some discussion happening now rather than people just shutting down.

"He never said anything," Booker said quietly, still watching Dex, who'd pulled out his cell to mess around with.

I heard the ding of a notification as Booker pulled his own phone out and scowled at the screen before he tipped it in my direction.

> Dex: Stop staring at me. I've told you before that I'm not making out with you.

"Idiot," Booker grumbled, but he couldn't hide his smile from me.

"It's going to be all right. We have six months to make some changes."

Booker nodded. "And until then, I might need a few things done to the ranch equipment," he said with a smile.

I had a feeling this was why Dex had said nothing to his friends. He knew they'd immediately find a way to send work his way.

What was wrong with that?

"I might have a slight accident in my car tomorrow," I said, snuggling into Booker's side as we listened to the town get serious about how we were all going to save this place. "And maybe the cheese smell is coming back."

Booker shuddered dramatically.

The meeting was drawing to a close an hour later, and everyone looked exhausted. The whiteboard that Delaney had dragged into the community hall was filled with ideas, and she was busy taking notes of people to follow up with.

It had been an epic brainstorming session, but the results were impressive. Dex wasn't the only business that admitted to struggling, but with the introduction of some new annual events and an expansion of the B&B in the cards, it was all looking more positive.

"We can expand the town visitors' accommodation by ninety-five percent in the next six months," Delaney said, sounding impressed.

"All of this won't mean anything if people don't know what's happening here, though," someone said.

"We can tell the internet about it," someone suggested, and Delaney smothered the smile on her face.

The thing was, they weren't entirely wrong.

"Reece has experience with managing events through social media. She can build you enough attention to have those beds filled in no time." The sound of his voice sent a chill down my spine.

Everyone looked around in confusion, clearly not knowing who it was that was talking.

Booker must have sensed the change in me, as every muscle locked up in my body. A wave of emotion flooded me from the feet up, but this time it wasn't fear.

This time I was just so fucking angry.

As Camden strode to the front of the room, he gently pushed Delaney to the side and stood at the front, smiling that smile I'd thought was so charming way back then.

His tawny hair was slicked back with way too much gel, and the country club chic look of polo shirt and chinos just didn't fit in with the people around him. Looking at him now, he exuded superiority, but not in a genuine way. In a way that screamed how he thought he was better than the people around him, no matter how far from the truth that could actually be.

"Ladies and gentlemen, allow me to introduce myself. My name is Camden Carter. You'll know my father, of course. He's the governor of this beautiful state. I've worked with Reece before, and she is excellent at drawing attention to a project she's passionate about. Isn't that right, Reece?"

That was all it took for Booker to realize who was standing in front of us.

"My father and I have come through your quaint little

town occasionally, and it has always charmed us in ways that only a small town can. We'd be honored to be part of your investors and help you build this town into something you can be proud of."

Camden opened his arms wide like he was preaching to his followers at a pulpit. He smiled that Cheshire cat grin and paused, waiting for what I'm sure he thought would be words of praise and gratitude.

"What makes you think we need more outsiders coming in here throwing about their money and trying to take over the place?" someone asked.

Camden's eyes widened in alarm, but this was a man who had grown up on the campaign trail. He wasn't done trying to control the situation yet.

"No one wants to take over. I'm offering you a lifeline. A cash injection to boost your little economy. There's a beautiful patch of land outside of town that I'd be honored to build a summer home on."

A snort came from behind us, and Camden's eyes narrowed in annoyance.

"No one's handing any land over to you, sunny boy. I've got some suggestions where you inject that cash of yours."

A ripple of laughter ran through the room, and Camden's arms finally sagged. You see, the thing with Camden Carter was that he wasn't half the man his father was. He had no finesse, no clever words to sway a crowd because he wasn't all that clever.

Camden stood at his father's side and absorbed everything that wasn't his to take. And he was just stupid enough to think that he'd achieved it all himself.

"Don't be mean to the boy," Marie from the bakery said, standing up and scowling at the crowd before her lips quaked as she tried to hold back a smile. "He's come here all on his big boy self to try to save us poor country folk with his daddy's money. That's a long way to cycle on your own."

She snorted then, unable to hold it in.

And then the insults flew. I had to give it to the people of Willowbrook. Most of them were hilarious.

But even with the rest of town taking great joy in making fun of Camden, Booker hadn't relaxed for even a second. When he surged out of his seat and Camden's real sneer came to his face, I thought for certain that a fight was about to start.

"We don't need people like you around here. People who get off on hurting women. On scaring them because that's the only way you can keep them at your side. Did you have fun at the ranch, tearing up her clothes and trying to hurt her again?"

The room fell deadly silent, and the laughter stopped as abruptly as if someone had flicked a switch.

"What's wrong, Camden? Not got anything to say for yourself?" Booker taunted. "Not so easy when it's someone your own size standing up to you." Then he looked down at himself and sneered at Camden. "Well, maybe not exactly the same size."

"I'll fight him," Cade piped up, already getting ready to climb on a chair as Delaney pulled him down and then hugged him proudly.

"No need, I've got this," Marie said, rolling up her sleeves as she strode to the front.

I actually thought she was going to punch him then, and clearly so did Camden, as he stumbled backward and scurried to the side of the room in search of the door.

"This is slander," he called out over his shoulder. "I don't know what that bitch has been telling you..."

"Nothing but the truth, you piece of shit," I suddenly exploded.

Camden froze and then slowly turned to face me. "What the fuck did you say to me?" he said lowly.

A shiver flashed through my body as the memory of him raising his fist for that first punch blazed into my mind. This was the exact face he made before he completely shut down.

"I called you...A. Piece. Of. Shit!" I enunciated as I strode closer. "I'm not afraid of you. What are you going to do, Camden? Are you going to hit me again in front of all these people? Are you going to run to Daddy and tell him all these mean people hurt your feelings? I don't care if no one's going to arrest you. I don't even care if you walk out of here and live the same nasty pathetic life you had before. But you come back here again, you even try anything to hurt these people, and I'm going to send all the pictures, all the emails, all the documents I took from your computer straight to dear Daddy and straight to the press."

Camden's face flushed white and then quickly went red with rage. "I don't know what you think you have..."

"I have everything," I told him calmly. "Now leave."

He stared at me for a second, and the town waited calmly to see what he'd do. I knew he could hurt me. Hell, I knew how much he wanted to. But he wouldn't risk the scandal, and just like I'd thought he would, he turned and left instead.

A breath of relief rushed out of me, and the crash of adrenaline that followed made me feel like I was going to vomit.

I felt Booker's presence at my back as he pulled me back against his chest.

"I'm proud of you, baby," he murmured. "But next time, let me hit him at least once before you chase him off."

I chuckled sadly then, and he held me tighter.

"You didn't tell me about the files."

"That's because I don't have anything," I told him honestly. "But he doesn't need to know that."

Booker kissed the top of my head, and I trembled in his arms. This wouldn't be the last we'd see of Camden. It couldn't end this easily.

"Come on, baby. Let's go home."

Home. That sounded nice.

CHAPTER TWENTY-NINE

BOOKER

Reece had been quiet since the town meeting and the confrontation with her ex. I knew it wasn't easy for her to see him again, and it was harder still for her to stand up to him in front of the whole town.

Honestly, I didn't think that guy could get away with showing his face anywhere around Willowbrook again. I wouldn't be the only one who wanted to show him what I thought of a man who preyed on a woman like that. He definitely wouldn't be getting his claws into the town by trying to buy his way in, that was for sure.

But there was something that was worrying me. Reece had bluffed with something she didn't have, and if he called that bluff, I didn't know what he'd do if we couldn't follow through. The only person I could think of turning to for help was the last person I wanted to go to.

I'd do it for her, though. There was nothing I wouldn't do for her.

"How is she?" Xander asked as he stood at my side in front of the window I'd been watching her through for the last ten minutes.

"I have absolutely no idea," I admitted.

We'd brought the mare out onto the sandy training ring this morning so she could have some time out in the sun. The skinny little thing was doing well. She was into a normal feeding routine and finally putting on weight like she was supposed to. Partially because of the sheer amount of treats that Reece kept sneaking to her, but it wouldn't do her any harm. The mare deserved to be spoiled after everything she'd been through.

"I need to go and see Dad," I told Xander.

He nodded quietly, watching Reece talk to the horse outside with Val sitting at her feet like a sentry. "If there's anything to dig up, he'll have someone who can do it," he told me.

I'd confided in the guys last night about everything I knew about the Camden situation and everything we didn't have to protect Reece if he ever came back.

"Stay with her. If she asks, I'm going into town," I told him, turning to leave, but Xander's hand came to my shoulder to stop me.

"First, you can't actually think I'm about to let you drive with that thing on your arm. Second, it's already done. Spend some time with your lady, Booker. Trust us to have your back."

I blinked in surprise. I knew Xander hadn't gone to our father because he hadn't left the ranch since we got back last night.

"Tell me Trace didn't—"

"There're such things as telephones, Booker," he said, sighing like I was the most exhausting person he knew. "I made the call. He's looking into it already."

I didn't know what to say. I knew Xander hated them both just as much as I did. The problem was they hadn't written him off yet, and that was why I was doing everything I could to keep him away from our parents. I didn't want them to pull him back into all the bullshit that constantly seemed to circle the pair of them.

"What did he ask for in return?" I asked suspiciously.

Whatever it was, I'd get him out of it. There was no price I wouldn't pay to keep Xander as free of the Farrington influence as I could. I wouldn't let him get dragged back into what had broken him in the first place just to help me.

"Nothing." I wouldn't have believed him if he didn't sound so surprised.

"You still shouldn't have done it."

"Booker, when are you going to accept that we're on your side? You don't always need to be the one who looks after everyone else. I'm here for you. We all are."

I didn't know what to say. My first reaction was to deny that I needed any help, but the closer we were all becoming, the more I could see just how untrue that really was.

The past few years had been tough. Trace had been trapped in an abusive marriage, and all I could do was watch from the sidelines and patch him up when he was finally ready to admit he needed help.

It had frustrated me more than I cared to admit, watching him try to solve all his own problems until he'd let me finally do something.

And now I was doing exactly the same thing to him and Xander.

We'd been brought up to be afraid of showing any kind of weakness. To close ourselves in and pretend there was nothing wrong in our lives at all costs. It was only now that we were grown men we were finally seeing how wrong it was to live that way.

It wasn't easy to set aside thirty-five years of trying to do it all alone.

"Go and be with your lady," Xander said softly when he no doubt realized I wasn't ready to respond.

He gave my shoulder a soft push, and I went willingly. It was hell trying to stay this far away from her. Especially when we didn't know where Camden had run off to.

My feet had barely made it to the porch steps when she turned and gave me that smile that was impossible to resist. She was like a magnet drawing me in, and it wasn't until I was pulling Reece into my arms that it felt like all was right with the world again.

"She's doing so much better," Reece murmured as she leaned against my chest. "What time is Cole getting here?"

"Should be here any minute," I told her, hoping that wasn't true.

I wasn't ready to burst this bubble yet, and as much as I hated sitting around and doing nothing like everyone wanted me to, I didn't want the distraction of work right now, either.

The headaches I hadn't admitted to were finally easing, and my head didn't feel quite as much like it was being crushed in a vise. I was taking it as a good sign. Strangely enough, my arm was bothering me the least. It helped that Reece had decided to be the one to spread arnica gel on my bruises. It made me almost grateful for them.

"I have a good feeling about today," she told me, her fingers absentmindedly tracing circles on my chest. "I think Cole is going to give us good news."

I knew the news she wanted, and where I'd been reluctant to tell her there was a chance of saving the foal before, I was feeling optimistic about it all, too.

"I think we should call her Spirit," Reece said softly, her

eyes watching the little mare who was starting the explore the training ring before coming back to the fence and nibbling at Reece's pocket.

She laughed and pulled out a chunk of apple and gave it to her.

"I like it," I told her. "It suits her."

I ignored the sound of Cole's truck for as long as I could, stealing every precious second I could with Reece.

I decided I liked the vet even more when he silently climbed into the training ring and didn't interrupt the moment we were having. But unfortunately, reality couldn't be ignored forever, and Reece stepped forward eagerly as Cole felt at Spirit's stomach, listening carefully with his stethoscope before continuing with a quick examination.

"Well," he said, stepping back. "Looks like you'll have a new addition to the ranch in about seven months."

He turned to me with a grin on his face, and Reece jumped in the air with a whoop of joy. Even Val pranced about like an idiot, joining in on the fun. Spirit watched on silently and then went searching in Cole's pockets for her next treat. I wasn't even surprised when he pulled out a chunk of carrot for her.

"Seven months?" I hated being the downer of the group, but someone had to warn Reece the fight wasn't over yet. "That's going to be a small foal."

"Yep. Looks like you're going to have some early morning bottle feeding in your future, Booker." He seemed far too eager for that prospect. "I'm going to have a check on Bullet, and then I'll come back and draw some blood. I want to keep a close eye on her hormone levels for the next couple of months. She's gaining weight nicely though," Cole said, retrieving another treat from his pocket and slipping it to Spirit.

"That's because she never stops eating," I told him, not owning up to the bag of apple chunks in my pocket.

"She's earned it," Reece said softly.

A breeze flowed across the ranch from the fields, pulling her long blond hair away from her face as it floated around her. Reece quickly put her hand on top of her hat to stop it from blowing away and smiled as she tipped her face toward the sun.

The bruising that she'd arrived with was gone now, and so was that forced happiness she thought she was fooling me with.

In its place there was a contentment I felt deep inside as well. It came from this place, and it was what I wanted to share with the people who needed it the most.

Cole climbed through the railings on the fence and went to head toward the barn. As he passed me, he clapped me on the shoulder.

"You're a lucky man, Booker," he mumbled, a note of sadness in his voice.

I probably wouldn't have noticed it before, and I turned to watch him make his way to the big barn doors.

Val looked up at me from Reece's side. "Go on then," I told her, and she trotted after him.

I was so conflicted over how I'd been before Reece had come into my life. There was a part of me that was almost ashamed of how blind I'd been to the people around me. But I was doing what I needed to get through the day. It was almost like I'd merely been surviving, waiting until Reece could come along and show me what it was like to actually live.

"You look sad," Reece said as she slipped an arm around my waist.

I looked down at the woman who had filled in all the

cracks in my heart and smiled. They came so much easier now that I couldn't imagine getting through a day trying to hide behind the scowls and muttered curses like I used to.

"I'm not," I reassured her. "I think I might actually be happy."

She squeezed me tight. "Me too."

"Come on. Let's check in on Bullet."

We meandered over to the barn, Reece tucked under my arm, enjoying the morning in a way that I'd never even noticed before. The sun warmed my skin, and the gentle breeze brought the smell of grass over the yard.

It would be time to cut the empty pastures soon. Maybe take a trip down to one of the livestock auctions and bring in some new horses for the ranch. We needed some working horses, especially with Bullet out of commission.

Cole was already on the way out by the time we reached the door. Bullet was more of a wait-and-see case for the next few days, anyway. There wasn't much we could do for him apart from managing any pain and monitoring the leg that he'd injured.

"He's a fighter, that one," Cole said, shaking his head. "I think he's got his eye on your little mare." He nodded toward Spirit, and I couldn't help but chuckle.

"Aww, a budding horsey romance," Reece gushed. "How's he doing?"

"Surprisingly well. Did he go down at all last night?"

"Nah, I kept an eye on him with the cameras, and he was up and moving about quite a bit, which makes sense now," I said, looking over at Spirit, who was prancing in the sand and looking happy to be outside.

"Cameras?" Reece looked confused as she spoke, and I realized how it might seem that I'd never told her about it before.

"There's a camera in the foaling stable which is the one Bullet's in," I explained. "Helps to keep an eye on the mares when we know they're imminently about to drop."

"That makes sense," she nodded. "Are you still wanting to have some put in around the ranch now?"

"This is because of the trouble you've had?" Cole asked.

He nodded at my arm. The story would be all over town by now, and after the town meeting last night, everyone knew exactly who the problem was. It was probably a good thing. If there was one thing Willowbrook was good at, it was being in everybody's business, and there was no way Camden could move through town with no one noticing him now.

"Mm-hmm. Plus, with the new business plans, it will help with the liability insurance."

Cole smirked, giving a little half-shrug as he did. "I'm so glad you brought that up," he said, trying to sound casual. "All these people and horses coming on board, sounds like you might need a resident vet."

I laughed. I had actually been meaning to talk to Cole about this but had never gotten around to it.

"Yeah, know anyone good?"

He tried to look offended, but we'd known each other for too long for him to even slightly get away with it. "I know a guy. Oof, he's expensive though."

"I'm sure we can work something out."

We walked Cole over to his truck, and he loaded his supplies into the back. "Email me some details, and we can see what we can work out," he offered. "The practice is quiet at the moment. I can put the time in now. It's actually perfect timing because I want to bring in a trainee next year so I can maybe get a night off once in a while."

Cole was the only vet in the area now. Most of them

had moved on over the last few years. Thankfully, he was also one of the best I'd ever worked with, so it worked out well for me.

I hadn't realized how much the town had slowly been losing over the years. The domino effect of the economy slowing down was leaching into every business around, and we needed a lot of them to sustain just the local population. We should have done this years ago. The more I thought about it, the more I wondered if the delay in my father's actions was down to him trying to turn a bigger profit.

I wanted to think better of my father than that, but he'd never really given me a reason to.

Hopefully, we weren't past the point of no return, but I had a feeling that things wouldn't pick up quickly enough for some businesses around here to survive.

"If things get too slow, come and talk to me," I told Cole. "I don't want to lose you if there's anything I can do to help."

"Awww, you getting attached to me, Booker?" Cole asked.

Reece sniggered, and I just shrugged. "What can I say? It's hard to find a good vet nowadays."

"Damn right, it is." Cole shook my hand and climbed into his truck before leaning out the window. "Thanks, Booker. It means a lot."

"No worries. You got much else on for today?" I asked.

I knew I was fishing for information, but I wanted to know if he was close to packing up the practice.

"Just heading over to the Barrett place." Cole's mouth snapped shut and then he half shrugged like it was no big deal as he fired up the truck. "See you around, Booker. Reece."

Reece waved goodbye to Cole, and I watched in confusion as he drove up the driveway.

"Trace and Delaney don't have any animals on the farm," I said.

Reece looked up at me and laughed. "Nope."

She grinned like she knew something I didn't as we turned back to the house.

"Come on. Let's grab some lunch," Reece said, changing the subject.

I made it three steps before I couldn't take it anymore.

"I don't get it. Tell me what you know," I demanded.

Reece laughed again, and I could see she was thinking about teasing me and withholding information.

It was time for the big guns.

"If you tell me, baby, I'll do that thing on page 187 you want to do."

"Have you even read page 187 yet?" Reece asked, slipping out of my grip and skipping ahead of me. "You might not like it."

Damn, I was pretty sure there wasn't anything I wouldn't like to do to her. It must have shown on my face because her breath hitched, and she gnawed on her lip as she got that look in her eye that meant I was about to be a very lucky man.

"Fine," she sighed. "Cole's interest doesn't lie solely in animals, you know? And there's a certain single someone who hasn't moved out yet with beautiful pink hair."

My face wrinkled in confusion because, of course, I knew who she was talking about. Poor Cole. He had no idea what he was getting himself into.

"Cole and Blake?"

"Blake and whoever she wants, I'm guessing. Have you not noticed the distinct lack of single ladies a certain age around here? Money isn't the only thing Willowbrook needs to bring into town."

She wasn't wrong there. Now I really felt sorry for Cole. It was desperate times if he was willing to put up with someone like Blake.

I shuddered at the thought.

She'd better not scare my vet out of town.

CHAPTER THIRTY

REECE

The ranch had been quiet for days, but I couldn't shake the feeling that something was off.

I'd been staying in Booker's house while Xander took the cottage. It was only supposed to be temporary, and then I noticed Booker had moved what was left of my things into his closet. Once I went through the wreckage, a few things had been salvageable, but I was desperately in need of a shopping trip soon. Otherwise, my future held a lot of laundry nights.

We'd fallen into a routine of waking up in the morning and making love until we couldn't ignore the world any longer. I spent my mornings with Bullet and Spirit, making sure they had everything they needed and their feed was made up for the day. Booker was in the process of hiring a new ranch hand and doing as much as he could to help Hank and Cliff while he had his broken arm.

Xander was less than impressed with him, but he was busy enough with some secret project that Booker kept slipping away without him noticing.

The afternoons were full of business planning and

social media content creation, and I was just about done with designing a temporary website for the ranch. Trying to persuade Booker to go full cowboy for TikTok was proving harder than I thought it would be, but the account was slowly growing without him.

I'd have to pull out all my powers of persuasion to get him to cooperate, though. And I was thoroughly up for the challenge.

"You need a name," I said, looking up from the computer and finding Booker staring at me in confusion.

"I have a name."

"No, a name for the ranch. You all just use your family name around here, and I get it. It makes sense when it was just a ranch. But you need a business name. Something that suits what you want to achieve here. And I need it by tomorrow so I can buy the domain name and launch the website," I added quickly before bolting from my desk and heading for the kitchen.

This was my soon-to-be patented approach to dealing with Booker. Information drop and then run. By the time he caught up with me, he was too distracted by the chase to go into full grumpy denial mode.

Not that I didn't love helping him work out the grumpy denial mood. It was a hard job, but I was here with it. When it came to Booker, I'd take one for the team any day of the week. Hell, any hour of any day. The man was a magician in bed, and even having a broken arm hadn't slowed him down.

"I don't want to change the name," he shouted from the office we'd put together. "I like calling it the ranch."

"The Ranch." I shrugged. "Maybe that could work. Sounds a bit dystopian prison thriller, though."

Booker wheeled his chair through the office door and glared at me. "It does not."

"Welcome to The Ranch," I said in the creepiest voice I could muster, hunching my shoulders as I tapped my fingertips together.

"Well, anything sounds creepy when you say it like that." He sulked, wheeling himself back into the office.

The seed was planted.

I was getting great at this.

"I'm going to change Spirit's hay net, and then I'm making lunch," I called out as I slipped on my boots and headed out the door.

It was so beautiful out here. Even the restless anxiety inside me couldn't fight against the peaceful atmosphere of the ranch. It would be beautiful out here when the full height of summer hit us. Hopefully, Booker's arm would heal well enough that we could take a picnic up the trail again.

My cheeks warmed with thoughts of our last picnic as I walked into the barn, heading into the shadowy back storage area where Booker had the feed stored and a little kitchenette set up. I'd already filled the hay nets this morning and had a line of buckets laid out ready with Spirit's feed. She was off the salt water and nearly solely on normal feed now that her weight was going up. I kept sneaking her an extra alfalfa hay net through the day anyway because she loved them so much.

I was probably going to make her fat, but I figured she deserved to be pampered, and I was pretty sure Booker knew exactly what I was doing and would have stopped me by now if I was doing anything wrong.

I heard a whiny coming from Spirit's stable and Bullet banging around in his. Maybe I could ask Booker if we could put them next to each other. That's what they seemed to want anyway, and Cole had already confirmed days ago that Spirit wasn't carrying any diseases or anything that she could pass to him.

It was cute that the two of them were getting so close to each.

A loud bang came from Bullet's stable as I lifted the hay net over the door for Spirit, and I turned to look at it with a frown.

He wasn't normally this aggressive.

"Do you want a hay net too, boy?" I asked, hoping just talking to him would be enough to calm him down.

Bullet didn't normally have another feed until this evening because he was already healthy and strong. But maybe an extra something wouldn't hurt. Lord, we'd have a whole ranch of fat horses if it was down to me.

I quickly secured the hay net and then decided to see if I could talk some sense into Bullet as another loud crash came from the stable. He was still healing, and having him injure himself more wasn't what anyone wanted.

"What's all the noise about, hey?" I purred as I walked over to his stable noise.

"Oh, it's just us boys getting acquainted," Camden's voice responded.

I should have run to Booker. I should have pulled out the damn cell phone in my pocket that he'd made me carry around. Instead, I rolled back my shoulders, and I let the anger that had been building inside rule my emotions.

I never claimed to be smart.

"Crawled back out of the gutter, I see. Nothing better to do than irritate the horses?"

Camden threw back his head and laughed as Bullet pranced back at the sound. Standing inside that stable wasn't the smartest thing Camden had ever done, but judging from the long piece of wood in his hand, I guessed he thought threatening the horses was the best way to get whatever it was he wanted.

"You always were amusing, Reece. Not that smart, though. You should have stayed off social media. It didn't take any effort to get a PI to track you down once you logged on," he said, tapping the wood against the palm of his hand. "Now, here's the deal, sweetheart. You're going to give me the files you stole from me, or I'm going to break this horse's leg."

"That hardly seems like a deal worth taking," I said calmly, trying not to let the panic show in my voice.

"It's his leg or yours." Camden turned to me with that smarmy smile on his face. He was enjoying himself. This was the sort of thing he got off on, and I couldn't believe I'd been so stupid not to see it before. "You have to be punished for the things you do, Reece. Don't you remember the first lesson I gave you?"

"I remember you beating me because you didn't get your way. Is that the lesson you're talking about?" I asked sweetly.

"You never used to have such a big mouth. Clearly, your first lesson didn't stick. You could always come home, you know. No one knows about this stupid fanciful vacation you've taken. All could be forgiven. You don't need to stay in this dump. You could stand by my side, and we could do something great..." His voice started that strange croon he did when he thought he was being persuasive, but really, it just turned my stomach at the sound.

But at least his attention was on me. I could see in his eyes how much he wanted me. The fervor had him licking his lips, and then he sighed. It made me feel like I needed a shower to wash away the feeling of his gaze drifting across my body.

"I'm going to stop you right there," I told him, holding up my hand. "I'd rather choke to death on my own vomit than allow you anywhere near me. The chances of me stepping foot into your home again are less than Bullet here bearing your first child. Now, this is what's actually going to happen. You're going to put down your stick and pretend for one moment that you can be an actual functioning adult. Then you're going to walk out of here, get in your car, and drive away. There's nothing for you here, Camden."

My heart was pounding so hard in my chest that I was sure it was about to leap out of my mouth. All I needed was for him to come out of the stable and away from Bullet. I didn't much care what was about to happen to me.

I'd healed from Camden once, and I'd do it again if I had to. But I wasn't about to let him hurt an innocent animal just because he thought it would make him a big, scary man.

Camden laughed, his arms resting over the top of the stable door as he rested the piece of wood over his shoulder.

"I've got a much better idea, baby."

"No one calls her baby but me," Booker growled from behind me, his arm coming over my shoulder as he grabbed Camden by the collar and then pulled him straight off his feet and over the top of the stable door.

I scurried to the side, my eyes wide as I watched Booker dump Camden onto the ground at his feet.

And there he stood, like my avenging angel, about to put all the wrongs in the world right for me again.

CHAPTER THIRTY-ONE

BOOKER

As soon as Reece had left, of course, I'd turned on the camera to watch her sweetly talking to Bullet as she fed the horses the snacks she thought she was hiding.

It was the favorite part of my day, watching her clucking around like a mother hen as she looked after her charges. I couldn't wait until she was doing it with our own kids. Reece was going to be an incredible mother, and for once in my life, I could see a future with a couple of rugrats tearing around the ranch while we chased after them.

I was already smiling as I turned to the camera, but the sight I found there had me freezing in my seat. My good hand gripped the arm of my chair so tightly that the plastic creaked beneath my fingers. Then I surged out of my seat, striding for the door.

"Val!" I shouted, and she was immediately on alert at my side. "With me."

This guy had to have been dropped on the head as a kid. He couldn't be so stupid that he thought coming here and threatening my girl was a good idea.

By the time I made it to the barn doors, I could hear him telling her to go home with him. I didn't doubt her for a second. I knew Reece's heart, and this guy wasn't even a memory in it. He was just a lesson from the past that would one day be forgotten.

"I've got a much better idea, baby," the idiot actually dared to say.

Every semblance of restraint I had inside me snapped at the sound of his words.

"No one calls her baby but me," I growled, lurching forward for him.

There was no way he was ever touching her again. He came here thinking he could threaten her, that he could hurt my girl, and I'd let him just walk away.

The yip of surprise he gave as I hauled his body over the top of the stable had me growling in satisfaction. His stupid little stick clattered to the ground as I threw him in the dirt at my feet.

"You've no idea how much I've been looking forward to this," I told him, a sneer coming to my lips.

Camden started crawling backward, scurrying toward the door like he thought he had a chance to escape.

"You can't do this," he hurried out. "Don't you know who my father is?"

"I seem to remember you mentioning...No, wait. I don't actually care." I reached down and picked him up by the collar again as Camden scrambled to his feet. "How many times did you hit her?"

All the blood drained from his face as dear old Camden realized what was about to go down.

"I don't know what you're talking about," he went with. "I never—"

"Don't waste your final breath on a lie, Cammy boy.

You're not that smart, are you? You keep your files on your laptop. You confess in places you don't even check for cameras. I have every word recorded."

I nodded over to the stable as Camden shook his head, his eyes darting about the barn as he desperately searched for a way out. For something that could save him.

I didn't know who this guy thought I was. Obviously, he was walking out of here. I wasn't going to sully the beautiful future I had ahead of me with the woman he hadn't been smart enough to appreciate. That didn't mean my fist wasn't meeting his face before I sent him on his way though.

"Here's what's happening now, Camden," I said slowly to make sure that he was actually listening. I stalked forward, slowly herding him out of the barn and away from Reece. "You're going to get back in your piece of shit car, and you're going to head back to whatever cesspit you crawled out of. I have a man in the city who's going to keep an eye on you. He's already digging into your past and pulling up all your dirty little secrets for me. I'm going to put those with what I already have, and I'm going to send them to your father. If you're quick enough, you might get home and cover up some of the worst of it, but I doubt you're smart enough to pull it off."

Camden started shaking his head. His hand went into his pocket, and he pulled out his car keys with shaky hands. Whatever this guy was into, it wasn't good. But it worked in our favor that he was scared of Daddy more.

"Daddy's going to put you on a leash, Camden. He can't afford to have an embarrassment like you running around in public. And do you know what you're going to do? You're going to thank me for letting him do that. For not finding a pretty little spot on the ranch where no one would find you and burying you there.

If I never see your face again, the matter ends there. But if you dare to even breathe in this woman's direction again, you won't like what I do next. Do you hear me?"

For a moment, it was almost like Camden found his balls as he gritted his teeth and actually hissed at me.

The dude was crazier than I'd first thought.

"You won't get away with this," he finally said, pulling his quivering shoulders back as he pretended to be a man. "I will *ruin* you. I don't need to be in this backwater town to do it. Are you really ready to throw everything away for *her*?"

Camden jutted his chin in Reece's direction, looking at her like she was trash, and I swear to god my heart leaped for joy when he did.

Because I'd just been waiting for an excuse.

My fist plowed into Camden's nose, which gave a satisfying crunch, and he sank to the floor, clutching his face and crying.

"I seem to remember telling you that you weren't allowed to breathe in her direction, Camden. This isn't a good sign for how your future's about to go if you can't even get that bit right." I tsked like I was talking to a child, and Val took that as her sign to let him know what she thought of the whole situation as well.

Hunching down, teeth bared, Val crept closer, snapping her jaws at the man who was crying on the ground. It totally went against her nature. She was usually so empathetic when she saw someone in pain. But apparently even Val could tell that this guy was no good, and she was ready to protect her own.

I squatted down, running a hand over Val's head as I met Camden's watery gaze.

"This is the part where you run away, Cammy boy," I mocked.

Thankfully, he found his common sense at that moment as Camden scrambled back to his feet with a sob and sprinted for the barn doors. Val darted forward, snapping at his heels and then barking as she came to a stop in the door, watching him running for the driveway.

"Good girl," I told her, fussing her ears when I reached her side. "We don't know what you'd catch if you put something like that in your mouth."

I heard Reece snort out a laugh, and I turned back to face her to make sure she was all right. Finding her bent over and clutching her sides as she laughed wasn't exactly what I'd been expecting.

"Oh my god, I think he actually peed himself," she said, pointing at a wet patch on the barn floor that definitely hadn't been there before.

I wrinkled my nose in disgust, knowing I'd have to clean that up because there was no way I was adding insult to injury and letting Reece do it.

She came to my side then, tipping up onto her toes as she kissed me on the cheek. "Thank you," she murmured, her hands clasping my shoulders as she laid her head against my chest. "Do you think he's actually gone?"

"Yeah, for now at least."

Even Camden wasn't stupid enough to not eventually figure out that we hadn't sent anything to his father and that we didn't actually have anything to send. Hopefully, he'd be so busy trying to cover up his tracks that it would at least buy us enough time for my father's guy to find something.

"I used to hope that he'd leave me alone when he found someone else to torment, but I don't think I'm as okay with that as I thought I was," Reece admitted. "I can't stand the thought of him doing what he did to me to some other woman who thought she could trust him."

"I know what you mean," I told her as we both walked out of the barn to head back into the house.

My adrenaline was dropping, and the throbbing in my arm was working in time with the pounding that had started up in my head again.

"Do you really have a guy in the city?" Reece asked, her face wrinkling in an adorable frown as we walked up the porch steps.

"My father does. Xander set it up. He's confident we should have something by the end of the week."

I didn't miss the relief on her face. Part of me was actually intrigued about what this guy had been up to that he was so worried about. He didn't seem like he had enough smarts to be into anything that illegal.

But I'd grown up in the same world he had, and I had a feeling that the threat of being cut off would be enough to make Camden feel like the world was about to end.

We just needed to find something that was big enough to cause a scandal.

Reece didn't look so confident, but surely the fact that Camden had beaten up his girlfriend would be scandal enough. I'd just prefer that we didn't have to involve Reece and that my father's guy could find something worse.

I wasn't so sure what it said about me that I was hoping this guy was out there ruining someone else's life as well.

I hated seeing her like this. Doubting herself and worrying about a guy who should have had the sense to leave her alone. I was here now, and there was no way I'd let him hurt her ever again.

"I need a favor from you," I told her as I steered us through the house toward the stairs.

Reece looked up at me with her beautiful blue eyes, and I fought the need to push her against the wall and kiss her senseless right there.

"You see, Xander tells me that if I'm going to recover, then I should be in bed. I can't remember what the second part of those instructions was. Head injury, remember." I pointed at my stitches and then shrugged in the universal what can you do motion. "So, for the interests of my health, I think you should accompany me upstairs and help me figure out how to stay in bed *all day long*."

She chuckled, but at least it had the smile back on her face.

"Well, if it's in the interests of your health, I don't see how I can refuse," she said, backing up to the stairs with a telling smile on her face. "Now, what could we do that could keep you distracted?" She tapped a finger against her lips as she pretended to think and then, before I could say anything, she turned and darted up the stairs with a giggle.

I was powerless but to chase her.

Just like I hoped to for the rest of my life.

Because if there was one thing I was willing to dedicate my life to, it was giving this woman every little thing she could ever desire, inside and outside of the bedroom.

CHAPTER THIRTY-TWO

REECE

Booker and I spent that afternoon lying in bed and trading stories about our childhoods in between soft kisses and gentle caresses.

It was possibly the best time I'd ever had in my life and the perfect way to push the memories of Camden aside.

All of Booker's stories were about the trouble he got into with his brothers, and we both pretended to ignore the sad look he got in his eyes whenever those stories involved Gage.

He hadn't responded to the message I'd sent him on Facebook, and I was thinking he maybe wouldn't. But we at least had a link to him now, and as soon as he was active on his accounts, it would be up to Booker to decide if we wanted to go to his brother and have a conversation that was long overdue.

For now, we had the ranch expansion to keep us busy and another Farrington brother who Booker was building a relationship with again.

Xander had been disappearing, working on something he said he wasn't ready to discuss yet. But when he was on the ranch, he was doing his best to fill in where Booker couldn't with his broken arm. And day by day, the city doctor image was slowly slipping away, and the boy who'd grown up in a small town was coming back.

"What have we got on for the rest of today?" Xander asked, striding into the dining room, which had turned into a full home office now.

I pulled up the calendar on the computer and checked our appointments. "The building inspector is coming to check the first two cottages that have been completed, hopefully, to sign them off. We have Cole stopping by later in the afternoon to check on Spirit and the foal, and the contractor wants to talk to you and Booker about the next projects that are on the board."

Booker had pushed up the timeline for the ranch. I didn't think it was a good idea at first, but everything was running so smoothly that we might actually be ready to open in the next three months.

"I've got a delivery coming at two as well that we all need to be here for," Booker said, wiping his hands on a towel as he came in from the kitchen.

He tossed it over his shoulder and then grabbed some papers from the desk to look through.

"I don't have that on the calendar," I said in confusion, shuffling through the stack of things that I still had to do.

Had I forgotten something? Damn it, it was all going so smoothly in a slightly chaotic fashion, and it would only take for one piece to crumble, and this shaky stack of organization I had was all coming tumbling down.

"It's something I arranged," Booker said evasively, turning to look out the window like he did when he was trying to hide something.

Xander looked between the two of us like he was getting

ready to referee an argument, and then his shoulders visibly slumped when I just went, "Okay."

"Ugh, come on, guys. It's gotten so boring around here. Can't we have a little drama? Something to give the rest of us to gossip about in town?" he asked, looking between us.

Booker glared at him like he'd lost his mind.

"No," he said, and then he stalked out of the room.

"Awww, I'd almost missed that," I said dreamily. "Say it again!" I shouted out of the office.

Booker grumbled. "No." Then he sighed when he realized what he'd done, and I sniggered.

Just like the good old days.

"Ugh, that's not interesting. That's you two being all lovey and crap." Xander sighed and slumped down into the chair on the other side of the desk. "I'm bored," he said dramatically.

"Oh, I know what. You could meet the building inspector. That sounds exciting, right?"

Xander rolled his head to the side to look at me. His nostrils flared as he rolled his eyes at me. "Sure, Reece. That's super exciting."

"Aren't you supposed to be some kind of mature city slicker doctor? What's gotten into you today?"

"Nothing," he huffed, scuffing his boots across the floor as he refused to meet my eyes.

"He's lovesick," Booker shouted from the kitchen.

Xander glared at the door, but then, when he didn't deny it, a grin broke out across my face.

"Xanderrrrrr, do you have a secret?" I asked, leaning forward and putting my elbows on the desk so I could prop my chin in my hands. "Is it a juicy one? Who is she? Ooooh! It's Blake, isn't it?"

"What! No! Have you met her? She's the most

annoying woman I've ever come across. Did you know that she actually asked me if she could paint me naked this week? In the middle of the bakery! Like it was a normal conversation. I saw Marie looking at my ass then like some kind of sex-starved predator. I've never been so objectified in my life."

Booker barked out a laugh from the kitchen, and Xander picked up the stapler from the desk, leaned to the side, and threw it out the door at him.

"Oh my god, this is amazing." I shook my head and leaned back in my chair. "You're going to do it, right? I mean, you're bored. What else do you have to do? Oh, she could turn it into a life drawing class."

I pulled my cell out of my pocket, and Xander physically dived across the desk to wrestle it from me.

"Don't you dare!"

He scurried across the office, clutching my phone to his chest with his eyes wide. "I'm going to meet the building inspector, and I'm taking this with me. You've lost your communication privileges, missy."

Then he strode out of the house, taking my cell with him.

I didn't care. It wasn't like I actually used it.

"At least Blake has found someone else to torment," Booker said from where he was leaning in the doorway watching me. "Wow, this is what it feels like when you have everything you need in life. It's pretty awesome," he said, rubbing his chest with his good hand.

It was weeks until he'd be getting the cast off his other arm, and I still hated it every time I saw it. I doubted I'd ever get used to the thing. It was a reminder of the single most frightening thing that had ever happened to me. And that was saying something.

But right now, the house was empty, and we had nothing urgent we needed to do for the next couple of hours.

I looked at Booker, a wicked thought entering my mind.

"I know that look," he murmured, standing straighter and taking a step closer, just as his cell rang. "Damn it. I need to take this," he said as he pulled it out of his pocket and glanced at the screen.

I stood from my seat and walked over to kiss his lips gently. "I'll be waiting for you," I whispered, slipping out the room to the sound of his groan as I left him to take his call.

This was perfect. It gave me time to have a quick shower and put on something I'd had delivered yesterday that I knew would blow Booker's mind.

I rushed through the shower, not knowing how long Booker's call was going to take and wanting to quickly give my legs another shave before it finished. When I came out of the bathroom and found him sitting on the end of the bed, I sighed in defeat.

"Damn it. I thought I had more time," I said, clutching the towel at my chest and then shrugging because this was as good as anything else.

But then I saw Booker's face and his look of annoyance.

"What happened?" I asked, sitting beside him on the bed.

"One of the backers just dropped out," he said, looking at me grimly.

That wasn't good, especially with the accelerated rate we were going for opening.

"Okay, did they say why?" I asked.

"He said that it didn't seem advisable in the current

political climate to be investing money in a project that could face issues in the future?"

I frowned, not understanding at first what he was talking about. What issues? There was nothing we hadn't covered, and when Booker had talked me through his business plan, it had seemed absolutely solid.

"No," I said when the wording he'd used ran through my mind. "You don't think..."

"Camden," Booker said grimly. "Or maybe his father."

"He can't do that!" I said, surging to my feet and starting to pace beside the bed as I gripped the towel to my chest. "Oh my god, Booker. I'm so sorry. This is all my fault. The ranch—"

"Is fine," he said gently, reaching out and taking my hand to draw me down into his lap. "The ranch will endure, no matter what. This is why I had investors, and we still have three more."

"But if he got to one of them, he could get to the others."

I'd thought Camden's threat was an empty one when he'd shouted it as he fled the barn. I didn't think he'd actually follow through. Mainly because it seemed too much like hard work. But if his father was behind this, then he was spinning some kind of story to make it look like he was the victim. We'd assumed he'd try to cover his back, but he was doing damage control in a whole other way.

There had to be a way to stop this. I couldn't bring down the business that Booker had put so much into. What he'd worked so hard to become a reality here at the ranch.

"Hey," Booker said gently, his fingers coming to my chin as he tipped my head up so he could see my eyes. "Don't worry about this. What we're doing here will happen no matter what the investors decide. It might just take longer. The important thing is that we're here doing it together. Got it. Nothing in my life is more important than you, Reece. And together I know we'll build something amazing here."

Booker leaned in and kissed me. The towel that had been wrapped around me dropped into my lap, and he smiled against my lips.

"See, my luck's changing already," he murmured.

But then his cell rang again and ruined it all.

I went to pull away, the panic of this being another investor dropping us making my heart pick up speed.

"Where do you think you're going?" Booker asked as he chased after my lips.

"You should answer that."

"There's nothing more important in this moment than me making sure you're okay," Booker told me, and from the look on his face, I knew he was being nothing but truthful.

Could the ranch plans continue without the backers? It would mean Booker investing everything he had. I should look over the financial projections again. Maybe if I could put out another social media campaign and raise our brand awareness...

Booker sighed. "You're in work mode, aren't you?"

I looked at him sheepishly and nodded just as his cell rang again.

This time when Booker pulled it out of his pocket, he grinned. "Get dressed. There's something I want to show you."

Okay, I was about to get whiplash with what was going on here today.

"Erm, okay." I stood reluctantly from Booker's lap, confused about what was happening, and he patted me on the ass before gently pushing me toward the closet.

I looked at him, grinning down at his cell, and picked up

the lacey little number from the dresser that I'd been planning on putting on before finding Booker in the bedroom.

"I guess I'll save this for another day, then." I shrugged dramatically as I tossed it into the closet over my shoulder.

Booker groaned as he watched the scrap of red lace fly away. "You're killing me, Reece."

Instead, I grabbed some jeans, slipping them on without any underwear, and then grabbed one of Booker's flannel shirts and slowly buttoned it up over my bare breasts.

Booker watched me hungrily and then audibly gulped.

"Okay...Yeah...We can be quick. Ten minutes tops," he rushed out before he grabbed my hand and dragged me out of the bedroom.

Men. So predictable.

Booker thankfully allowed me time to put my boots on, and as he charged out of the house, we found a confused-looking Xander standing there, staring at his phone.

"What's so important?" he asked, looking from Booker to me and then frowning again when it became apparently obvious what we'd been interrupted from the beginning. "If this is you wanting to show off about your sex life, then I'm not sure I want to be involved. And it's a bit creepy, honestly," he huffed.

Booker rolled his eyes and laughed, not even bothering to deny it as he tugged on my hand and led us down the steps.

"Come on, we can take the truck," Booker said, climbing into the driver's side and then whistling loudly as he leaned out the window.

Val came charging out of the house and jumped

through the passenger door as I slid in behind her. Xander watched in outrage.

"I know you're not thinking I'm sitting in the flatbed while your dog takes the people seat," he said.

"She called it first." I shrugged and closed the door while Xander huffed.

"I'm taking the other truck," he said, spinning on his heel and getting in the ranch truck he must have just arrived in. "I'll follow you," he called out the window as he started the engine.

Booker turned his truck toward the driveway, and we headed away from the ranch. He'd said it would only take ten minutes, but I had no idea where we could go in that amount of time.

The question was solved as we pulled up to the road and found Dex on a ladder fitting a sign that had definitely not been there the last time I'd come down the driveway.

"What the...?"

"Close your eyes," Booker rushed out.

I glanced at the excited man at my side and then did as he asked. It wasn't often that I saw Booker get so excited about something, and I was intrigued enough that I'd have done anything he asked. Not that I wasn't just about to do literally anything he asked, but most of that you couldn't do out in public.

"Stop thinking sexy thoughts," Booker grumbled as he brought the truck to a stop and killed the engine.

"How did you know?" I asked, not even bothering to deny it.

He leaned closer, and I felt the ghost of his lips brush against mine, making me gulp as he whispered, "You get this cute little blush on the tops of your cheeks, and your breath quickens."

Booker kissed me, leaning forward as he wrapped his hand around my neck and deepened the kiss to the point where I was squirming in my seat, desperate for more.

"Don't open your eyes until I tell you," he growled, nipping at my lips, and I felt my breath catch in my throat.

Damn. This man could turn me to liquid in an instant.

I heard Booker climb out of the truck, and then the door opened next to me, and his hands came to mine. Booker guided me out, steering me a few steps away from the truck before he turned me around and placed his hands over my eyes.

"Are you sure you've done that right?" Booker asked someone. "I don't want it dropping off and killing someone."

"Are you doubting my work?" Dex asked in outrage. "Here I am balancing on a ladder with no help at all so you can pull off this epic surprise and what thanks do I get? Nooo, let Dex risk his life for—"

"Will you just shut up already and get down here," Booker growled, but I could hear the grin on his lips in his voice. "You're ruining the view," he teased.

There was the sound of two feet hitting the ground, and I jumped. "Please tell me he didn't just throw himself off a ladder to make a point?"

"Awww, I knew you loved me, Reecey baby. Don't worry. When the time is right, I'll free you from this brute, and we can run away together."

I felt a breeze whisper past my face, followed by a grunt from Dex as he stumbled away from us laughing. I didn't think I wanted to know what they were doing.

"Okay, ready?" Booker asked.

"I don't know anymore," I said nervously.

"Trust me, you are," he whispered in my ear.

When Booker pulled his hands away from my eyes, I

blinked against the bright light that momentarily stole my vision, and then I focused in on the new sign that hung over the driveway.

"Oh, Booker, it's perfect," I said happily.

He wrapped his arms around me and hugged me against his chest as we both stared up at the timber sign, which was framed by two horseshoes, displaying the name...

Second Chance Ranch.

It was for me, and it had been for Booker too. Now we were going to share that with anyone else who needed it, too.

CHAPTER THIRTY-THREE

BOOKER

I straightened my shirt and ran my fingers through my hair again, making sure that it was as perfect as the unruly blond lengths could be. Maybe I should have gotten a haircut.

I looked down at my jeans, wondering if I should change, and then remembered that I didn't, in fact, own anything other than jeans and cursed.

Damn, why was I so damned nervous?

Ever since Camden had trashed the cottage, Reece had lived in my house and slept in my bed every night. We ate every meal together. She was the last thing I saw when I fell asleep and the first thing I saw when I woke. I knew her better than I knew myself. Every inch of her body, everything that makes her breath hitch and her toes curl.

Reece was my favorite subject, and when it came to her, I'd been a diligent student.

So why was I so damned nervous to be taking her to the carnival?

It was just a town carnival. It was barely a date. The picnic at the lookout had been a better date.

Oh god, was this a bad date?

Reece had been over at Delaney's today, but she should be back soon. They were setting up the social media accounts for Delaney's business and talking over what the plans were for the next couple of months.

I had no idea about this stuff, but Reece obviously did. The accounts she'd set up for the ranch were doing well, and we had people following Spirit's story and asking for updates nearly every day.

There was no way I was shaking my ass on that thing, though. Social media was for kids, and I wasn't about to set myself up to be the laughingstock of town.

I looked in the mirror again and cringed. Maybe I should wear a tie. Except I didn't own one of those either. I stared into my closet and cursed my past self for not being organized enough to know that I'd need stuff like this.

Damn, it would have to do.

I came downstairs to the sound of Reece moving around the kitchen, and the smile came to my lips automatically. I loved having her here in the house. In my space. *Our space.*

When I reached the doorway to the kitchen, I found Reece dancing in front of the sink as she washed the lunch dishes that had been left there. Val yipped and pranced around Reece's feet, making her head fall back as she laughed at her antics.

She was wearing a simple flowery summer dress, and she was the most beautiful woman I'd ever seen.

I stood leaning against the doorframe watching the picture of everyday life in front of me, wondering what I could have possibly done to deserve this in my life. To deserve her. When she realized I was standing there, she came dancing over and held out her hands to me.

The old Booker would have turned around and walked

away. He'd have grumbled about how only idiots danced when there wasn't any music playing.

But this Booker looked at the vision standing in front of him and did what the old one never would have dreamed of.

So I reached out, taking hold of her hands, and grabbed onto my future with both hands, spinning her across the kitchen before doing my best imitation of a shimmy which had Reece cackling in glee.

And I knew that no matter what came my way, it would all be all right.

Because I had her at my side.

And what else could I possibly want?

"A Ferris wheel!" Reece squealed, jumping up and down on the spot with a stuffed unicorn under one arm that I won for her on the ring toss.

I'd officially hit the peak of manliness.

Tucking her under my arm, we walked over to the Ferris wheel where the others were waiting for us.

"Aww, what! I want a unicorn!" Blake gushed when she saw the fuzzy pink monstrosity that Reece had been instantly smitten with. "Booker, pleaaaaaaaaase win me a unicorn."

"Maybe later." I kissed the top of Reece's head, and she smiled up at me. "I've got a Ferris wheel to ride first."

"I never thought I'd see the day," Dex mused, looking at me wide-eyed. "I want to make fun of you for going soft, but I'm genuinely too happy for you to bother."

Dex shrugged like he hadn't just said one of the nicest things I'd ever heard him utter.

"Thanks, man."

He coughed awkwardly. "Yeah, manly feelings and all that...Trace, let's go and win the girls some stuff with our big muscles." Dex struck a muscle-man pose, and Cade looked at him, unconvinced.

"Don't worry, Dex, I've got this," Cade said confidently.

"I always knew you were my hero, Cade," Blake said happily, taking his hand that he'd offered to her and doing a little curtsy as she did.

"Come on, Dad," Cade shouted over his shoulder as they headed away. "I need you to spot me a twenty."

"Spot him a...We need to stop letting our son hang out with Blake," Trace grumbled as he followed them, digging in his pocket for his wallet as he did.

Delaney just shrugged. "I think he's learning valuable life skills," she argued.

"Forgotten about again," Dex grumbled, sulking after the rest of them.

He was always the dramatic one of our group, but at least it broke the tension that usually always followed us around and had been strangely lacking for the last couple of days.

I looked down at Reece, who was still tucked under my arm, "Ready to ride the Ferris wheel, or do you want to go with the others?"

"Let's do the Ferris wheel," she said, looking up at it as her eyes glistened in the lights. "I've never been on one before."

"How is it possible that you've never been on a Ferris wheel?" I asked as we got into the queue with everyone else.

She shrugged. "I dunno. I guess the opportunity never really came up."

It was easy to forget that Reece hadn't had a good time growing up, either. She hadn't let it affect her, or at least not in any way that seemed to show. Reece was one of those people who always had a smile on her face and was ready to help everyone around her. I couldn't help but wonder over the years how many times she'd let people help her, though.

That didn't matter now because she'd found her way to Willowbrook, and when you lived in this town, there was one thing for definite. You were never alone.

"Make a hole, people!" Mrs. Shulster called out from the queue in front of us before turning to a confused-looking Reece. "Reece has never been on a Ferris wheel, and we need to rectify this injustice immediately." She jostled the strange little dog she always carried in her arms, and it just flopped about lifelessly.

The surrounding crowd cheered, and we were ushered to the front of the queue. This was just like the people I'd grown up with, and as we were bustled into our seats, I realized I'd never appreciated how lucky I'd been to have them around me growing up.

"Was that dog..."

"It's best not to think about it," I told her, not wanting to get into the Titus situation.

"Take her twice around and stop for the view at the top," Marie told the operator firmly, slipping him a five-dollar bill.

He looked at it disappointingly and then shrugged, reaching over to check the safety bar. "Hands inside the carriage at all times," he half-heartedly said, and then we were moving.

Reece gasped, peering over the edge before she wiggled in her seat and giggled in excitement. "This is so cool."

I missed the entire first loop. I couldn't take my eyes off her. She radiated happiness, her blond hair whipping up in the wind as we reached the top and then tipped her head back and stared at the stars.

"I wish we could have one of these at the ranch and ride it every day," she whispered.

"If you want a Ferris wheel, I'll buy you a Ferris wheel," I told her earnestly.

There was nothing I wouldn't do for this woman.

She laughed and nudged me with her shoulder. "Don't make fun of me."

"Who's making fun?" My hand came to my chest in faux shock, and she giggled before I leaned forward and kissed her, wrapping my arm around her shoulders as I pulled away. "I'd do anything to see this smile on your face every day, Reece. To come down to the kitchen and see you dancing across the room. Finding your books tucked behind my couch cushions that definitely don't belong to me, and your strange bottles and potions in the shower. There's nothing I wouldn't do if it would keep you at my side."

"Booker," she whispered, leaning her head against my shoulder. "I don't need a Ferris wheel. All I need is you."

"Move in with me," I said, pulling her closer and running my fingers along her jaw, my thumb brushing over her pouty lips that always seemed to be begging to be kissed.

"I don't know if you noticed, but I kinda already did. Or rather, you moved me in, thinking I wouldn't notice."

"True. But let's make it official. Get you a key, your own hook by the door to hang your hat."

"I don't think I've ever seen you lock the door."

"It's symbolic," I whispered, finally giving in and kissing her softly. "Say you'll be mine, Reece. Let me spend the rest of my life trying to prove to you that I deserve you."

"I love you, Booker," she said when I pulled away,

looking deep into my eyes. "I wish you could see the man that I see when I look at you."

"Is that a yes?" I asked, ignoring the part that I wasn't quite ready to think about. But I'd work on it. I'd work on anything if it would make her happy.

"Of course, it's a yes."

We missed the entire next circuit of the Ferris wheel, and it was only when the carriage jarred forward that I realized we'd stopped. There was nothing in the universe that could have stolen my attention from the woman in my arms at that moment.

My fingers pushed into her hair, and she sighed happily as she tipped her face up. Her beautiful blue eyes looked like they shone with the light of the stars as I pressed my lips against hers.

The crowd below us cheered, and Reece smiled against my lips.

"Ignore them," I muttered, kissing her again. "They're cheering at someone else. They definitely can't see us from down there."

She peered over my shoulder, and then that cute blush touched the tops of her cheek as she did a little wave.

"No, they can definitely see us," she said, ducking her head down. "In fact, I'm pretty sure someone is filming us."

"Then we should definitely give them something to look at."

I kissed her again, pulling her close as I did. Everything else in the world faded away because all that mattered was the woman in my arms.

This was perfect.

She was perfect.

And I had to be the luckiest man alive.

CHAPTER THIRTY-FOUR

BOOKER

I hung up the phone and then kicked my feet up on the desk, leaning back with a sigh.

That was it. Another two backers were gone, and we were down to the final one. The project was officially out of funding. I could maybe mortgage the ranch, raise the capital that way. There was no point in looking for new investors. Camden and his father had put out the word, and we were officially on the blacklist.

And yet, there was a part of me that didn't care.

I looked around the makeshift office that we'd set up in the dining room and found myself strangely accepting of the end.

I felt bad that Reece had worked so hard only for Camden to come in and break something else she had claimed as her own. It was the last flailing act of a pathetic man.

He probably thought it would break us. That I'd look at Reece and decide she wasn't worth the trouble.

He really was stupid.

The ranch would continue on just like it always had.

Maybe we wouldn't expand this year, maybe we would. For once in my life, I was content, and I knew we'd figure something out.

"What's going on?" Xander asked as he walked into the office. "I thought we were meeting with the contractor today about the next stage, but I got your message saying that it was canceled."

I rolled my head to the side to look at my brother. He'd changed so much since he'd come back to Willowbrook. Hell, he was talking about selling his sports car and buying a truck. If that wasn't the symbolic shedding of his city life, I didn't know what was. He'd even dug out the old, battered leather jacket that he'd worn for most of his college years. I couldn't believe it actually still fit him. It was like having the echo of the brother I remembered from back then sitting right in front of me.

"We're done," I told him. "I just lost two more backers. The project is over."

Xander looked surprised as he slumped down in the chair on the other side of the desk.

"Just like that?" he asked. "There's nothing else you can do."

"Not right now. No one else is going to risk investing in us with the governor out for blood. Maybe in a couple of years we can pick it up and try again."

"Why aren't you angry?" Xander asked. "You should be pissed, man. You've been working hard for this."

I shrugged, turning to look out the window at the barn where I knew Reece would be sneaking more apples to Spirit and Bullet. She hadn't asked why we suddenly seemed to always have a bowl of them in the kitchen.

"I guess I'm reassessing my priorities," I said, not really knowing how to explain myself.

Xander whistled through his teeth. "It's good to see you like this, Booker. But don't throw everything away for her. You can have more than one thing go right in your life, you know. Or at least that's what I've heard. I've yet to actually figure out how to do it myself."

I looked at Xander then, took in all the changes, and felt guilty that I hadn't made more of an effort to talk to him about it.

"How are you doing, Xander?" I finally asked the question I should have asked weeks ago.

He seemed surprised that I was. "Me? Fine, I guess."

I pulled my feet off the desk and sat forward, leaning against the tabletop as I did. "Don't bullshit me," I said sternly. "I'm your big brother. I'm allowed to be worried about you."

"I think once we pass the thirty-five mark, you lose the right to pull the big brother card," Xander laughed, evading the question.

"I didn't get that memo. Now answer the question."

Xander sighed and lurched out of his seat before striding to the window and leaning against the frame as he stared outside. I didn't care what he was looking at as long as he answered the question.

"It's...strange being back here. I don't know if it's good for me, and yet I can't bring myself to leave either. It's not like there's anything but an empty apartment waiting for me in the city."

His shoulders slumped sadly, and I felt the part of me that wanted to fix things for everyone surge to the surface. But I couldn't do this for Xander. It was something he needed to do for himself.

"So...sell it," I said simply.

The city wasn't the answer to Xander's problems. If it

was, then he wouldn't have found the bottom of his spiral there.

"Yeah, I think I will."

"I thought you'd fight harder than that, if I'm honest."

I pushed out of the chair and moved around the desk, sitting myself on the edge. This was probably the part where I should hug him or something, but I didn't know if either of us was in a place where that sort of thing made sense.

Xander glanced over his shoulder and gave me a sad smile. "I think I'm done fighting," he told me. "Right now, I'm trying to figure out who I am and what life for that version of me looks like. Now, tell me what you're going to do about the ranch so I don't have to think about my depressing life for much longer."

A breath whooshed out of me, and I tipped my head back to stare up at the ceiling. "Hell if I know. The cottages are finished, so I'll probably rent those while I figure the rest of it out."

"Is this where I'm supposed to offer to pay you rent?"

I shook my head and laughed. "Nah, man. The cottage is yours for as long as you want it."

"There isn't a certain young lady who wants it back."

I grinned then. "Nah, she stays in my bed where she belongs."

"Happy suits you, Booker," Xander said, clapping me on the shoulder as he left the room.

"It would suit you too, brother," I murmured sadly, watching him go.

Xander would find his way in the world again. I knew he would. I was just hoping he wouldn't go through hell while he was trying to figure it all out.

CHAPTER THIRTY-FIVE

REECE

Booker had been quiet all day, and I knew something had happened that he wasn't sharing with me. It didn't take a genius to figure out that it was the loss of another backer.

I looked around at the ranch I'd come to love so much, wondering if my coming here was the worst thing that had ever happened to it.

Booker had told me that the ranch would continue on as it was without the investors. But he needed them to expand. To build the cottages and hire more staff for people to be able to come here and figure out their problems in the peaceful fields of horses. The rentals and the extras Booker planned to offer to the people who came here were enough to not only pay for the staff but also to expand the number of horses he could help.

And all of that had ground to a halt now.

I'd been going over the figures for days now, trying to find a solution, but I just couldn't see one. Not an immediate one, at least.

Booker came out of the house, heading to the folding tables by the grill with platters of meat.

"I can't remember the last time we had a proper cookout here," he told me. As he put the plates down, he looked around and sighed. "This is something we need to do more."

"Why do you look so happy?" I asked in exasperation, the guilt over everything that had happened finally getting to me.

His eyebrow ticked up in question before he strode across to me and wrapped his arms around me. "What's wrong?" he asked.

I turned my head to lean against his chest as I stared out at the empty fields. "Did I ruin this?"

His laughter wasn't exactly the empathetic response I'd expected, and I looked up at him in shock.

"Oh, right. You're not joking," he said, looking sheepish. "Reece, I wish you could have seen this place before you turned up. It was...really depressing," he admitted, shaking his head.

"Yeah, you should have seen him sulking all over the place," Xander called out, carrying two bowls of salads out to the table. "It's the only reason I stayed away. Couldn't take him pouting and that weird growl he did." Xander shuddered dramatically as Booker rolled his eyes at his brother.

Before he could say anything, we heard Blake call out, "Booky bear!" in that sing-song way he hated so much.

Strangely, it was Xander who did an about-turn and tried to make a run for it back to the house. Booker chuckled, and I realized there was something else I'd missed.

Cade came charging around the corner giggling as Blake chased him, Delaney and Trace strolling behind them, looking as happy as always.

"Can we go on the quads?" Cade shouted, doing a lap of the tables as he did. "I told Blake I can totally smoke her in a race!"

"Please. If anyone is going to smoke Blake in a race, it's going to be me," Delaney scoffed, and Cade ground to a sudden stop, his mouth hanging open in shock.

"You can ride a quad?" he asked, impressed.

"Your mom was the first one brave enough to launch one off the hill out by the pond," Trace said all misty eyed and then seemed to realize what he said and winced as Delaney pinched his side.

"Coooool." Cade fist-pumped the air and then ran to the barn, whistling for Val, who charged after him.

"I'm exhausted. It's your turn," Delaney told Blake, sinking into one of the chairs and pushing her with one foot.

Most people would have at least argued a little, but Blake looked like all her dreams had come true as she skipped after the kid who seemed to be her best friend.

"It's like you have two kids," Xander muttered.

He was too busy watching Blake skip away to catch the look that Trace gave Delaney.

"Oh my goodness," I rushed out.

Delaney grinned and then put a finger against her lips, and I snapped my mouth closed before I said anything else.

"What? What just happened?" Xander said, looking around.

"I just realized that we're missing the garlic bread. Can you check it's not burning for me, please?"

Xander huffed out a sigh of exasperation and then turned around and reluctantly headed back to the house. He wouldn't be impressed when he got into the kitchen and realized I hadn't even put it in the oven yet.

"So tell us the big news," Trace said, quickly changing the subject in possibly the worst way he could.

Delaney seemed to hold her breath, hoping that Booker wasn't about to take up the questioning where Xander had left off, and I frantically started to rack my brain for some other excuse to occupy him.

"The ranch expansion is off," Booker said, shrugging like it was no big deal. "You'll have to count me out of your regeneration plans."

"What?" Delaney suddenly bolted upright, concern lining her face. "What do you mean, it's off?"

"Burger? Hot dog? I thought I'd wait for everyone to get here before I threw on the steaks." Booker turned to the grill, clearly thinking that was the end of the conversation.

Men could be so oblivious at times.

"No!" Delaney said sternly. "You don't get to drop that bombshell and then pretend it's no big deal. And I want a burger, please and thank you."

"Burger coming up. Trace?" Booker pointed some tongs at his brother, who looked just as shocked as Delaney did.

"I'll take some answers with a burger on the side and a hot dog for Cade."

"Blake will want a hot dog too... wait, no, back to the answers first." Delaney shook her head, clearly trying to get past Booker's apparently flawless distraction method.

"We lost most of the backers. The funds are gone. We've got two of the cottages up, so we can add to some of the accommodation numbers you wanted. The rest is going to need to wait a couple of years until the drama dies down." Booker shrugged and then turned back to the grill as I sighed and went to sit down.

Damn, this was all my fault, and Booker might seem to

think it wasn't a big deal, but I'd feel guilty enough for the both of us.

"Camden," I said sadly, wincing as I did. "He or his father or someone has gotten the investors to back out."

"That little piss weasel ex of yours?" Trace asked, surprised.

Booker snorted at Trace's accurate description, and Trace looked at his brother like he might have lost his mind.

"Apparently, he didn't appreciate me making him piss himself in fear before I punched him in the face."

"To be fair," I added, "I think you actually punched him in the face and then threatened to bury his body out on the ranch somewhere."

"Nice!" Delaney chimed in, grabbing a cherry tomato out of the salad bowl and popping it in her mouth.

She groaned like it was the best thing she'd ever tasted and then sank back into her chair as she chewed in satisfaction.

Trace smiled softly as he watched her before sitting down and pulling the salad bowl in front of him.

"So—we're not angry?" he asked as he picked out the cherry tomatoes and put them on a napkin.

"Nah. It will all come together at some point. For now, I'm just going to keep doing what I was doing before. Maybe keep the extra ranch hand on and take a bit more time off." Booker shrugged, waving the tongs in the air to make his point, and then went back to the meat.

"Okay. That doesn't sound terrible," Delaney admitted, giving Trace big, dreamy eyes as he placed the napkin of tomatoes in front of her. "So—we're happy then."

"Super happy," Booker said. "Especially now we've got that new rugrat of yours to add to the family."

Trace ducked down and kissed the top of Delaney's

head before she tipped her head back, and he kissed her lips as well. Apparently, Booker was a bit more observant than I gave him credit for.

"It's going to be a big family," Trace said, looking around at us all.

For the first time in my life, I felt like I belonged. And as I watched Booker grilling our lunch and Cade and Blake chasing each other around the yard, I decided that maybe I'd like to add to this family, too.

CHAPTER THIRTY-SIX

BOOKER

Dex looked around at the group of us sitting at the table as he chewed on his burger. His hand kept moving around as he pointed to everyone including Val, frowned, and then repeated the process again.

"What are you doing?" I hissed when I couldn't take it any longer.

Sometimes his strange antics drove me crazy.

Dex frowned again. "Who's missing?"

I winced at how much it felt like that cut deep. Of course there was one of us missing. He'd been missing for far too long.

I didn't know if he realized what he'd said, or if it was the confusion on everyone else's face, but Dex quickly added, "Who's that?"

"Oh god," Blake muttered, sliding down in her seat. "Someone hide me. I can't take it anymore."

Delaney chuckled and patted her friend's arm. "Is it hard being popular?"

"I'm used to being the weird girl. Don't these people know they're supposed to just politely humor me and keep on walking?"

"I'd be happy to fill them in," Xander muttered.

I looked between the two of them, and Reece squeezed my knee in excitement. When I glanced in her direction, she was beaming in excitement, and my head snapped back in Xander's direction.

Oh, little brother. This one was going to be painful.

I laughed, making Xander look at me in shock, not understanding why Reece and I were staring at him.

Then I remembered what Dex had said.

"Who's who?"

Dex hitched his thumb over his shoulder, and then it was my time to slump down in my chair, wishing that someone could hide me because the car Dex had noticed before any of the rest of us was my father's.

"That can't be good," Trace muttered.

His eyes went to Delaney and his son, and I knew he was trying to decide whether to send them inside. I doubted it was an argument he'd win with Delaney.

"Cade, you wanna come and help me raid Booker's freezer to see if there's any ice cream?" Blake loudly whispered in the kid's direction.

She might act like she didn't have all the cogs turning, but when it came to Cade, like everyone else, there was nothing she wouldn't do for the kid.

Delaney smiled at her gratefully, and Cade jumped from his seat and charged for the house. Hopefully, she'd find some excuse to keep him inside for a while.

"We're going to listen in from the porch, though, right?" Cade asked loudly, making Blake cackle, and Delaney just sighed in defeat.

The kid needed to learn subtlety, or he'd never make it through his teenage years.

"I wouldn't blame you if you wanted to go with them," I told Reece as my father's car pulled up outside of the house. "This is probably going to turn into some kind of shitshow."

Reece bristled at the thought. "I think I'm good where I am, thank you."

I could see her fierce determination in her eyes. Reece had my back, and she was ready to leap to my defense if needed. I'd never really had that before. Yeah, Dex and my brothers always had my back. But I was the eldest, and it had always been expected that I'd be standing in front of whatever trouble came our way. Or, maybe it was what I'd always expected of myself.

And here was this beautiful woman ready to push me to the side and take on the world by herself if that was what I needed.

Damn, I didn't think it was possible to love her any more than I did, and then she went and did that.

I kissed her lightly on top of the head before standing and striding over to my father's car. I had a moment of gratitude when he climbed out, and there was no sign of my mother. Then I almost laughed at the thought of her ever willingly coming to the ranch.

"Jasper," I said, stopping a short distance away from him.

It was close enough for me to see the wince on his face.

"I have a copy of the information I could gather on Camden Carter," he said, getting straight to the point and moving to pass the papers to me. "My associate has already delivered a copy to the governor with a message from me. He sent this for you."

Jasper pulled an envelope out of his pocket and passed

it to me. It was made from thick paper, and I was too intrigued not to open it. At this point, it could have been a threat that needed dealing with.

It wasn't.

I slid out the check for a hundred grand, then folded it in half, and slipped it in my back pocket, not wanting to think about it right now.

"The governor sends his apologies. Apparently, the situation was misrepresented to him, and this is his apology for any inconvenience."

I nodded slowly. It didn't cover what I'd lost in investors, but it was a start. It also helped that it had Camden's name signed on the bottom, and I knew signing it would have hurt more than the punch I gave him to the face.

The one thing rich dicks hated the most was reaching into their own pockets.

"Thank you," I muttered, not really sure where to go from here.

My father shifted uneasily, and it had my spine straightening, preparing for the blow. This was the part where he'd tell me what I owed him for his help. If it got Camden off Reece's back, anything would be worth it.

"I'd like to speak to you all for a moment if that's acceptable," my father said, looking over my shoulder to where I knew the others were probably standing.

My brothers wouldn't have let me come to face my father alone, and I doubted Reece or Delaney would have either.

I was proved right when I felt Reece's hand slip into mine and give it a gentle squeeze in support.

Jasper took a deep breath, looked around, and smiled. "I missed this place," he said, and my stomach nearly dropped out of my ass. If he wanted the ranch, there was absolutely no way. "There are so many happy memories here. Happy times. I wish I could say the same of the ones from our own home."

When Jasper looked back at us, there were tears in his eyes.

"I failed you boys so completely that I don't think I can ever come back from it. I knew your mother was hard on you, but I never knew...the things you said, Booker. I made her tell me everything. Apologies can never be enough, but I need you to know that I am so very sorry."

His voice hitched, and I knew he was trying his best to hold back his tears.

I'd never seen my father cry. I'd never seen much of any emotion from the man. He was this figurehead of our family who only appeared on rare occasions because he was too busy making his money to actually spend any time with us.

"I was a selfish, stupid man. Nothing can change the past. But I need you to know that it's done. It's over. I'm divorcing your mother. The papers are being drawn up, and she's already packing her things. She'll be moving back to Washington, where the rest of her family is. I'm hoping to stay in Willowbrook. I know I can't possibly right any of the wrongs that have happened between us, but I'm going to try to do what I can for the town."

No one said anything, and Jasper seemed to take a moment to look at each of us like he was trying to memorize our faces one last time.

I didn't know what to say. His absence and inattentiveness didn't excuse what had happened. Then I looked at Reece standing at my side, and I wondered if there was any chance of forgiveness in our future.

Since I'd found her, I was seeing so many things in a

different light. I just didn't see how there was possibly any way to get past everything that had happened to our family.

But I wanted to be the type of person who looked for a way.

The type of person who didn't shut down any possibility.

I might not leave a door open for my father, but I could leave a window open. I could at least decide that I was willing to look for *a chance* of forgiveness, even if I wasn't ready to give it yet. Even if I maybe never would be. It wasn't a step forward, but I was at least looking in the right direction.

"We're having family dinner at the farm on Sunday," Delaney said from behind me. "If you're serious about what you said, if you can honestly tell me, hand on your heart, that you're leaving her, then you're welcome to join us. Cade would love to see you. But that woman will never be welcome in my home, Jasper. And if you decide that you can't not have her in your life, then I don't want you there either."

No one else spoke. We were probably all as surprised as Jasper was. Out of everyone here, I didn't think Delaney would be the first of us to extend a hand to him. She'd possibly been hurt by our parents the worst of any of us.

"Thank you," Jasper said, looking down at his feet. When he glanced up, the tears had finally slipped free from his eyes. "I can assure you that there's no going back. I can't ever forgive her for what she did to you all when it was me she was trying to punish."

There was too much happening. More feelings than I was comfortable with and a glaring look at the past that was perhaps a long time coming.

The Farrington family wasn't just broken. It had been shattered into a million pieces years ago. Trace, Xander, and I were slowly putting our family together again. But now we needed to figure out if we wanted all the pieces, and how to go about finding the ones that were still lost.

CHAPTER THIRTY-SEVEN

REECE

After Booker's father had left, everyone else had drifted back home. No one really knew what to say or how they were supposed to act. Delaney's offer had taken them by surprise. The guys needed to figure out their feelings about their father before they were in any kind of place to decide if there was a chance for a relationship with him as well.

Booker had been quiet for days, and Xander had been stomping around the ranch, fighting just about everything he had the chance to. I was staying well away from him, but Booker didn't seem to have the same luck, and they'd been snapping and rubbing each other the wrong way the whole time.

It didn't seem to affect their relationship. If anything, they both seemed grateful to have the other to take their frustrations out on.

Men were weird.

But tiptoeing around the two of them was getting old, and there was a lot to do, and I was the last person around here who could figure it out.

So I pulled on my big girl pants and told Booker that it was time to look over the cottages and decide what he wanted to do with them. I never thought the subject of the failed expansion plans would be one I'd grab onto out of sheer desperation to start a conversation. It felt like the one thing we should have been avoiding the most. And then Jasper had turned up at the ranch and flipped our world upside down.

"Your contractor did a good job," I said, grasping for something to say as we stood in front of the two cottages and stared at them.

Booker grunted in agreement.

His hands were in his pockets as he stared ahead, but I knew he wasn't really seeing the two cottages. He was too lost in his thoughts.

They really were lovely, though. This was the first time I'd been up here, really. I loved how they were far enough apart that they had their privacy, and yet the shared yard meant that if it was set up right with some patio furniture, it would be a lovely area to socialize if they wanted to, or if a large enough party booked out both cottages.

"The view is nice."

Wow, I really was grasping at straws now.

Booker looked up and that old smirk I remembered from when we first met ticked across his lips.

"I'm being a total ass, aren't I?"

"I wouldn't say a *total* ass." I winced, trying to soften the blow. We both knew the real answer was yes.

Booker and I hadn't been together for long, and we'd moved fast. I didn't know whether to leave him to his thoughts or just jump in with both feet and try to help him wade through them.

The old Booker was definitely a hands-off emotions

person, but the man in front of me had changed and softened. He was dropping his shields and molding the life he wanted.

I was just lucky enough to be part of the process.

Booker wrapped an arm around me, and I nearly sighed in relief. We headed toward the nearest cottage, and Booker fished a key out of his pocket. The need to make a sarcastic comment about how he'd figured out locks was on the tip of my tongue. I didn't think I'd ever seen him lock a door until now. Small-town living, I guessed.

I held it back, though. Now wasn't the time to poke fun at him when he was opening up.

Obviously, I was saving it for later, though.

"This one is two beds, two baths," Booker said as we stepped inside. "The one across the way has an extra bedroom. They're both wheelchair accessible."

There wasn't any furniture yet, but I could already see it set up as a cozy space. The open plan downstairs even had a fireplace, which would be so nice in the winter. Especially when there was snow outside.

"We could probably furnish them for a reasonable cost," I said, peering around a door and finding a small laundry room which already had the machines plumbed in. "If you wanted to rent them out."

I looked over my shoulder to see Booker peering up at the fireplace, and then he straightened again, nodding like there was something up there that he'd expected. He had to be faking it, right?

I didn't think he was going to answer me at first as he walked over to the window to stare out at the view.

"I was going to let the expansion plans sit for a couple of years. Just spend some time on the ranch like I used to, but this time I'd have you with me." He looked over his shoulder at me with a soft smile and held out a hand so I'd join him at the window. When I reached his side, he continued. "I love this land. I love having you here and seeing the future I want us to build together. I'm...content. And I don't think I've felt that before. But the happier I get, the more grounded I feel, and the more I think I might want to fight for the expansion too. Do you think that makes me selfish?" He looked at me in question, and I surged up on the tips of my toes to wrap my arms around him.

"Why would that make you selfish, Booker?" I asked in surprise.

"Because I have so much. Because life is perfect, and yet I still want more." He genuinely looked like he was struggling to understand if he was doing the right thing, and I thanked the universe for giving me this man who couldn't be any further from selfish even if he tried.

"Booker, you want to show people the ranch and how it can help them. I've seen your plans. I've seen the numbers. If you were a selfish man, you wouldn't be working your business based on charging people a fraction of the cost that you could. You wouldn't be looking into animal therapy and hiring staff experienced in rehabilitation. You'd have structured a business you could have actually made a profit from rather than just trying to cover the costs."

"I don't need any more money," he said quietly.

"So why can't you see how selfless that makes you?" I asked him softly.

I knew the answer. I think he knew the answer too. He just wasn't ready to admit it. Booker had been told his whole life that he was a disappointment, that he wouldn't amount to anything. That the things he wanted were wrong. And he'd heard it so many times that he'd forgotten to remember it wasn't true.

"Will you help me?" Booker asked. He looked around at the empty cottage, and a shy smile came to his lips. "I don't have a clue how to make this look nice."

"I'd love to."

Booker gently kissed my lips, then tipped his forehead to press it against mine. "I don't know how I got so lucky to find you, Reece."

"We were both lucky. Everything that came before was worth it because it led me here to you," I whispered.

"Don't say that." Booker held on to me tightly. "Nothing was worth that."

"I'd have paid that price a thousand times over." I looked up and met his gaze. "Can't you see how lucky I am to be this in love with you?"

"Even with all the stuff going on in my family?"

"Everyone has their baggage, Booker. I think the family you're pulling in around you happens to be a pretty great one."

"My dad..."

"Will have to earn his place in that family if you all decide you want him to," I told him firmly. "He doesn't have to be in your life. Even if Trace and Delaney decide they want him in theirs. You're allowed to have your own boundaries."

Booker nodded, turning me to tuck me under one arm as we headed out of the cottage. "I never thought I'd be in a place where I'd think this, but I think I'm ready to hear him out. I'm not sure I can offer him more than that, but I'm willing to consider it. That's all I'm ready for at the moment."

"I think he'll understand that, and at least he already knows he's got a lot of hard work ahead of him, and he seems prepared to do it."

Booker hummed in agreement as he stopped to lock the cottage door and then held out his hand for me, which I gladly took. He fell quiet as we headed home, lost in his thoughts, except it wasn't as worrying this time around.

He had a lot to think through, and some decisions were ones you had to make yourself.

I trusted Booker to figure out what was right for him. He was the only one who could, after all.

CHAPTER THIRTY-EIGHT

BOOKER

I shouldn't have been as nervous as I was. Hell, I wasn't the only one. Strangely, it was Blake who seemed to watch everyone closely, waiting to see if anyone looked even slightly too uncomfortable.

I hadn't noticed how much she looked out for the rest of us until today. She always hid behind her jokes and laughter. It was easy to not look too closely at the pink-haired dynamo in our midst.

Family dinner had been the strangest experience of my life because it was exactly how I'd imagined a family dinner would have been if there had ever been a moment in my childhood that was remotely happy.

After the initial awkwardness when Jasper had turned up at Delaney's farm, we seemed to have settled into a strange atmosphere of just ignoring the issues no one wanted to discuss.

But as soon as we'd sat at the table, and as soon as the food was passed around, it was like everyone finally took a breath and relaxed.

The conversation flowed. There was laughter and smiles.

By the time Delaney stood up to get dessert, it was almost like it had always been this way.

"Pops, do you want to play catch with us?" Cade piped up. "Dad has an extra glove you can use."

It was an unexpected offer with the innocence of a child. Jasper looked shocked, but then a smile broke across his face.

"I'd really like that. If your dad doesn't mind," he quickly added, looking at Trace almost pleadingly.

"Sure." Trace nodded once and then stood from the table.

"Let's have dessert outside," Delaney declared, following Trace into the kitchen to have a hurried, whispered conversation.

This seemed too much and too fast for Trace, but he'd do whatever it took to make Cade happy. That was what you were supposed to do for your kids.

My gaze found Reece, and for the first time in my life, that thought made me happy. Because I'd do anything to make her—and the kids I wanted us to have one day—as happy as they could be.

And I couldn't wait.

"Come and play, Uncle Booker," Cade cheered, and I waved my broken arm in his direction with a sad expression on my face.

Finally, a good reason to be wearing a cast.

Some days I forgot I had it on, and others, I was seconds away from finding a saw and taking the damn thing off myself. Reece would probably kill me, though. I dreaded to think where I'd be right now if I didn't have her as an excuse to look after myself for once.

We'd all only just stood from our seats when someone hammered on the front door of the farmhouse, and Delaney came through from the kitchen, her eyes wide in surprise.

"Who could that—"

The door flew open, slamming into the window as it did, and a huff of distaste flowed through the house that could only have come from one person.

Xander froze, and that wonderful woman I was so in love with stepped in front of him, shielding him from the harpy that was invading Delaney's home.

Only Regina Farrington would have the nerve to step foot into a house she couldn't have been less welcome in like she owned the place.

"I didn't," Jasper rushed out, pale at the thought of getting the blame for being the one to bring her here.

For the first time in my life, I actually believed him.

"There you are," Regina hissed as she stormed into the kitchen. She looked at the table we'd just been eating at and sneered before she turned her glare on my father. "Here, I'm not signing these."

She threw a file of papers across the room, and then Regina looked around at the people silently watching her. There was no sorrow on her face that she'd walked into a family gathering she'd been excluded from. Any semblance of propriety she might have had before was completely gone, and there was nothing but hate on her face.

No one spoke. Xander silently picked up the papers that were now strewn across the table and shuffled them into a pile.

"You're not welcome here," Delaney said firmly, stepping forward while the rest of us stood in shocked silence. "If you don't leave immediately, I will take an enormous amount of joy in calling the police to remove you from my property."

Even I felt the corners of my lips twitching at the thought of poor Ethan, our police chief, having to drag Regina out of the house.

"There's no need," the woman answered, lifting her chin a fraction so she could look down on everyone like she so loved to do. "I'm leaving for Washington immediately. I just had to come and deliver your father's ridiculous papers. I'm not signing them, Jasper."

"They're more than fair," Jasper said, finally stepping forward and putting himself between the family he wanted and the woman who'd driven them away.

Regina scoffed. "Oh, dear stupid Jasper. If you think I'll just sign your documents and leave without a fight, then you never did really know me, did you? You can have this tiny insignificant town, but I'll be taking the rest. Everything. When I'm finished with you, you'll be nothing but a penniless fool in the gutter with the rest of this trash."

"Enough," I growled, stepping to my father's side.

I was so done with this woman. Why had she stayed all these years when she was clearly so unhappy? Why make the rest of us as miserable as she was? Didn't she have even the smallest shred of decency inside her?

"*You*," Regina sneered in response. "At least you're not the only failure of a son now." Her eyes darted to Xander, and I saw Reece stiffen out of the corner of my eye.

But Regina's attention came squarely back to me, and I was actually relieved about that for once. This was my place in the family. Standing up for them against anyone that wanted to hurt them. Even if it was our own mother. And it was a place I'd gladly stand in any day of the week.

"I should probably finally confess that I'm your mysterious investor," she said smugly, an evil smile touching her lips when I gritted my teeth. "I would have enjoyed taking that patch of land from you, but obviously, I'll be pulling my money, along with the rest of them. I'm almost impressed that you could upset someone as important as the governor, Booker. Maybe you're not the biggest disappointment of the family after all. Knowing that your project is dead in the water is nearly as good as breaking it myself, though. You should know by now, Booker. You're not meant for success. If you could just learn your place in life, things would go a lot smoother for you."

My mouth opened to finally tell her exactly what I thought of her, but Xander took that moment to gently move Reece aside and come to stand with me.

"The ranch project isn't dead in the water. I'll be investing," he said firmly.

"And so will Delaney and I," Trace said, coming to stand on my other side.

I looked at both of my brothers in shock. "You don't have to."

"We can't let you always be the one that gets to save the day," Xander said, shaking his head as he laughed. "What else have I got to do? Besides, you need a doctor, and I need a job. It's a match made in heaven."

"I don't know what to say." They couldn't know what this meant to me. Not just because the project was going ahead, but because it would be a family project. For once, we were putting the Farrington name on something good. On something worthy of a legacy.

"If there's anything I can do," my father said. Then he held his hands up in surrender as if he was trying to hold me off from arguing with him. "I might as well sign it all over to you than let your mother have it."

Delaney barked out a laugh, and I took the opportunity to look at Regina, who had come bursting in here thinking she'd be the center of attention and was now basically being ignored.

My father looked at her and shrugged. "You should have signed the papers, dear. It was a generous offer while it was still valid."

Xander passed him the paperwork he'd collected, and my father tore it in two.

"I'll have my lawyer contact you with a new proposal more fitting of our future financial position."

"This isn't over," Regina seethed, taking one last look at the people who would never stand on her side.

She didn't wait for a response. Apparently, that was all the goodbye our mother had for her family because she spun on her heel and stormed out of the house, slamming the door behind her.

I should say something. This was probably the part where I was supposed to try to reassure my father. Tell him that the money didn't matter. We'd help him fight her.

But Jasper surprised us.

He turned to Delaney with a look of relief on his face and smiled. "Now, did you mention something about pie?" he asked, rubbing his hands together.

Everyone moved at once. The conversation started up, and we walked to the porch like we'd intended before.

As soon as I had the chance, I grabbed Reece's hand and drew her to a stop. When she looked back at me in surprise, I tugged her back into the dining room and pressed my lips to hers as I backed her up against the wall.

She hummed happily against my lips as her arms wrapped around my neck.

"You're incredible," I whispered against her lips.

"I'm not sure what I did to deserve that, but write it down or something so I can keep doing it."

"I saw the way you were ready to stand up for Xander."

"Well, he's family, right?"

"Yeah, baby. He is."

I kissed her again, my teeth nipping her bottom lip, so she gasped, and I deepened the kiss just the way I wanted.

"Ick, put the girl down, Booky bear, or I'm eating your pie for you."

I ignored Blake, and kissed Reece again. Damn the pie. I had something else much better, and I couldn't wait to get her home to take another bite.

ABOUT THE AUTHOR

Piper Wylde is an author who writes small town, contemporary romance that will make you feel all the feels. She lives with her husband, son, two neurotic golden retrievers, and a put-upon cat who rules the house.

Piper is from England and living the dream of her own small town existence in the countryside. She spends her days in imaginary worlds and drinking as much tea as physically possible.

Printed in Great Britain
by Amazon

60518315R00201